CW00551661

Nightshade

Nightshade, Volume 1

Percy Cadaver

Published by Percy Cadaver, 2024.

This is a work of fiction. Similarities to real people, places, or events are entirely coincidental.

NIGHTSHADE

First edition. May 13, 2024.

Copyright © 2024 Percy Cadaver.

ISBN: 979-8224666485

Written by Percy Cadaver.

To my loves:

Arbel Ben-Abraham, Eli Piller, Lara-May Coetzer, and Sophia Danis

TRIGGER WARNINGS: Queerphobia, horror elements, violence, abusive relationships, child abuse, unhealthy family dynamics, animal gore, panic attacks, needles, hair pulling, mentions of seizures, psychosis, drugging

Part One

NIGHTSHADE

Chapter 1
Veronica

I'm getting married today. It's about time. I have been waiting for this day my entire life, after all.

Today, they're all going to see me. Soon enough, they'll regret not seeing me sooner. They'll regret the snarky headlines about me that long ago prevented me from having any semblance of a positive or formidable reputation.

I take a deep breath and stare at myself in the mirror. My braids fall down my shoulders, sapphires and diamonds woven and hooked between strands. My face is hidden behind a thick white veil, concealing my gray eyes. They're the single physical trait I've inherited from my mother. The tightly fitting white dress seems to glow against my dark golden brown skin, embedded with diamonds meant to shine once the light hits me correctly.

For once, I'll be in the spotlight, the dazzling presence, all eyes on me, as it should've been from the start. The one problem with my dress, other than how it was far too tight, is that it falls past my feet, meaning it is very likely that I'll trip on the aisle.

I cannot afford a slip-up like that, not today of all days. I'll finally be receiving the attention that I'd far long been denied, only to be made a fool of The Two Kingdoms, just as I was deemed as a child.

Not that their laughter will be long-lived. I intend to allow the heads of those who once mocked me to roll and rot once I've married into the neighboring kingdom. Everyone will think twice before they even consider laughing, and they'll have no choice but to respect me. For now, I'll have to deal with pre-wedding jitters. I am a lady of seventeen, I'll have to learn to grow up eventually.

I secure a diamond necklace around my neck.

"It's odd seeing you in something other than blue," says my guard, Sabine, stepping into the room.

I tend to abuse the color blue, however, blue looks fantastic on me, so no harm no foul, I suppose. The fact that it's my favorite color certainly has no significance.

"I really will miss Your Highness," Sabine sighs.

"I will miss you too, my friend," I admit, wrapping my arms around her.

That is the only thing I'm going to miss about the kingdom. Sabine is the one person I feel like I can trust. Even the staff seems to have an agenda. I can't wait to get out of that star-forsaken castle. I can't live like that anymore.

"You look beautiful," She smiles.

High praise. I believe she is the prettier of the two of us. She is the personification of the romanticism movement, which is ironic considering that she has no interest in romance. Her gold armor was bright against her dark skin, her eyes a light brown, with flakes of blue and gold at the center. She looks like something out of a fairytale.

"Thank you," I look down, heat rising in my face.

"You're going to be the main attraction today," She grinned, taking my hands in hers. "After today, you'll be all anyone in the two kingdoms talks about."

The room is massive, all grandeur and splendor. The walls are a violent crimson, the glossy black, banners hanging from columns a velvety purple. The columns are ivory, gold cracks running up them. The orchestra, with instruments of white, lavender, and rose red, is drowned out by the sounds of people talking, and a slight buzzing in the back of my head.

Sapphire and diamond chandeliers hang low from the yard-high ceiling, dousing the hall in fragments of light. I grip my bouquet tightly, reminding myself not to screw anything up. The child in front of me sprinkles an assortment of flower petals on the aisle ahead. I step forward, bracing myself. My life is about to change, forever.

Good.

As I walk down the aisle, rows stand up as I walk past them. All eyes are on me. The attention, the captivation of the crowd, all of it is intoxicating. Daman stands impatiently at the front, staring me down. In the spot of best man is his younger brother. The eighteen-year-old, socially inept prince, Noah Henry Acacius Woods. Daman and Noah forsaken, it's *my* moment to shine, and Daman's impatience is *not* taking that away from me. My father links my arm in his, leading me away from my past, and into my freedom.

"Do you, Princess Veronica Helena Isolabella Belladonna of the Kingdom of Couteau, take Prince Daman Zagan Woods of Kingdom Mortem Venenum, to have and to hold, from this day forward, for better, for worse, for richer or for poorer, in sickness and in health, to obey and serve, till death do you part?"

I'm finally going to be free. I'll have everything I ever dreamed about, everything I've ever wanted.

"I d-" I begin.

The lights flicker, before being summoned into a larger flame, shooting out towards the windows.

The windows shatter completely, a horribly beautiful rain impaling the audience, blood and glass now splattering all over the white flooring. Wind blusters in the room, sweeping my parents into the air and smacking them against a pew. My heart pounds in my chest, and my first thought is to push through the screaming crowd and sprint out the giant doors before another gust of wind slams them shut. Stifling a scream, I grab onto Daman, who pushes me aside, the force knocking me to the ground. Daman turns to the back wall, tugging one of the decorative swords out of its slot. Noah covers his mouth, stumbling backward. He's quickly grabbed by his guard.

There's a laugh that comes from the rafters. A woman's voice, deep, raspy, with a twinge of a rough accent and a lisp. As she speaks and even as she laughs, her voice offers a ghostly warped, echoed quality. She has the voice of a shadow-blood, one who has cursed powers of the dead.

"Oh, what a shame," She says. "We seem to have missed the objections."

"Show yourself!" Daman commands, his threatening stentorian voice echoing off the walls.

Her laugh reverberates around the room, overpowering the echo of his scream, only seeming to grow into a menacing crescendo. A tall figure, clad in a black cloak steps into the light, only her tailbone-length ginger mess of curls peeking out. I can only imagine her menacing fanged grin hidden behind the mask covering the lower portion of her face. It's *her*. It's Nightshade, in the flesh.

Nightshade is a terrorist who has plagued The Two Kingdoms, Couteau and Mortem Venenum, for too long. She's a shadow-blood, one who speaks with the dead, one who can move objects midair, who can knock people unconscious with a simple snap, kill them with a single contact with their skin. Not only is she a sickening Supernatural, cursed with illegal, disgusting abilities, but she is both a shadow-blood and a vampire. There's been a price on her head ever since she instigated her dirty rebellion of leeches and scumbags.

"Miss me?" Nightshade sneers at Daman, now sitting on the rafters, one knee propping up her arm.

She snaps her fingers, followed by an echoing snap in the distance, causing the entire audience, including our parents, the priest, and a majority of the guards, to fall unconscious. She laughs at our terror, unclipping her cloak, and letting her somewhat torn bat-wings spread, before leaning backwards, falling from the rafters. She flips midair, and swoops to grab me.

I let out a strangled scream, erupting after holding it in for so long. I kick her in every way I can, trying to worm my way out of her grasp before we get too high off the ground. Daman will catch me. Probably. Maybe. Yeah, no that isn't likely, but I force myself to have an inkling of optimism so I won't spiral out of control. Nightshade grunts, trying to grab me tighter as she flies up to the rafters, before setting me down on a beam, sighing in exasperation.

"Beckett, make sure the princess doesn't try anything," Nightshade orders, before opening up her wings, and plummeting in Daman's direction, her fist extended.

A boy stands up from the audience, sighing as he summons wind from the windows, propelling himself to where I am, sitting beside me in the rafters. He is young, probably not much older than thirteen, if even that, with darker tan skin. He has a mountain of disheveled curls on his head, sharply pointed ears peeking out from them. Two different colored eyes, one green, one brown, with a scar over his right one, gaze through bronze goggles. I realize with mounting horror that he's an elf.

"Well, if it weren't for the fact that heights are *terrifying,*" He says, grabbing onto a pole as tightly as he can and kicking his legs. "I'd say we'd have the best seat in the house!"

Daman is on the ground, his knuckles whitening around his sword, as he growls in frustration, blood dripping down from his nose. A dragon girl grabs him from behind, keeping him in place. I can't see the girl too well from up high, but I can faintly make out her puffy blue hair. Nightshade nods at her, and the girl summons fire to her fist, striking Daman right in the jaw. Daman roars in pain, sweeping his leg and knocking his captor to the ground. She quickly rolls over, and as he stands, she flips herself to twist midair, kicking him in the face, and uses fire to propel herself up. She quickly settles back into a fighting stance.

"If it isn't the prince of the night, still finding disappointments in his journeys to discover a woman's pleasures," The dragon says. "It's been awhile. Wish I could say it was nice to see you– but it's not."

Daman removes his hand from his face, now a broken canvas, covered in ash and blood. He twirls his sword, stepping toward them, nothing but fury in his emerald eyes.

"Well look who's still a dick. What's it like being mommy's obedient little manipulative bigot boy?"

"Don't speak ill of my mother," Daman sneers.

"You know, I'd say I did your mother, but she doesn't deserve me."

Daman swings a fist at her, and she catches it. She's quite tall–just slightly shorter than Nightshade–and incredibly built. Nightshade approaches him from the other side.

"Oh my stars," I whisper. "They're gonna *kill* him."

"No, not yet. Maybe eventually, but not yet," Beckett mutters, watching the scene intently. "But if my calculations are correct-"

8

"Screw you, *Jinx,*" Daman spits, blood ricocheting from his mouth.

"Oh why don't you screw yourself?" Nightshade shoots back, kneeing him in the gut, forcing him to double over. "We all know how much you'd enjoy it."

He plunges his sword into her chest, breathing heavily and shaking as he tries to dig it in deeper. I find myself gasping, startled, to which Beckett just chuckles. Nightshade screams, exaggerating her breath as she falls to her knees.

"I can't... believe... you," she gasps, before her pained, labored breaths turn into laughter, "*fell* for that. Oh, was that supposed to hurt? You do remember those swords are pure decoration, right? Why don't you try silver next time, imbecile?"

The sword hits the ground with a clang. The metal is bent, none of it having punctured her.

"Why do you have to make this so hard?" He growls between his teeth.

"'Cuz she's stubborn like that," The dragon grins, disappearing and reappearing behind Daman.

"Daman, look out!" I scream, but it's too late.

The girl douses the flame of a candle behind her, and whacks the back of his head with the candelabra. Daman falls to the ground, defenseless. I scream and nearly jump, without thinking, when Beckett grabs me.

"Aha, *boomshot*, take that, Daman," He says. "Well, it was nice meeting you! Uh-"

"Nerd boy, let's *go*!" The dragon yells.

"I know, I know, give me a second! Anyway, as I said, nice to meet you, wish this could've been better circumstances! Sorry that I have to leave you up here, but can't have you following us. Bye!"

"Okay, JJ, what's the plan?" The dragon asks Nightshade once Beckett hits the ground. "Do we light the place up, grab the prince, and leave?"

"Not while there are people inside," Nightshade says.

"Okay, yeah, good point," The dragon says.

She turns, and Nightshade snaps once more, leaving Noah's guard unconscious before they strike. Noah offers an expression of pure terror, and the dragon grabs him, slinging him over her shoulder. They leave without another word.

I'm gonna get caught, I'm gonna get caught, I'm gonna get caught-

It's the only thought running through my mind. I've been trailing them for the past hour. My legs are *killing* me. I tossed my shoes behind me forever ago, which was a bad choice, as now sharp pebbles and twigs continuously are injecting themselves into my feet. It's a miracle that none of them have detected my footfalls or used their powers to discover me- or heard my incredibly loud thoughts.

This is stupid, this is stupid, this is so stupid.

Eventually, they reach the end of a village, near the start of a forest, in front of a library. Nightshade stomps her foot on the concrete, and a hidden trap door is revealed. I wait for a good few minutes after they hop down it, before sighing in spite of myself. I rip a dagger out of the holster on my thigh– I always keep one close, just in case, and begin hacking at the train of my dress, and eventually shortening the skirt. It isn't pretty, and my mother would have my head on a platter if she saw me wearing it, but I can't have this dress continuing to weigh me down.

I nearly slip climbing down the rungs of the ladder in the darkness. I land on my feet, nearly cutting my feet on the jagged rock. There's a system of tunnels I didn't know existed. Down the tunnels, the stalactite-covered walls are illuminated by the dragon, who is, quite literally, on fire. In front of her are blue lasers that protrude down the darkness, and I assume they're coming from Beckett, seeing as his goggles are now hanging around his neck.

I follow as quietly as possible, as the three of them talk. Eventually, they stop, and the tunnels shake as Nightshade slowly lifts her head up. A circular trap door slides sidewise from above, and a ladder drops down. The three make their way up, Noah still slumped over the dragon's shoulder. I decide to wait underneath, watching as they forget to close the entrance behind them.

I wait for a while, just sitting there. I get bored of just hearing them continue casual conversation, and climb the ladder myself, peeking out from the top. Sitting there is Noah, except, his posture and overall demeanor have changed. He's got a soft smile on his face as he listens to the dragon yell something from on top of a table.

And the longer I look, the more... *terrifyingly* familiar the dragon looks. She's tall, and I'm short. She, somehow, has built quite a bit of muscle, while I have not, and her skin is slightly darker than my own. My own eyes are gray, her eyes being a bright carnelian.

I'm unscathed, and yet there is a noticeable scar that juts up from the side of her face and upwards toward her nose. Even with these differences, there's no questioning that that is my mother's judgemental expression. The one I've inherited.

Though changed with such detestable, inhuman features, as well as years of age, I remember that face all too well. Both from paintings around the castle, and my own memories. Memories of playing with another little girl, just two years older than me. Playing with her until the room had caught fire, and I was nearly burnt to a crisp. I hadn't known why, and I'd never put it together. That's when my parents had claimed Aella had a deadly illness to be cured of, and I hadn't seen her since. Until now.

There is no mistaking Aella. The first-born. The sister who's destroyed my entire life. I forgo all thinking entering the room.

"So much for 'not giving the princess any intel,'" Beckett sighs, saying the last bit in a mocking French accent. Likely trying to imitate Aella.

"Giving... me- what? I didn't hear anyone say anything about-" I start.

"Telepathy, *bitch*," Aella says, lighting her hand on fire, and turning to Beckett. "And, in any case, she can't say anything if she's dead."

"If you kill me, you'll only be proving that you're monsters," I warn, hating the way my voice shakes.

I slowly tilt my chin, trying to prove superiority.

"I don't give a damn what you think, princess," Aella says, fire extending to both of her forearms.

Noah puts a hand on her shoulder, and she shoves him off. I just close my eyes, and raise my chin higher, now foolishly determined not to give her satisfaction. I convince myself that I'm too stubborn to be scared, though my heart jackrabbits in my chest. I open my eyes and see her standing right in front of me, fist still aflame, though Noah's hand is wrapped around her wrist, the other arm grabbing her waist. Not that it would do much.

"It's not worth it," He says softly.

She sighs, and the flames extinguish. He lets go, and she steps back.

"So... you're with them?" I ask Noah.

"Uh, no?" He says, pushing up his glasses.

Noah picks at his nails, tearing a piece off and shoving it in his pocket. Aella laughs, leaning her elbows on her shoulders and resting her head on his.

"You're so bad at lying," Aella teases.

"I'm technically not lying!" He says, continuing to pick at his nails. "I'm not part of the rebellion. And in any case, it'd be best if she *didn't* know about my involvement. My parents hate me enough, thank you!"

"I won't tell," I say. "I don't agree with this, but I won't tell. Also, Aella-"

"*What?*" She spits.

"Your hair is blue," I say.

"Astute observation, princess."

"Can you stop calling me that? You are literally *also* a princess."

"The only difference is I don't actively agree and associate with mommy and daddy dearest."

I scoff, and she sneers.

"Well," Nightshade says, re-entering the room. "Now that this... reunion is over-"

Noah turns to her, and his face absolutely lights up. He walks over and throws his arms around her.

"You jerk, I was so worried about you," He says.

She hugs him back and I just stand there extremely confused. Why on earth would he be worried about her? Why does he know her at all? What in the names of the constellations is going on? He's hugging her so impossibly tight, so tight that I doubt she's breathing. It's a good long while before they pull back, her hands on his shoulder.

"Did you manage to sneak the shit? Did Hazel have it, and could you grab it before-" Nightshade asks.

"Glad to see you too," Noah crosses his arms, and she waves him off.

He reaches into a bag, and not knowing quite what to trust at this point, I take a step backward, hand hovering near my thigh, in case I need to grab my knife. Instead of pulling out anything dangerous, he pulls out a stack of books. Nightshade grins and sets them on the table, before giving him another quick hug.

"What are those? Secret plans?" I demand.

"They'll shoot her if she goes to the library," Beckett supplies, holding a blowtorch and removing a welding mask from his face, leaving behind only his goggles.

Aella shoots him a look and he sticks out his tongue. He lowers the mask back over his face, and goes back to whatever it was he was doing on the cave floor.

"Noah, do you care to explain... what in the names of the constellations is happening?" I ask.

"Not really, sorry," He says, apologetically, scratching at the back of his neck.

"How about now?" I say, grabbing my dagger.

While I don't know much, I've convinced Sabine to teach me to fight, lest I end up in a situation in which I needed to defend myself. Situations such as this. Situations in which people thought they could take things away from me, and then ignore me without a second thought.

"Oh *finally*," Aella says, lighting her arm on fire.

I stumble backwards, grabbing a shield from off the wall. Nightshade sighs, and hits a lever on the wall of the cave. A large chunk at the front of the cave rises upwards, emitting a loud whirring noise. I lunge for Nightshade–rather than Noah, because I do like Noah well enough. I feel a gust of wind push me down, and then out of the cave.

"Sorry!" Beckett yells, followed by a quiet, "Not really, though."

I hit the dirt. Rising quickly, I dust the dirt off of my dress. Aella disappears, reappearing in front of me. I jab at her. She disappears before I can land the blow, appearing behind me. I spin around, striking the dagger into her right shoulder. She jerks in pain and I grab it back, spinning it in the air, and attempting a high kick. She grabs me with her left arm, throwing my leg to the ground. I hit the ground. She doesn't make a move.

"You sure you want to mess with me? Because I've just been itching to do this," Aella looks down at me, crossing her arms. She seems... unphased that she's been stabbed. Which is the exact opposite of what I was going for.

"You don't have to do anything, if you're dead," I respond.

I sweep my leg around, hoping to knock her off of her feet. It doesn't work. Of course it doesn't, why would it? She leaves the dagger in her shoulder, and I get up. She doesn't stop me. Nightshade slowly emerges from outside of the cave. I turn around, facing my back to Nightshade. I reach under my dress, fingers lingering over the dagger attached to the holster on my other thigh. I draw it out slowly, tilting up my chin and keeping eye contact with Aella as I twist the handle between my fingers. I wait for the right moment, taking a step backward so that Aella thinks I'm ceasing.

I jolt my fingers backwards. For whatever reason, I know exactly where it's going, as if I can feel the surrounding energy of the objects around me. Which shouldn't be possible, but that's an issue for later. Right now I need to fight two impossible foes, grab Noah, and hopefully make it out of this alive. However when I turn around I see–

Nightshade standing there, the dagger between her teeth. Though her fangs seem to be hidden within her mouth, her teeth are stained a dark red. She places the handle of the blade between her fingers, biting down hard on the blade and dragging it out agonizingly slow. There's a high-pitched squeak, grinding out slowly as she edges along as slowly as she could.

If she scratches my dagger with her stupid teeth, I'm going to make her beg for mortality. A slight sinister smile spreads across her lips, which are now dripping with a black ooze that I can only assume is her own blood.

"I guess we're doing this then," She says with a bow, eyes turning black, and voice warping.

I turn back to Aella, who's now gone invisible. I watch in horror as the air around me grows warmer and warmer, a wild raging ring of flames walling me in. It surrounds me from all sides.

Two arms grab me from behind, grabbing my arms firmly and holding me in place.

"Struggling is pointless," Nightshade says, voice still warped and betraying no emotion, her black eyes chillingly empty. "Try to fight us, and despite your efforts, you will fail."

I know at this point that I am in over my head. Despite that, there is no way that I'm giving up. I'm stubborn, and I have a need to prove myself. So I decide, idiot that I am, that I am, in fact, going to fight Nightshade and Aella. Relying on Aella continuing to hold me in place, I kick upwards at Nightshade, hoping to knock her backwards. It doesn't do much. I kick Nightshade in the stomach, and though she grunts out in pain, my efforts are to no avail. She stays in the ring. Aella drops me to the ground once I meet air, and I fall to the ground *hard*.

"Wow," Aella laughs, mockingly. "Stars, princess, sit down before you hurt yourself."

"No," I spit, standing back up. "I'm not about to let you monsters take this from me. Not when *you've* already ruined my life enough as it is."

I reach for my blade and hoist it backward, preparing to throw it at Aella. Deathly cold fingers wrap around my wrist. For a blissful moment, I'd forgotten Nightshade entirely. I drop the dagger, catch it in my other hand, and strike Nightshade in the side. While she recovers, I kick her in the knee as hard as I possibly can. When it buckles, I shove her into the flames, which momentarily open for her. I use the moment the flames are open to make my escape.

"Noah, c'mon," I yell to the cave. "I don't know what they did to mess with your head, but we gotta *go* while they're distracted."

"Oh my stars," He says, looking at the scene ahead with a disturbing amount of concern. "What happened?"

"I happened," I say, picking twigs and rocks out of my bloody foot.

"... Veronica, for the sake of the stars," He sighs, picking at a chipped nail.

"Noah, we both know the implications of what they've done. I had to do *something*."

"You really didn't," Nightshade says, suddenly behind me.

Lovely.

"My deepest apologies, princess," She says, holding me in place as Beckett tosses her a vial.

She catches it, almost effortlessly. I shove my mouth closed. No, no, no, no no. This can still go my way. I can still salvage this situation. I'm in charge, I can do it, I just have to get it under control. I can still be the hero here. I'm not useless, they'll see, they'll *all* see. I have a purpose. I'm not helpless, I'm not the scared princess in the shadows everyone thinks I am.

At least, these are the thoughts running through my head as I squirm helplessly. Managing to keep me in place, Nightshade pops off the cork, pouring a shimmering purple liquid onto a patch of fabric, which she holds against my face. It smells of poppies, and chamomile, of chemicals, and of failure. I am so sick of being helpless. I am so sick of being exactly what everyone thinks I am. I want to be better. I want to be fought for.

"Stop fighting, darling. Rest now, we won't hurt you. You weren't supposed to be here," Nightshade whispers, words becoming more and more distant.

My body becomes lethargic, and I go limp. I try to fight it. I really did. I try so hard. But my eyes get heavier... and heavier... and heavier. It's impossible. And who am I to continuously try to fight the impossible?

Chapter 2
Veronica

I awake in my own bed. My mother is crying. Apparently I'd "worried her to death."

Maybe I should make stupid decisions more often, I think.

What's less surprising is that my parents are not as concerned about my wellbeing, and more concerned about the political implications of the wedding. Parents of the century. They've been known to neglect many things. My people would've starved the previous few winters if it weren't for myself secretly attending to their duties. They don't seem to realize having a kingdom means having to run it. Or having an heir means having to raise it.

After all, my parents are supposedly too busy trying to cure my older sister, the future queen, of an incurable illness. My role in the family is to secure our peace with the kingdom Mortem Venenum by marrying the crown prince and future king, Daman. I hate the entire idea that my worth is only determined by submitting myself to marriage, yet what needs to be done needs to be done. Especially when this would be the act to officially secure our kingdoms together. I'm just lucky to have fallen in love with him. Sometimes he can be... intense and rather frightening or controlling, but he has a lot going on. And I love him. It's expected of me anyway.

If anyone from any kingdom knows anything, it's that the Woods get their way. They have a well-run kingdom because they rule with an iron fist. I'm told my parents and ancestors ruled the same way until my parents neglected their duties for Aella.

Things would've been different by now. If it weren't for those horrid scumbags.

I decide I'll figure out the entire Aella situation on my own. I'll admit, it is for a bit of self-indulgent revenge against everyone. Today my parents are out, doing some fake charity event that would only benefit them.

I don't know much of what happened after my attempt to fight Nightshade and Aella. After my mother left my room, Sabine sat on the edge of my bed and told me everything she knew. Guards had been called, causing Nightshade and Beckett to flee the scene. Aella was taken captive, kicking and screaming, cussing them out. Beckett had tried to run back for her, but Nightshade forced him to keep running.

According to Sabine, there's been rumors that she's been living with some peasant family in Mortem Venenum, and has regularly been escaping the castle. What's worse, is this has been happening for years, and of course, I knew nothing of it.

Once I no longer felt as sick, I decided I wanted answers.

"Everything's secure," Sabine reports. "No one is following us."

"Good. Absolutely no one is to know about this, understood?"

"Yes, Your Highness."

We remain mostly in silence, only the tapping of our feet against the floor echoing in the halls. We creep into the strategy room, staring suspiciously at the fire across the room, the one rumored to be fake. My heart is stuck in my throat, a volcano erupting in my stomach, an impending sense of doom only increasing with every step. Every nerve in my body twitches, begging me to run away. I have to betray all logic to satisfy my curiosity, whatever the cost. I brace myself, sticking my arm into the fire, clamping my mouth shut so I couldn't scream. I pull my arm back in pain and horror, expecting to see it charred to a crisp, only to find myself completely fine.

"It's... fake," Sabine whispers in disbelief.

I gulp and step through the fire, immediately tripping down a flight of stairs. My flesh is torn through by the stone, leaving fresh blood dripping down my knees and elbows, my lip now split. I cover my mouth, trying to hold back a whimper, the pain of the sting rising like a crescendo of fresh, raw violence. I grab a railing, the metal nearly freezing to the touch, though traces of warmth become noticeable as I continue to stumble down the flights of spiral stairs. Aella's voice can faintly be heard. I don't know how either of us got back to the castle, or how Aella got out in the first place. I've been told that wherever she was being kept in the castle, my parents were getting top scientists to figure out how to fix her. However, she and her stupid magic are stubborn, so it never worked. However, all beakers, all the science shit, the experimental tools were all left on a table, not in use.

A familiar person, a girl barely a few months older than Aella comes into view. I know who she is. I don't know her personally, but I've seen her in passing. Her name is Leona, and she's been working in the castle for the past five years. She's one of the few knights trained in interrogation and torture, I know that for a fact.

"Oh my stars," Aella says, just out of view "Pull harder."

"Stop that," Leona snaps. "Are you always such a disappointment?"

"Sorry Leona, I don't have a degradation kink," Aella patronizes.

Stars, Aella is annoying. Part of me is glad I didn't grow up around her.

"This isn't a joke, Aella," Leona says, and I can hear Aella yell in pain, something creaking from the room. "You won't think this is so funny when I'm tearing you limb from limb."

"That sounds real sexy," Aella breathes. "Maybe on our next date."

I step to the side, managing to find a crack in the wall in which I can take a small peek. Aella's wings are torn, and she looks disheveled and bloody. She's shaking, beads of sweat falling down her face. It's hard to tell whether or not the awkward flirting was all a ruse... or if she's just... like that.

"I don't get paid enough for this," Leona groans.

Aella laughs, licking her teeth, hands lighting on fire.

"Aww, were you not having fun, Leo?" Aella asks.

"I'm going on break," Leona shakes her head, leaving the room. "I'll get answers eventually."

Leona is gone before Aella can make a prod at that. Aella winces a bit, seemingly now able to react to the pain. Despite this, she's laughing her ass off once Leona is out of earshot.

"Well," Aella says, breathing heavily. "That hurt like a bitch."

"You're lucky that worked," Nightshade says, stepping into view.

"Eh, these people have no backbone. I was bound to push her to a breaking point at some point," Aella dismisses, as Nightshade gets to work removing her from the Catherine wheel.

"Y'know, this would be easy to dismantle and use for parts," Beckett suggests, giddy, tapping his fingers together in glee as he stepped into view.

"Don't even think about it, nerd boy," Aella shakes her head, rolling her wrists. "I'm getting the hell out of here."

She steps down, leaning her hand against a piece of foundation and taking a breath. Beckett grumbles in disappointment, his eyes darting between the Catherine wheel and the tools in his pocket.

"I wouldn't be so sure about that," I slide into the room, my sapphire cape trailing behind me.

"Oh, good, a distraction!" Beckett giggles, leaning down to start disassembling it. He groans in disappointment as Aella drags him away.

I tsk, chuckling, my hand to my lips as I step toward them. Pieces on the chessboard, I've got them in a check. Aella lights a hand on fire, and Nightshade grabs an arrow from the quiver resting on her hips. She loads the bow on her back and infuses it with black tendrils of death-energy.

"Did Evsaphine and Lucius send you down here to spy on me?" Aella sneers.

"Mother and Father are elsewhere," I say. "I'm here because I want answers."

"Too bad," Aella says, grabbing Beckett by the collar, lifting him into the air like a cat.

Beckett gives a sad sigh, and drops several gears on the ground. I take another step in, and Nightshade raises an eyebrow. Aella rolls her eyes, and keeps dragging Beckett out of the room.

"I think I'm entitled to some answers," I say.

"You think you're entitled to everything, princess," Aella says.

I stop walking. This isn't fair. None of this is fair. She's working for Nightshade and her stupid little rebellion. She's going to be queen. My parents know about her involvement. Of course they know. Apparently it's common knowledge among many outside of the castle. And yet... they still love *her*. No matter what *I* sacrifice, no matter what I do.

They

Favor

Her.

There's a faint humming in the back of my head. I don't think much of it, I never do. I just assume it's something everyone else experiences, and if not, it must be some weird supernatural mind trick. It's annoying, and it doesn't matter.

"That's not fair," I say.

"Yeah? *Nothing's* fair. That's why we're doing shit about it. Grow up, princess," Aella says.

"Hey," Nightshade says, putting a hand on Aella's shoulder.

Aella winces and Nightshade retracts her hand, quietly apologizing. Aella continues to walk, stumbling. Nightshade bends over slightly, Aella throws an arm around her, and the three of them walk out.

I don't follow them. I call for Sabine once they leave, and explain what I'd seen. How quiet Nightshade had been. How Aella had gone through pain with a smile. Beckett wasn't much different from the last time I'd seen him. I don't tell my parents. I don't tell anyone else. Daman knows that I know. He can tell I'm lying about something. How I get quiet whenever he asks about Nightshade, about Aella, about the rebellion. He's angry, he calls me a liar. He knows we're both liars. It isn't my fault. It isn't his fault.

All of this, everything, is Aella's fault. It's Aella's fault, and Nightshade's.

And I...

I want to hurt them. I want to hear their relinquished screams. I want everyone to know that I was the one to bring them to justice. I have to be graceful. I have to be perfect. I need it, desire for it, lust for it. I lust for the power, for the attention, thirsting for it as if it's air taken from my lungs far too long ago. I need to be perfect, I need the attention. I want to be loved. No. No, it's too late for that.

I want to be *feared*. Then they'll look. Then they'll listen. Then they will *all* see. And... maybe someone will even be proud.

Chapter 3
Veronica

I lay in the bath, every part of my body seeming to sting and burn in the warm water, as I sink deeper and deeper still, the water slowly turning crimson. I can't tell what is real. My roots are stiff with blood, as I scrub it out of my braids. I try to scrub the blood off my body, but I only seem to be making more. I can't stop screaming, even as I sink deeper and deeper into the bath, that now feels more like an ocean, submerging myself. I can still see them. They ruined everything. They will still be after me, as long as I live, unless I snuff them out first, I'm sure of it.

Daman had taken me out for the night, without guards. In comparison to the forests of Couteau, the forests of Mortem Venenum are relatively harmless, granted you don't provoke the surrounding plant life. We'd been drinking, I forget what Daman had given me, but whatever it was, it was strong. It just so happened Nightshade and her little rebellion were out for the night— however Aella and Beckett were absent this time. A dragon with purple wings, an elf with white hair, and someone else with bright green hair stood in their absence. I don't remember much of what happened, I was tired, my mind foggy. I just remember swords, and arrows and this... awful energy. The buzzing in the back of my head returned...

I remember pulling out my dagger. I remember swords hitting my skin, though who's I cannot remember. I remember Daman shouting a little at Nightshade, a little at me, barely regarding the others at all. I remember Sabine yelling at Daman, and I remember yelling at Sabine. I can't remember the squabble. I can't remember how I got here.

Stars, I wish I did. I hope I taught the rebellion I wasn't one to mess with.

But... the blood is sticking to my skin. Warped memories stick too, sinking in the bath with me, disappearing every time I get close enough to reach them.

I'm losing Daman. I'm losing the one thing I have. The Two Kingdoms are laughing at me. They are laughing at me, I swear to the stars, I know they are. I'm not enough.

I'm nothing special. That's why they won't look. That's why no one ever stays. That's why I'm alone all of the time. I try. I try to be more than mediocre. I'm a princess, for the sake of the stars.

I sink beneath the water, only realizing I'm screaming once water enters my lungs. I have to be imagining that. After all, my chest is already *so* tight. It's not like that is unusual. Sometimes... sometimes my chest tightens, and I get lightheaded and have trouble breathing. I used to be scared, sometimes that it would kill me, but eventually it just became normal to me.

"Your highness, are you alright?" Sabine asks, walking into my room.

I slowly raise my head, resting it against the edge of the bath. I look at her for a while. She just stands in the dim candle-light, staring idiotically.

"Obviously, I'm doing just fine. My life has never been so wonderful. I love getting my freedom and marriage stolen from me, and then nearly, y'know, getting murdered. Are you kidding me? Stars, and you people think *I'm* an imbecile."

"I'm sorry, Your Highness," Sabine lowers her head.

"Don't be, I misspoke, I'm sorry. Why are you here, exactly? Shouldn't you be finishing your hours outside my door?"

"I heard you screaming."

"I could've sworn that was only in my mind," I whisper.

She shakes her head. I take a shaky breath, and she tosses me a towel... I could swear I'm still caked in layers of blood, holding in a scream as I watch the towel become soaked in blood. I squeeze my eyes tightly as I drag the soft white towel across my body, though it becomes coarse and rough, as if the fibers had become spikes. I drop the towel in the bath, collapsing to my knees. All I can hear is screams. Though, again, I can't tell whether or not my voice is leading the horrid chorus, let alone if it's a part of the choir at all. Vaguely, I can hear Sabine calling my name.

It grows further, further, further still, as if I am beneath the water, beneath the waves, drowning in my own terror. It will never get better. They are going to get me- Nightshade is going to kill me one day– and everyone will laugh and look away. The buzzing in my head grows louder and louder, as various objects fly around the room.

On their own, I swear. The objects are moving on their own.

The only noise in the dining hall is my silverware scratching against the plate. I have my head lying on the table, dragging my fork back and forth across the plate, idly. Once again, I'm used to this. Once again, my parents are always too busy with "breakthroughs" or "training Aella" to show up to dinner on time. As I grow older, I don't care as much. I have other company at most times. An occasional conversation with a maid, if they feel like it. Long chats with Sabine. Things will change. We'll capture Nightshade, I'll marry Daman, and things will be different. The Woods seem to care for me, at least.

And so here I sit, and I sit, and I sit. I'm not going to let my food go cold again. I stopped waiting for them when I turned twelve. After seven years of getting stood up on family dinners, you get used to it. You stop waiting. You stare at the rose gold plates, and the feast that will go to waste of food the rest of the kingdom likely wouldn't be able to afford to even *look at* within their entire lifetime.

That night is different. That night, Aella isn't in the castle. So, as a result, that night, they show up. I almost wish that they didn't. They seem as faceless as ever as the candles dim. That's all they are, shadows upon the butterfly pea flower tea colored walls.

"Well, look who decided to show up," I murmur to myself.

"We talked about the mumbling, dear," My mother says. "Would it kill you to sit up straight?"

I sigh and sit up as straight as I possibly can. My mother nods in approval. Servants walk alongside my parents, pulling out chairs for each of them. The servants place food on their plate, and not so much as a word is exchanged between them. The servants bow, and leave the room. My parents don't thank them, barely even acknowledge their own presence. Part of me wonders if they know how to acknowledge anything without judgment, if they can acknowledge things at all.

"How's the search for the golden child?" I ask, poking at my food.

"Manners," My mother says, nodding at my plate.

I groan. My parents give me a sharp look. I don't care. Neither do they, clearly. They never answer my question. It's like I'd never spoken. We eat in silence for a good majority of the dinner. It doesn't matter. Really. I don't care, I promise.

The doors open once again. Another servant, one I don't recognize. Still, complete silence. The servant bows, and hands my mother a letter. The servant isn't acknowledged. Not once. My mother peels the wax off the seal of the letter and sets it beside her plate.

"Well, the Woods certainly don't delay," My mother mumbles.

"What is it, my queen?" My father asks.

"Another ball. Likely trying to raise spirits in lue of... that girl," My mother says, sneering at that last bit.

"That doesn't seem safe," I say. "We're not going, right?"

"Don't be ridiculous, of course we are," My mother says, dismissing me with a flap of her hand.

"Nightshade *just* broke into the castle. That in itself is a major security breach, and she usually doesn't try to pull crimes in *our* kingdom. Not to mention she took Aella with her, breached my wedding, and attacked me and Daman!" I say, exasperated.

"Don't worry, we're going to locate Aella," My father says, staring down at his food.

"I don't care about Aella! I'm concerned for *my* safety, quite frankly! Aella is clearly working with them, and they're out to get me. Stars, it's like I'm talking to the air!"

"Stop being selfish," My father says.

"We have to go, we have to show the public that everything is fine and we're not afraid."

There it is. Making sure they impress the Woods, keeping public appearances for the commoners that they don't give an honest shit about. No one in this star forsaken family has an honest bone in their body.

I can suck it up. I can fake a smile. I can put on a show for the kingdom. Perhaps I'll get wrapped up in this magnificent lie. Maybe, just maybe, if I stick myself in the tide long enough, I'll be pulled somewhere better. Maybe I'll become someone better.

I sigh as I stare at myself in the mirror. I force myself to be composed. I'm pretty enough. I'm wearing a dress made exclusively of sapphires woven into a light blue silk gown. Beneath it are layers of petticoats made of pure silver that just barely peek out from beneath my gown. The laces of my corset, as well as the bones of the underbust are also silver. Hopefully this will protect me from her. I insist that there be more, so I also wear a cape of silver. The metal hangs like a waterfall from the top of my neck, laced like a choker with strings of sapphires. Matching earrings fall to my shoulders.

In fact, strands of blue had been woven into my braids, along with bits of silver, half of my braids put in a neat bun resting on top of my hair, accompanied by a tiara. The rest of my braids fall just over my shoulder.

If Nightshade manages to invade the ball, she won't be able to lay a finger on me.

I take a deep breath, and Sabine takes me by the hand. She leads me out of my chamber, down the stairs. She lets go of my hand, as neither of us are prepared to explain our friendship to my parents, as we reach the front door to the castle. There are two carriages waiting in front of us. One is a soft blue, the other a faded, dusty rose, both adorned in gold. My parents are already in carriages. A few minutes later, Sabine scoots closer to me as the carriage jostles along on route to Mortem Venenum. She leans close, lips nearly touching my ear, leaving prickles of goosebumps up my arms.

"Noli timere," she whispers. "Ego te incolumem custodiat." *Don't be afraid. I will keep you safe.*

In the Two Kingdoms, everyone is fluent in English, our native sign language, and Latin, though the latter language is used often for emotional emphasis. Some individuals in Couteau also learn French, usually as a status symbol showing connection to the original rulers. I know enough to carry a conversation, but not much beyond that. My parents had always prioritized Aella learning. After all, she's going to be queen of Couteau one day.

"Promise?" I whisper.

Her left hand slides behind her back, but her right hand gently closes around mine. She runs her thumb over my hand, hestating a moment. Eventually she smiles at me, gently, something hidden behind her eyes.

"Promise."

Balls are always disgustingly loud, and the noise almost causes me to crumble each time without fail. But I can't crumble, no, cannot fail, not when I have to make them damn sure they know who the hell their future princess is, hell, who their future *queen* is. To make them aware of the blood she's not afraid to adorn herself with. After all, Aella was to inherit a kingdom of swamps and fog, and I was to marry into a kingdom of gold and blood.

"Now presenting," A man shouted above the crowd, as I descended down the stairs, relishing the stares. "Her royal highness, Princess Veronica Helena Isolabella Belladonna of the Kingdom of Couteau."

Beautiful people, all in masks littered the black ballroom floor, moving inwards away from the red velvet walls. Gowns spin to the tune of the orchestra, gloved hands clasping together. Gold flakes and rubies are engraved in the floor, and adorned the low hanging chandeliers clad in lit candles.

They're all watching. Don't mess this up. I think. *Oh stars, they're all staring. They're whispering. They're all judging– is that person laughing?*

I try to shake off the thoughts, straightening my posture and providing my practiced smile. Hours spent in front of the mirror, just for my stupid face to look presentable to these leeches. I give a wave, hoping for the motions to fall into place as I descend down the stairs. I keep my head up, resisting the urge to watch and make sure each foot hits each stair.

Steady yourself. If you're not perfectly careful, you'll twist your ankle, and you'll fall down the stairs, and everyone will see, and they'll all see how pathetic you really are. They'll know. They'll be right.

I stop halfway down the stairs, as I've practiced many times before, as I always have done. Just as always. The creak echoes throughout the room as a woman steps out.

"Now presenting his royal highness, Daman Zagan Woods of Kingdom Mortem Venenum."

Daman steps out, wearing a deep red tunic and a dark black cape, a crown made of spikes and wires as dark as a starless night sky sitting upon his blonde hair. He shoots me an eye roll as he is announced, and I respond with a mockingly pretentious curtsey. I can see him laugh– just slightly. It's validating. I continue to descend down the stairs, the ballroom separating as the two of us move to meet one another. My white gloved hand falls neatly into the black silk that covers his, as he pulls me into position.

The sound of a low violin note fills the ballroom as Daman bows, his charming smirk glinting in the moonlight as I follow with a curtsey. He firmly places my hand on his shoulder, leading me into the dance. At some point, he forces me backwards, his chest on top of mine as he drops me into a sudden dip, nearly dropping me for a second as he grabs my waist and lifts me into the air, spinning me above him.

"What-" I started.

"Shh, don't question it," He says.

I feel like I'm flying. I hope I don't look stupid in my reaction to this sudden adjustment. He moves my body to the front of his, threading me to fall beneath his legs, lying on the floor as he spins me around. Eventually he picks me up and flies me through the air once more, bringing me back down to my feet, but steadying me so I don't fall. He grabs me by the finger, jerking my body as he spins me around, and around and around. As I begin to fall he grabs me roughly, sending me into a dip, one leg extending into the air, as the band plays one final note, signaling that our dance is over. Our breaths became the only audible noise, before applause rings throughout the ballroom once more.

I close my eyes, soaking it all in. The attention, the glamor, all of it. I stay enthralled by the adrenaline and adoration even after the applause ceases and the others move to take their own places on the dance floor. At last, he jerks me up, my silver eyes meeting his emerald eyes.

"That was different," I tease.

"It's only a start," He says, and I try not to tense when he grabs me by the chin. "It's only a taste of what almost was."

"And what will be," I say. "We're not going to let that sickening supernatural get in the way of our future."

"Your optimism is naive. Sometimes, it's safer not to have any hope at all," he says, twirling me around. "Stay where I can see you, I have business to attend to."

He leans forward, planting a kiss on my cheek. And just like that, he's gone, and I am beside myself once more. I make my way to a nearby couch, lifting the hem of my dress as I sit, trying not to slouch and spread my legs. Act like a lady, look like a lady. Be just the way they molded me to be. I just have to stop being so useless.

After I suffer a few minutes of sulking, she approaches. She's in a black ball gown, covered in crimson laces, and jewels resembling bats pinned to various pieces of her dress. Strands of her dark ginger hair seem to hang to her knees. Behind her bright red mask covered in red lace and bat gemstones, are two all too familiar bright, icey sapphire eyes.

"Stars," I sigh. "You're so... *annoying*. How did you manage to get in here?"

"I'd almost think you aren't pleased to see me," Nightshade drawls, wearing a smug look.

"I'm not. Answer the question."

She chuckles to herself, voice echoing for the first time during this conversation. She looks different than I'd expected. Her ice blue eyes are piercing, cold, freezing me in place, dark shadows surrounding them. Her face is softer than I thought it would be, though her nose is sharp. She sits down beside me, swinging one leg over the arm of the couch, one arm resting on the cushion behind my head.

"The Woods are simple minded, particularly when it comes to extravagance such as this. Security is lower than you'd think, darling. Also, I have eyes and ears within the castle."

"Don't call me darling," I strike, scooting away from her. "And no one in their right mind would spy for you."

"You'd be surprised, darling," she states.

Oh that *bitch*. She stands slowly, before extending her hand out to me. She is the harmony in the song of agony, and anarchy, yet she has the audacity to reach for my hand and ask,

"Waltz with me?"

And what's worse is that I don't think to put up a fight. Daman is somewhere on the opposite side of the room, some nobleman's rich daughter with her arm around him. I force myself not to be jealous. That, and I'm painfully bored. So, I sigh, roll my eyes, and oblige. The worst part of it all is that she's a good dancer. All of it is so perfectly practiced, moving in time, as if she's done it before. I keep expecting her to step on my feet, or to miss a beat. She doesn't. Not once.

Stars, she's annoying.

She laughs, spinning me around. She slides her hands around my waist, still perfectly in time to the music. That *bitch*, why can't she just make *one* mistake?

"Whatever you're doing," I say, careful not to miss my steps as I tilt up my chin. "You won't get away with it."

"Oh darling, I'm afraid you won't be able to stop us," She pulls me into a gentle dip, her lips hovering a hair's breadth away from mine.

"You're evil," I whisper, ashamed as heat rises in my face.

She pulls me back up into a twirl, before placing her hands against my waist once more, pulling me closer as we spin about the floor.

"Oh darling, evil is in the eye of the beholder," She whispers, her breath cold.

"Beauty," I snap my eyes up to meet hers.

"What was that?"

"You misquoted," I step toward her, abruptly taking the lead.

"Did I?" She asks, pulling me closer.

"The phrase is 'beauty is in the eye of the beholder,'" I shoot, heat rising in my face.

She dips me back down, "Evil, beauty, it's all relative, all a construct. Sweetheart, we created a world, we can destroy and rebuild in an instant if only we have the power to manipulate others. Isn't that in itself beautiful, yet also inherently evil?"

"You're speaking utter nonsense."

"Oh, our world is utter nonsense, darling. Come with me."

I find myself listening to her yet again. I don't want to. At the same time, it's so painfully loud in here. It's loud and hot, and not to mention the putrid smell of hundreds of bodies all too close. I roll my eyes as she offers her hand, taking my hand in hers. She flings open a dark purple velvet curtain, pulling me beside her and shielding us both with the curtain. She turns to the arched glass doorway, slowly creaking it open. She quickly shuts the door behind us as we step out onto the courtyard.

"What is this for, exactly?" I ask. "What is your plan here? Why did you-"

"You seemed overwhelmed," She shrugs.

She saw right through me. I need to get better at hiding it, especially when Nightshade is such a present threat.

I've never seen the courtyard at night. It's lovely, I'll have to admit. The vines wrap around the arches leading out of the ballroom, glowing a light violet, green flowers glowing somehow brighter than the vines. The gravel path is covered in sparkling stepping stones, the sides lined with glowing teal rose bushes. I hear bubbling from nearby, as a large fountain presents itself, circled by five benches. The air is prickling, so cold as it bites at my skin that it nearly seems to burn. Despite it all, it's better than the humid, putrid smelling, incredibly loud ballroom.

From up here, the image of the kingdom burns into my eyes. Not because of anything in particular. Only because here it's floral and beautiful, and down there... down there is the city. A city that looks so dull, diluted, and decrepit from up here.

"Never snuck out, I take it?" Nightshade asks, one eyebrow raised as her lips settle into a smirk.

"I'm not a delinquent, like you," I awkwardly cross my arms, tossing my braids backwards and lifting my chin. "I have no need to leave things, as *I* am *always* honored with an invitation, unlike dirty *villains* such as yourself. However, it seems as if it's certainly not your first time sneaking out of one of these..."

"You're so cute when you try to act superior. And to answer your question, no not in the slightest. You have no idea how many of these ridiculous balls I've had to sit through."

31

"Like you'd be invited," I cross my arms.

"Who said I had a choice?" Her features darken, as she steals a glance back to the castle. Her lips mischievously quirk up. "Although, I have crashed most of them."

I scoff and shake my head, though her attention is no longer on me. Not that I care, because I don't. I don't need validation, especially not from *Nightshade* of all people.

"Why are you here, Nightshade?" I sharpen.

She doesn't respond, simply turns her blue eyes up to the stars. She hums to herself, attention seemingly fixed on the moon. She walks along the path, kicking at gravel with her heels. She mumbles something about it being a clear night, her eyes remaining on the sky. Her eyes quickly turn to the windows, and a grin spreads across her face. She's far more expressive than I'd imagined from behind the lower mask and the hood.

Then there's shattering screams from overhead, red glass raining onto the courtyard.

Nightshade grabs me by the arm, pulling me away. She holds onto me, covering me with her wings. If she taught me anything, it's that mercy is a lie. A beautifully morbid lie. Although I'm a master of deception, I have not become proficient in the puppetry of mercy, always getting terribly twisted in my own intangible ties.

"You still have the ring," Nightshade mumbles.

"Yeah, no shit," I say.

She folds her wings back in, but doesn't let go of me. I shove her, but it does nothing. I try to step on her foot, and she calmly moves it. She lets go of me with one arm, and as I try to struggle out of her grip, she continues to hold me tightly with the other. She uses her free arm to inspect my hand– the one with the engagement ring on it. When she grabs for it, there's a hissing noise and she winces, letting go.

"Stop that," I say. "Let me go."

"I'm afraid I can't do that, princess."

I look down at my ring, flipping it between my fingers so that the jewel faces upside down. It presses into my palm as I close my finger into a fist. I pull my arm backward, before launching my fist into her throat. She falls backward, still holding onto me, a mark now firmly burned into her throat.

It sizzles and bubbles, the smell of burning beginning to seep into the courtyard. I place my knee on her chest, trying to figure out my next play.

"Stars, you're stubborn," She breathes.

"And you're a bitch," I say.

She flips me off of her, hopping to her feet. She grabs me by the wrists, and I try to twist out of her grip, to no avail. I dig the point of my heel into her foot, and she doesn't even wince.

Stars, I hate vampires, I think, and she chuckles.

"Why are you like this?" I sigh.

"It's more fun this way," She shrugs, extending her wings and stretching.

There's more crashing noises from overhead.

"Ow," Beckett says from above.

Beckett winces, grabbing something out of his satchel, pouring something from a vial onto his hand, and then wrapping a cloth around it. Aella emerges behind him, a teasing look on her face.

"Y'know, you could've just used your laser eyes, nerd boy."

Beckett pauses for a moment. He then immediately facepalms. She laughs, grabbing his tophat so she can ruffle his hair.

"I may be stupid," He says. "I'm not jumping."

"Okay," She shrugs.

He looks down, waves at me, and then turns to leave. Aella simply grabs him with her arm, flipping him around and slinging him over her shoulder. He yelps and tries to squirm out of her grasp, which in turn distracts me from trying to escape Nightshade. She covers Beckett's mouth with her free hand, running backward and leaping out of the window. His scream is muffled. She spreads out orange wings, which were hidden under a black waist length cloak. She lands on her feet, before gently lowering Beckett to his.

"You okay?" She asks.

Beckett is literally shaking. He still gives her a weak smile and a thumbs-up.

"JJ, we gotta go, we got caught," Aella says, turning to Nightshade.

She doesn't even look at me. Bitch.

"And the others?" Nightshade asks.

"Beck and I made sure they got out," Aella says.

Okay, well, they're leaving now. That's a good sign, right? I can go back inside, and find Daman and pretend that nothing happened. Right?

"The princess is still wearing the ring. I was sure Isolde would've held it for safekeeping, but luckily for us, my theory was incorrect. Unfortunately, it's silver, so I haven't been able to slip it off. It'll be difficult to cancel the wedding, let alone postpone it as long as she still has this."

"Well... I'm not gonna take it off," I say, closing my hand into a tight fist, the jewel digging into my palm.

Beckett frowns, and Aella shoots Nightshade a look. After a minute of complete staring, I realize that they're all speaking telepathically. I just stare at them for a minute, inhale, and start screaming. A few seconds pass. Aella opens up her mouth to say something, and I just scream again.

"Nightshade and the others are out here!" I yell as loud as I possibly can, running for the doors.

"Shit," Aella sighs.

It's mere seconds before Nightshade catches me.

"You two can go, please get somewhere safe and transmit to me wherever you're going," Nightshade says, a hint of laughter in her tone. "I'll handle the princess. Beckett, can you hand me the-"

"Mhm!" He smiles and digs through his satchel.

He tosses a vial over to Nightshade, and another cloth. Then he and Aella walk off without another word. It's just me and Nightshade now. What she doesn't know, however, is I have something... something besides daggers and silver, hidden under my layers of hoops and petticoats.

Legend says that if you drive a wooden stake through the heart of a vampire, they will die. No revival, no afterlife. Just a simple death. Quite painful death actually, as I've been told. I just so happen to have collected several in my years of collecting... well... a variety of speared objects. I have built a bigger holster to attach the stake to my leg, and I slowly unsheath it.

"Beg for mercy," I whisper.

"Why should I?"

I pull out the stake, holding it shakily. Her eyes widen, her brows upturning, yet her pupils continue to dilate, eyes turning completely back. Her breathing shakes, seeming to vibrate with my trembling fingers.

"You wouldn't," She gapes.

"Oh, I *would*," I grin. "Now, you're gonna listen to me, and, if I feel in a good mood, I'll let you live."

"You know darling, you're adorable when you're on a vengeance rampage."

"I'm going to kill you," I grit, trying not to scream in her face.

"You see, that's where you're wrong," She grins.

"Wanna test that theory?"

I plunge the stake towards her heart, squeezing my eyes shut at the last minute. Her ice-cold hand grabs my wrist, nearly breaking it, stopping my arm mid attack. I open my eyes to see hers wide and afraid as she looks back at me. For a moment she looks almost human, almost vulnerable. She clearly didn't think I would do it.

"Forgive me, but I can't die right now, and I need the ring."

She unscrews the vial, pouring half of it onto a cloth. I hike up my skirt and turn, preparing to hit the ground running. But before I can, I can hear a whooshing from behind, and the cloth is pushed against my face.

"Again," She whispers. "I truly am sorry."

I squirm, and I try to scream, but there's no use. And still... no guards have come. I immediately feel my heart slow, my breathing retreating to match it. The stake hits the gravel below in a clatter.

"Why-?" Is all I manage to say before my head becomes too heavy to carry.

My hands fall, and I hiss in pain as tiny rocks seep into my skin. My head falls onto Nightshade's chest. She lifts her hand, her head cocked in confusion when I flinch. She uses her hand to cradle my weary head, her touch almost like a twisted lullaby. Slowly beating is her heart, the metronome that plays to the intricate yet wild waltz that now plays the role of our livelihoods.

Beside us the fountain hisses and swishes, bubbling in sorrow as it laments my failure, my inability to aid my kingdom. The birds sing the melody, her breaths take the harmony in the orchestrated concert of shame. Even the stars themselves glare at me, their disappointment burning through me, hot and heavy. I stare through blurry eyes at the stake, the orchestra dimming as everything becomes warped and fuzzy. If only I had reached her heart faster. If only she were lying dead on the ground, instead of holding me in her arms. I let my own reality crumble as I close my eyes.

Chapter 4
Veronica

I awake, bound to a chair, a glaring light stabbing into my bleary, blinded eyes. The light clicks out to reveal Beckett, notebook in hand. Well, if one could even call it a notebook. It's a mess of light bark and old wanted posters, though he seems to try to use the blank sides. He runs to the desk behind him, inking his quill and restitching his so-called "scientific notebook," all while examining me. And then come the relentless, pestering questions.

"Okay, list your symptoms," He grins, plopping onto the floor in front of me, sitting criss-cross.

"I haven't a clue. Now leave me alone."

Beckett looks disappointed, as he dips his quill in the ink that now sits beside him.

"Symptom list, trial sixteen, irritability," Beckett murmurs.

I groan, throwing my head back and hitting a wall. The pain vibrates through my head, seemingly amplified.

"Watch your head," He snickers. "Should I add clumsiness to the list of symptoms, or are you just always like this?"

My eyes slowly start to adjust to my surroundings. All lighting comes either from Beckett's little machine, or from candles attached to the walls of the cave. This main room of the cave is almost completely empty. I am on one side, a small rug and a little table by where my chair was. Somewhere not quite center of the room is a long table with a chess set. And... *her*. Nightshade sits, legs open wide, on top of a table, her feet resting on a chair. She crosses one leg over the other, pulling a black glove over her hand. She picks up my ring and spins it around on her finger, before her eyes land on me.

"Looks like sleeping beauty is finally awake. How was your coma, princess?" Aella teases.

She's seated on the ground, head leaning on the back of the chair Nightshade is resting her feet on. For the sake of the stars, did no one teach them how to sit properly?

"Oh, how wonderful," I grumble. "Just when things couldn't get any worse. How long was I out?"

"Three days, give or take," Aella shrugged.

Three days. Three days, and no one came.

"I'm sorry, but we didn't know the dangers of waking you too early," Nightshade says. "We wanted to see if they'd come for you. Seems not."

"You're exactly what they say you are, you know," I say. "Nothing more than a wretched monster. You're the scum of the earth, simply put, and one day you'll be nothing more than a worm speared by my heel. You'll see. The Woods will come for me, and when they do, you'll regret ever crawling out of what demonic hole labored in the creation of your horrid wickedness."

"Well well," Nightshade says, a slight chuckle in her tone. "It seems I've struck a nerve. There's desperation in your tone, in your prideful boasts. Who are you really trying to convince, yourself, or me? Admit that they don't care about you, then we'll let you go."

But then I give it more consideration. No one had come in three days. Daman was... well, he had appeared to be flirting with other girls at the party. And my parents don't give a shit about me.

No. The Woods care, they have to. They're the only ones who do.

My freedom is just out of reach, taunting me gently, as its smile rips into the flesh of my soul. The choice of admitting defeat, whether I believe it or not, hangs in the air, and yet I desire so strongly to have it. I'm a wonderful liar, I can lie again. Just let her think she's won, and move on.

I don't want her to have that kind of validation. I'd sooner die. But I also don't really want to die, not when I'm so close to marrying into the Woods and having everything I've ever wanted. I can't do that if I'm trapped here.

Maybe I can escape on my own. I'd certainly show The Two Kingdoms that I'm capable. Show them I'm more than just a damsel in distress, the product of their failed king and queen. I know deep down, if I try, I could do it. I know I'm so close to having control, having power over my own life.

Each side of the decision has a piece of me teetering on its very edge, yet, there seems to be no balance.

I fight the temptation to play to her demands. I am more than aware of the fact that Nightshade wants me to give in, to beg for mercy, no matter the cost. Again, I'd sooner die rather than let her have what she wants.

"They'll come," I say. "Just watch."

"You don't seem very sure of that, darling," She says.

"Hey, wait, maybe we shouldn't-" Beckett starts, and Aella quickly covers his mouth.

"While we're striking each other's throats," I say. "I'd like to point out the fact that you're horrible at your 'Nightshade' act, and you'll inevitably fail. I cannot wait to watch you fall to pieces. I'll laugh at your funeral."

"Pardon?" She crosses her arms with her palms out, her arms more hovered together than crossed. "Please explain to me how I'm 'horrible at my Nightshade act.'"

"You have literally nearly cost yourself your own secret identity, which, mind you isn't very secret, *Jinx*, I've literally seen you in and out of your mask, and the others literally say your name around you, you're not as slick as you think you are. Also, you're just dramatic. You're not scary, you're not a hero, you're just drama. The best you can do is continue your stupid little fantasies with your little meaningless attacks. Attempting to psychologically torture me, or whatever it is that you're doing won't give you any advantages, nor any progress on your so-called 'mission.' Instead of doing petty things like... *this*, why not just go for an attack on Daman? Or a more direct siege on the kingdom?" I suggest, then slam my mouth shut, realizing I probably shouldn't be giving them ideas.

"Ah, that's so overdone, so cliche. And, to be perfectly candid, princess, we haven't the power needed for that. Ah, no *that* would be imbecilic, Veronica. And after all, darling, you're just as much of an attention seeker as I. And now, you get to be part of the biggest ploy against the kingdom, no matter what side you're on, a part of the narrative. And, afterall, what is chaos without an audience, and a little bit of drama?"

"I would hardly refer to your actions as, 'chaotic.' They are deranged, down right malicious. You are evil."

"That all comes down to perspective, darling. Remember the conversation we had earlier? Evil really is just in the eye of the beholder," She shrugs. "But, as you're currently of no real use to us, I may as well return you. Beckett, get the sedatives. Can't have her knowing how to get here."

She stands up on the chair, and Aella moves out of the way as she tips it downward to walk down it. Aella rolls her eyes and picks the chair back up after. I tense as she stands behind me. Her fingers brush against my wrists, and the ropes around them loosen.

"Untying her before drugging her? JJ, are we having a dumbass moment right now?" Aella asked, then looked me up and down. "Oh. Right. I forgot that it's *Veronica*."

"I'll stab you," I try to lunge at her. Seeing as I'm still tied by the ankles, I only succeed in falling on my face.

"Sure you will, princess," Aella says, a grin on her face.

That bitch. I'm going to get her one of these days. The ropes drop beside my ankle, and I grab the chair, pulling it off of me, huffing. The three of them are going to pay for this. Well, maybe not Beckett. Even if he is annoying, he is still, unfortunately, just a kid, and the most tolerable of the three. I look away from them as I stretch, everything sore and tight.

For once, I desperately want to return home. I begin to worry about what'll happen if I let them sedate me. Will they attack me with their demonic abilities? What if they attempt to brainwash or alter me? I wouldn't put it past them if they have the ability to do so.

An arch-like portion of the cave begins to rise up with a whirring noise. Nightshade pulls her hood over her face, raising up the mask that now fell against the cloth on where it connected to her neck. Her face is, once again, completely hidden.

The second Daman steps inside the cave, Nightshade lunges for him, knocking him to the ground. She lands on top of him, launching the bombs that are her fists, exploding onto the minefield that is his face. I watch as his face flings to each side as it receives the blow. As horrific as it is, there is nothing I can do as Aella seizes my arms. I can't react, can't help, can't look away. Throughout it all, not once does he scream in pain or horror.

He kicks her with enough force to send her ricocheting into the ceiling. She comes crashing down, her hood falling backwards. She lifts herself up, brushing herself off. She pulls down her mask for just a second, spitting black blood on the floor. She pulls it back on, forgoing re-adjusting her hood. Her eyes are now black as a raven's feather, as she prepares to strike once more.

"What you're about to get, is what you deserve," Nightshade grimaces. "Karma's quite the vixen, isn't she?"

Daman spins his sword, running toward her as she finally makes her way to her feet. He launches the blade into one of her wings, and she screams out.

"I took your advice," He smiles, turning his sword and moving to stab her in the other wing, evoking yet another pained scream from Nightshade. He kicks her in the forehead as she struggles to her feet.

She falls backward onto the ground, and runs her fingers over her forehead. She wipes the blood from her forehead, panting and looking at Daman with an inhuman, blank face of pure fury. He raises his sword upward, preparing to plunge it into her chest, when she raises her palm, fingers turning black as a green fog surrounds them. Daman is then blasted backward, blinding green light momentarily filling every crevice of the cave.

I watch as Daman's body is slammed, repeatedly, between walls. I can hear him crying out in pain, yet she doesn't stop. Nightshade stands, rigid, her face now void of her sinister grin as her brow furrows in concentration. Daman continues to berate her, though his attempts to belittle her into leaving him alone are futile. His blood now paints the cavern walls. I scream his name, as if it'll do anything. As if she'll leave him alone.

Tears sting in my eyes, my chest tightening as I watch the man who I am infatuated with be tormented. I try to run towards him, to assist him, to do anything, but my body is frozen, not allowing me to escape Aella's grip. I watch as he is slammed against a wall one final time, with enough force for it to crack a bit. His body begins to rise, his legs kicking as he puts his hands to his throat, as if trying to rip something off of him. I turn to see Nightshade making a choking motion near her chest, black tendrils surrounding her wrist.

"You're a fool," Daman chokes.

"For letting you live?" Nightshade flicks her wrist, slamming him against the wall once again, before choking him harder. "Yes, I suppose I am."

"Jinx, don't push yourself," Beckett cautions.

"I'll be fine," Nightshade trembles a bit, dropping Daman and falling to the floor.

Aella groans, letting go of me. She gives me a firm look, then looks between me and Beckett.

"Stay," She commands, pointing to me. "Don't kill the kid."

Aella hurried to Nightshade's side, helping her up. Nightshade nearly collapses, the black looking more like a light cover over her blue eyes, lime green wisps surrounding her body. Aella quietly mutters something to Nightshade, who shakes her head, falling back to the ground. Nightshade's eyes shut, and somehow, she stands, a bright white light filling the room. Still glowing white, Nightshade's eyes snapped open, expanding black voids once more. The light now becomes dim, surrounding her as she walks towards Daman, the black tendrils now disappearing. She looks almost... ghostly.

"Oh no," Beckett whispers, as Aella groans again, facepalming.

"Oh, so you went and made yourself into more of a monster?" Daman coughs.

"I may have beckoned for assistance," Jinx says, then her voice changes into something else completely, "Call her a monster again. I dare you."

"She always was one," Daman hesitates, grabbing onto the side of the wall to steady himself as he tried to stand. "We did what we had to do."

"You made her into this. She'd be happy if it weren't for you."

"Is she possessed?" I whisper to Beckett.

"Basically," Beckett whispers back. "Sometimes she summons ghosts to help as a last resort."

"Are you allowed to tell me that?"

"I don't think so."

Nightshade, or the ghosts, or all of them for that matter, crumple over for a moment, beginning to cough uncontrollably, blood spewing from her mouth. Nightshade grabs onto the wall for stability, forcing the cough to cease. She takes a few deep breaths, ready to fight.

Daman's face is beaten and bruised already. Nightshade lunges at him, picking him up by the throat and slamming him to the ground. Aella gives

Beckett a look and he sighs, rolling his eyes at me. He runs to the side of a room, hitting a switch. The ground opens up from beneath Daman and Nightshade, dropping them into a room below us.

"Sorry!" Beckett called after them. "Not to Daman, though! Daman, you're a jerk!"

"Yeah, that'll show 'im, Nerd Boy," Aella teases.

I can hear Daman and Nightshade's fists colliding against each other from the other room, which continues for a while until I hear a loud thud from the room. Daman's body comes flying back into the room, and Nightshade hovers slightly above the ground. Daman pushes her with all the force he can muster, and Nightshade hits the table. She knocks the chess board off as she slides across the table. She rolls off the floor, standing up and taking a breath. She readjusts her hood, whispering something to herself in several voices.

"Thank you for all of your assistance, but I believe I'll be able to take it from here," Nightshade pants.

"It's only fair we help," a voice says from her mouth. "We could kill him. It wouldn't count as-"

"Out," Nightshade commands, coughing up black sludge.

Her eyes slowly turn to blue, the black tendrils returning as the white light around her disappears. She trembles as she walks forward. While it's evident that Daman is exhausted, Nightshade looks awful. With every step, she looks like she's going to crumble. After just a few weak steps, her eyes roll back into her head, and she collapses to the floor. Daman scoops her up, and I tense up.

"Jinx!" Aella and Beckett both shout.

Beckett charges towards Daman, who slings Nightshade over his shoulder. As she hangs from him, Beckett tries to grab her. Daman grabs Beckett's throat with his arm as he pulls a pistol from his side.

"Veronica, get over here. Now," Daman spits.

I quickly run to his side, but Aella stops me, grabbing me tightly. She lights her fist aflame, holding it all too close to my face. I shut my eyes, as I hear Daman turn the safety off his pistol. The flames are so close to my face, they're nearly licking me. Across the way, I can hear Beckett hyperventilating.

"Touch her, and I'll pump his skull with silver," Daman growls.

"He dies, and I'll burn everyone in this star-forsaken room," Aella threatens.

"And here I thought you hated me," Beckett teases, yet his voice is still tight and strained in fear.

"Shut it," Aella snaps.

I don't see what happens next. All I know is there is clambering, and gunshots, and when I open my eyes Aella and Beckett are both laying sprawled on the ground, as Daman catches his breath.

"Oh, stars, are they-"

"They're alive. For now. We'll kill them later. Now let's *go*," He grabs me by the wrist, tugging me out as he keeps his grip on Nightshade.

Chapter 5
Veronica

Unlike my parents, the Woods are typically on top of things. Once they'd caught Nightshade, there was little hesitation to set up her trial. If it had been my parents, Nightshade would still be in some rotting cell. Or, rather, would've escaped it by now.

It's been one week since Daman rescued me. Likely, today Nightshade will be condemned to death. Unfortunately, I won't be staking her myself, although I could always ask for that to be part of the sentence. Alas, that request would likely be denied. The trial takes place in the same chapel in Mortem Venenum that was supposed to hold the union of Daman and I, until she ruined it. It's quite fitting. Quite fitting indeed.

It's never much of a trial with the Woods. No one gets out of these alive. They rule almost as strictly as Robsepierre, and love their guillotine just as much. Stars, how I idolize them. If only I could get people to listen and adore me, yet fear me as much as they do. That's all, I don't exactly approve of the mass murdering bit. However, there is always room for improvement, and one day I'll have the ropes. I'll be able to keep things just a tad safer for the human citizens, without as much violent condemnation of the supernaturals. Maybe exiling rather than execution, though only the criminal supernaturals are executed.

Her royal majesty Queen Isolde Andromeda Woods stands to the left of the stand. To me, she's a woman in power actually taking charge, so I cling to her to be the idol my mother could never be. She has her chin high, layers of pearl necklaces adorning her neck, diamonds dangling from her ears. Her jet-black hair is in a neat bun, not a single strand of hair out of place. A black tiara rests on her head, the crimson jewels dripping downward in a v-shape down her forehead. She's in an onyx dress, which swishes with each step she takes, her heels clicking menacingly all the way to the stand.

Behind her, stands His Royal Majesty Dietrich Alador Woods, a man in a dark suit and a deep red velvet cape. He's taller, his wavy, shoulder-length black hair swept back and gelled. His crown is far bigger and more regal than my father's, and seems to be a more extravagant version of Lila's tiara. I believe I've forgotten to mention the lost princess.

Her royal highness, Princess Lila Aylin Woods. She was the princess of Mortem Venenum, the daughter of the king and queen, and sister of Daman and Noah. She went missing seven years ago, at the age of ten. No one knows what happened. A funeral was held not long after her disappearance, just in case. Soon after, she wasn't of much interest in the two-kingdoms rumors, and became nothing more than a forgotten memory. A forgotten memory to everyone but Noah, who, sadly, is still looking for her.

I've seen pictures of her, a sad young girl in a frightening crown, long black hair cascading in braids down her back. The poor girl looked absolutely miserable, though no one knows quite why. Most pictures of her have been sold, burned, or destroyed, again for reasons no one knows.

Nightshade stands on a stage, being held to the back of the room with silver handcuffs. She is barely conscious, having only been forced awake a few minutes before the trial after being in a power-drained coma for the past week. It's a delightfully ironic, albeit a pathetic scene.

She's wearing a charcoal collared black tea dress, with ruby bat-shaped crystal buttons running down the top of the dress, and stopping at the skirt. Her dark ginger hair is pulled into two little braids atop her head that recedes down her back into a low-hanging ponytail.

She's visibly falling in and out of consciousness, only waking up to wince when she burns herself on the handcuffs every so often. She looks anything but threatening, in fact, she just looks vulnerable. Part of me almost feels bad for her. Almost.

The beginning of the trial isn't of too much interest. Daman stands beside me as I speak, keeping his hand tightly around my wrist. Anytime I get off track, he gives me a squeeze. I sit when he speaks, on his request. He beckons me to stand beside him once more once he's finished speaking.

More accusations of things she's done come to light, and I can see Nightshade standing there, looking down, a sly grin quickly sweeping her face with each one. At one, I can swear she's laughing, if only slightly, before making eye-contact with me and rolling her eyes.

"You're just begging me to tell them the truth, aren't you, Isolde? About what you're really doing, and why I do what I do?" Nightshade grins, her voice rougher than usual.

"What is she talking about?" I whisper to Daman.

"Keep your star-forsaken mouth shut," He whispers back.

I put my head down and obey, nervously twisting my braids between my fingers. Daman forcefully takes my hand in his, squeezing it just a bit too tightly as he laces our fingers together. He takes his other hand, putting it against my head, petting it before pressing my head against his chest and putting his arm around me.

"There are no secrets, you disgusting liar," Daman says.

"You'd know more about secrets than anyone," Nightshade retorts.

Daman grabs me tighter, and I can feel his heartbeat pounding ferociously, his nails digging into my skin. Nightshade scoffs, rolling her eyes. Two guards unhook her chains from the floor, grabbing her. She groans, pulling the chains from their grip, then putting them behind her back herself in a more dignified manner, wincing at the silver as it moves against her wrist. She lifts her chin up.

"Agony to the Woods," Nightshade grins, lips closed. "May the stars fall and lay waste to them and their rule. Isolde, Dietrich, Daman, I truly hope karma makes you pay for all that you've done. If I had it my way, you'd be facing hell in the streets, Noah upon your throne."

The crowd breaks out into a frenzied uproar, and the guards quickly seize her, pressing the silver forcefully on her skin. Nightshade just shuts her eyes and laughs at the chaos she caused. But after all, that's all she is. She is chaos, she is death, she is destruction. She is everything I'm against. Her laughter continues to echo the room.

It's haunting. It's the only sound in the silent vacuum of the room, just her deep laugh echoing incessantly. How can she just laugh in the face of certain death? When death surrounds you, do you take comfort in knowing it's coming for you? She's nothing but some lie, a beautiful, traitorous paradox. I despise her. I want nothing more than to use her onyx blood to ink my quill, her corpse on display.

Although, if I'm being honest, her words have been echoing around my mind. What is the 'truth' she'd previously mentioned, and why won't Daman tell me?

Following the chaos, the trial is moved, and execution seems to be the only option fitting her existence and constant rebellion. Dietrich tries to argue otherwise, which feels incredibly uncharacteristic for him. The trial is moved to the town square. The town square is beside a seaside port, and often is covered in soot, due to pirate cannons attacking local shops and trading centers, as well as other ships. The square is more of a semicircle, the southside being the clear turquoise water and docking ports, the outer circle being covered in shops. Though the crown jewel of the town square is the gallows, the body of some unfortunate pirate now rotting as it hangs in plain sight, a warning for citizens not to step out of line.

"I have an announcement to make," Nightshade proclaims, her dark ginger hair tossing as she violently shakes her head for emphasis. She flicks her wrist, which shoots into the air. "I know where the missing princess is."

"She's lying," Dietrich shouts over the calamity of a crowd.

"Gag her," Isolde commands through gritted teeth.

Though they never address her, it's clear that Lila's disappearance is still a raw wound to the Woods. Whenever her name is mentioned, they all grow very quiet. And yet, there are pictures of her all over their castle. Some have been torn, some have splotches of paint on them. Some are in rooms you wouldn't expect a painting to be. I once asked Daman why there was this surplus of unsettling paintings. His response was that his younger sister seemed to be haunting them. He never elaborated. All I know is that Lila and Daman were very close. After all, why else would he save her things to be used for our future daughters?

The two knights standing beside Nightshade suddenly fall unconscious, as she throws her head back and continues to laugh. The crowd screams, and disperses as green fog emerges from Nightshade's body, falling from the wood of the gallows and cascading like a waterfall.

"Thanks for the power-nap," She muses.

Her shackles break, clattering beneath her. She jumps down, and in a blur, she's in front of Dietrich and Isolde. Daman grabs me, protectively, before sheathing his sword and pushing me to the ground in an attempt to protect his parents.

Afterall, they are his parents. They're the king and queen of his kingdom. I'm not all that bothered that he pushed me aside. Nightshade's eyes dart to me, and she sighs, approaching me. She kneels beside me, and all Daman does is put a hand in front of Isolde. Nightshade hoists me up, though it isn't in haste.

"Are you alright?" She whispers.

"Yeah, I'm fine," I mutter, taken aback by the gesture.

"Good," She nods, before turning back to Daman and asking, "Is this how you treat your ladies? How chivalrous."

"I was trying to push her away from you," Daman says.

"Keep telling yourself that," She crosses her arms.

A flame seems to form in Daman's eyes. He flips his sword, getting into a battle stance. Nightshade lets out an exasperated sigh, rubbing her temples. She puts a hand on my shoulder, gesturing for me to get back.

Whatever attack Nightshade was planning is halted by Daman plunging his sword into her gut. She screams in pain, a horrible banshee-like sound. He keeps digging it deeper as she falls to her knees, until the blade has found its way through the center of her wings.

"That was uncalled for," She chokes, black blood dribbling down her lips.

"It's a justified threat, dear," Isolde reasons, her arms not fully crossing. "After all, you're a terrorist who just resisted punishment. And you've just laid a hand on a princess of whom you've harmed multiple times. And we know how you treat princesses."

"Do *not* blame me for Lila's death," Nightshade spits breathily. "Her blood is on your hands just as much as it is on mine, if not more."

She continues to choke, coughing up more and more blood. I look to Daman for some kind of explanation. Why wouldn't they have told me Lila was dead? I mean, I never knew her, as I was only allowed to play with

Daman as a child, but it felt like I'd been lied to. And why is Nightshade so upset over her death?

"After all," Nightshade laughs bitterly, wiping blood from her lips. She removes the sword from her gut with a squelch, wiping the blood off with her cape. She points it loosely at Daman once she makes it to her feet, eyes turning red as she fixes her gaze on Isolde and Dietrich. "According to her, you're the one who kicked her out. You hurt her and took away what little of a home she had, and she grew so hopeless that she took the plunge."

"*You* finished the job," Daman says, lowering the sword with the tips of his fingers.

"*I* kept her safe," Nightshade snaps, raising the sword once again. "The three of you broke her."

"Well *maybe* she had it coming," Daman says.

"She was just a kid," Nightshade says, voice warping and eyes turning black.

Ice covers the town square, narrowly missing the guards, but wrapping around my ankles.

"Um, you might want-" I start, trying to warn the Woods.

"*Quiet*," Daman snaps.

"Now isn't a good time, Veronica," Isolde says.

"Oh, I'm sorry, would you prefer I freeze your sorry asses a different time, when it's more convenient?" A voice asks.

Someone steps out from behind the gallows, a sweet smile on her face. A girl, no older than fourteen, with umber skin and vitiligo. She wears clothes fitting for summer, purple with white lightning bolts and flowers painted on. Upon closer inspection, there are purple scales scattered in patches on the side of her neck, and her arms and legs. She has a cloud-like halo of fluffy black curls, curling purple horns peeking out from the front of them, dozens of flowers seeming to peek out as well. She grins at Daman's dumbstruck face, before spreading out purple wings.

"Good timing, Icylyn," Nightshade mumbles.

"You guys were so close!" the girl teases. "Welp, sucks for you, bye assholes!"

NIGHTSHADE

The ice spreads up to our hips, rendering us unable to move. It's cold, and wet, and seems to stab and jab into me, though, that's just the temperature of the ice. The girl gives a little wave and the next second...

All of the ice disappears, along with the ice girl and Nightshade.

Chapter 6
Nightshade

Daman is an asshole. There isn't much more to say about that. Thank the stars that Icylyn happened to be in the library nearby and had heard the commotion. Otherwise, for once, I think I would not have been able to make an escape. She'd held them still as she froze time itself. As time remained still, we'd made our way to our base. Aella had found us as we'd gotten closer. I'd coughed, my legs giving out beneath me. I'll survive this, but *stars* will it be a painful week.

"We'll meet you back at the base, alright Ice-storm?" Aella asks.

Icylyn nods, and disappears in a blizzard. Snow rests on the ground even after she is gone.

"I'd welcome death," I groan.

"I'm sure you would, JJ. Unfortunately for your sorry ass, I'm not letting that happen," Aella grabs my wrist, and pulls me to my feet. "Do you want me to get us there now? Are you good to walk?"

"I'm fine," I say, and continue forward, trying to straighten myself. I can't, and just continue onward, crouching slightly.

"JJ," Aella says. "You're doing that thing again."

"What thing?" I wince.

I stumble forward once again, holding onto a nearby tree branch. I take another breath, and when I breathe out, it feels like my insides are ripping apart.

"That thing you do when you pretend everything's fine," Aella says.

I give her a look and she matches it, before putting my arm over her shoulder. For one moment, we're engulfed in flame, and the next we're in the base. Not the cave, but the secret base belonging to the rebellion.

"Alright, go sit down, JJ," Aella says.

"I'm fine, Aella," I mumble, before sitting down on the table.

Three of the rebellion members walk into the room shortly after. Raven, a shadow-blood with bright green messy hair and brightly colored clothes, walks in first. Their skin is peach, and they wear a crown of roses, bare feet trailing blood on the floor, one eye completely black, the other blue. Following them is Sage, an elf with choppy white hair, black lipstick smudged on her lip, a spiked necklace fastened tightly around her pale neck. Following them is Hazel, yet another elf. She wears a white sweater with a blue cloak, her white and blue half up in two buns. She's still in her armor.

Hazel works inside Cazlamenta as Noah's main guard, and makes up most of our intel.

Beckett and Icylyn sit side by side in the corner, reading over a blueprint they'd sketched together.

We work in almost complete silence. I put my hands up and Raven tosses me my sewing kit. I have two, one back at the cave, and one here. Internally... it'll heal on its own, eventually. Hopefully. It'll be fine, I'm a vampire.

The team desperately needs a medic.

"Are you really about to stitch that up without someone looking at it?" Hazel asks.

"I do not need to worry about that, I'm a vampire, though I appreciate the concern," I answer.

"Oh holy shit!" Beckett says, taking a look at me for the first time.

"Fucking language," Aella holds him in a headlock and ruffles his curls.

Beckett makes a face, trying to squirm out of her grasp. He laughs, trying to fight her, biting down on his thumb. Icylyn looks at them, shakes her head, and returns to looking over the blueprints.

"Jinx, stop that," Hazel says, signing as she speaks.

"It's perfectly fine, I have to close the outside wound before anything can infect the inside before my healing can kick in," I brush her off, momentarily dropping my needle and thread so I can sign as I speak. Most of the time in the base, we'll sign while speaking if Sage is in the room, because she's Deaf.

"You are being an idiot," Sage signs.

I lack most of my notoriously public charisma or appearance of any intelligence around the rebellion members. It's nice, in a way. One less part of myself that I have to disguise. I look down at my stitches, satisfied for now, and patch the two holes in my wings.

"You know, it's sundown soon," Beckett says. "Icylyn, Aella and I were gonna head home for dinner, I'm sure my mom would want to take a look at that."

I open my mouth and Aella instantly shakes her head.

"You're coming with us. You don't get a choice."

Introductions come later. Beckett's mom starts evaluating and fixing the wound where she can almost the second I get in the door. She has a tan skin tone slightly darker than Beckett's, and glowing purple eyes. Her face and ears are covered in an assortment of piercings. She has wine red choppy curls that hang inches above her shoulders, complete with an undercut. Rebecca leaves for a moment, then returns after washing her hands.

"Now that that's taken care of," She smiles. "I'm Rebecca Acosta."

"Jinx Athanasia," I say, voice shaking, against my will extending my hand.

"It's nice to finally meet you, Beckett, Icylyn and Aella talk about you all the time," She smiles, then pauses, thinking for a moment. "Did you say your last name was Athanasia?"

"Athanasia," Rebecca echoes, smiling a bittersweet smile. "I haven't heard that name in a while."

"They're dead," I spit out.

I have the sudden urge to tell her everything. Things I couldn't tell anyone, things only Aella and Lila know. It scares me.

Beckett, Icylyn, and Aella walk into the room, all shouting over each other, completely unintelligible. Beckett plops onto the couch on one side of me, and Aella plops down on the other side. Icylyn sits on the other side of Beckett.

"I knew them," Rebecca nods, smiling fondly. "We were in a rebellion together. I dated one of them for a while, and her older brother was my best friend," Rebecca smiles fondly. "Remind me to show you the cave someday, Beckett. It has a lot of my tech in it."

I don't think any of us were really expecting this information.

"Holy *shit*, Becca!" Aella grins. "You mean the one up north?"

Rebecca nods. I can't look Rebecca in the eye. I feel as though I've stolen something from her.

"Hold on, you were in a *rebellion?*" Beckett asks, eyes wide.

"How do you think I met your dad? He was a pirate," Rebecca grins, gently messing with Beckett curls. "There's Yuca con mojo in the kitchen if you kids want any. I'll leave you alone for a bit."

She turns toward the kitchen and then veers to the side, going down a corner leading to a hallway, which I assume leads to her room. Aella, Beckett and Icylyn shoot each other a look and start pushing at each other, racing to the kitchen. Beckett's journal drops open, to a page where a small glowing dagger has been sketched out.

"...Beckett, do you mind if I take a look at your journal?" I ask, eager to get my mind onto a new project, rather than processing any of that.

"Go ahea-" He starts, and then there's the sound of screaming and clattering from the kitchen. "*Aella!*"

Aella laughs, and more crashing comes from the kitchen. I laugh in spite of myself. I don't know how Rebecca manages those three. I know I sure as hell cannot, although, I don't want to. I set the book in my lap. The blade of the dagger shines a lime green, and the handle is made of stone. Impenetrable stone.

The blade would be made from the bark of a senroom tree, in a forest in the neighboring kingdom Couteau, not-so-cleverly named Fear Forest. It will make it so that the blade can cut through quite literally anything.

"Please tell Mrs. Acosta I'm grateful for the hospitality, but I must be on my way," I say, standing.

"JJ, you're not about to do something stupid, are you?" Aella asks.

"Depends on your definition of stupid," I say, pulling my lower face mask up over my nose.

I pull my hair into three sections, quickly braiding all three sections, and then braiding it all together. I really do enjoy superspeed in many cases. I pull my hood over my face, and leave before another word can be exchanged.

PERCY CADAVER

Nevermind that I got stabbed this morning, the idea of sitting and doing nothing is far more painful than any wound. I need something to do.

And so, I make my way to Couteau.

NIGHTSHADE

Chapter 7
Veronica

I venture to Fear Forest, just southeast of my castle. It's quite a beautiful forest, though extremely dangerous. In fact, it's too dangerous. I'd managed to catch a glimpse of a dagger Beckett had sketched, and re-sketched it in my notebook. I could always use more protection, especially if it means getting to throw it in the face of those Scumbags.

It isn't long before I find myself in peril. Unfortunately, that's becoming a very regular event lately. I step too close to a tree, the bark being a beautiful lavender.

"Veronica, darling, I wouldn't get that close if I were you," Nightshade warns.

Of course she's here. As if things couldn't get any worse.

"Now I'm just going to get closer to it to spite you," I say, taking a step closer.

I feel a tingling sensation and look down to see orange and purple vines wrapping around my ankles. I'd not realized that I'd stumbled right into the trap of a pipunch tree. Nightshade groans, her face in her palm, shaking her head.

"I told you not to get close," She berates.

"Well, you told me not to, so obviously I'd want to do it!" I yell back.

The plant pulls tighter and tighter, until I find myself nearly forgetting I have feet at all. As I lose feeling in my legs, a vine begins to wrap around my waist. I cover my mouth, trying not to scream. The last thing I want to do is appear weak, especially in front of Nightshade. I have a dagger hidden in a holster behind my shoulder. All I have to do is grab it, but when I reach for it, nothing is there.

"Did you steal my dagger?" I shriek.

Nightshade shrugs, "It was fair game."

"If this thing kills me, I am going to haunt you so hard."

"You'd have to be willing to have your soul tethered to mine."

"Ew."

Nightshade rolls her eyes, grabbing an arrow from behind her back. As the black tendrils return, circling her pale skin, she pricks her finger on the tip, black blood dripping down the arrow. She loads it onto her bow, taking her sweet, sweet time aiming her shot.

"Stars, could you load that thing any slower?" I ask.

The tree's mouth begins to open, and I brace myself as its warm, sticky breath gropes at my skin. Soon will come the bright turquoise poison, which will paralyze me instantly. It isn't already enough to have defensive poison in its vines, apparently.

"I'm trying not to hit you, you narcissistic ignoramus." She yells, lowering the bow.

I try not to let fear grip me as the vines squeeze me impossibly tight, cutting off my circulation. I see my limbs turning purple, and swear I can hear my bones cracking, as my vision blurs, little white dots clouding my sight. Two arrows come for my waist, just barely missing me. The tree screams out, as it recoils its vines. It nearly sucks me in as it draws a deep inhale, and I hit the dirt, praying the tree's poison sap won't hit me.

I lie there for a minute, catching my breath, then stand without another word, brushing myself off as if nothing happened. Nightshade, to her credit, remains silent. I continue through the forest, and she seems to follow close behind. I'd prefer someone other than Nightshade to be here, but at least I'm not alone. The forest is nothing but an endless void of flesh-eating monsters, covered by a facade of leaves, and the hues of pink, blue, and purple. Nightshade abruptly sits on the ground, staring up at me.

"What are you doing?" I demand.

"Oh, just seeing how long you last."

"Until?"

"Oh, until you crack, darling. I'm quite interested in seeing how far the stubbornness goes."

"Says the one who was stabbed this morning," I roll my eyes. "Why? Are you trying to get something from me? Because I'm not helping your stupid rebellion."

I continue trudging on, without another word. I don't want to be alone, at least, not now, but she still won't budge. So I figure, I'll keep walking until she gets scared and alone in the forest and comes running to me. The only flaw in my plan is that she is immortal and stubborn. So I figure, screw her. It just means I'll make it to the Senroom tree before her, to gather materials for the dagger.

I figure I'll manage to find the tree and face its challenges on my own, but even the forest seems to be against me. I notice after about an hour of walking that the rock I've passed three times is all too familiar, or that there can't be multiples of an exact tree. The worst part is when the forest warps its path once more, leading me back to Nightshade.

"Give up?" she instigates.

"You'd like that, wouldn't you?" I cross my arms.

"Watching you walk in circles is incredibly nauseating, and, in any case, I'm starving," She says, not moving from her spot.

"You bite me, and I will bite you back," I threaten.

"How forward of you, princess," She grins.

"Stars, you're such a vampire."

"Don't stereotype me."

"Then don't be stereotypical."

She huffs, but can't seem to find something to retort with. Finally, I've managed to make her shut up. I've achieved the impossible. Despite the silence, though, she continues to annoy me. Nightshade always seems to be walking too slowly, and the forest seems just too dark. Below us, the periwinkle dirt grows more and more damp. I take one step, and as the mud sinks into my heels and socks, I am grabbed from behind. I twist around, trying to escape, but the grip only tightens.

"Veronica, darling, quit being stubborn for just a second, you're going to get yourself killed," Nightshade says.

"Please," I mumble. "As if you care."

As if anyone cares.

"Now's not the time for that. Believe it or not, I'm not heartless, and I am concerned for your wellbeing, even though you clearly don't care for your own."

I roll my eyes. "I'll be fine."

She pulls me back, putting her arm in front of me as she takes a cautious step forward. She slowly bends down, grabbing a small shining pebble. She then tosses it into the mud. The pebble, in turn, catches fire, freezes, and then immediately sinks as the mud bubbles around it. She turns back to me with a stubborn: *See, I told you so* expression. She then backs up, crossing her arms as she stands beside me.

"So what do you propose we do?" I ask, at a loss for ideas.

"I could fly us over," She suggests.

Oh, yes, and let her touch me? Absolutely not. I don't want her or her disgusting supernatural wings anywhere near me. So what if they look good on her? They are inherently wrong and against what was planned by the stars so very long ago.

"Absolutely not," I say, crossing my arms and lifting my chin.

"Then what do you propose we do, darling?" Nightshade asks.

"I'll- I'll figure it out," I mutter. "And stop calling me that."

I sit down on a rock, half expecting it to shoot me into the air. It doesn't, to my relief. I figure this will be a good spot to at least attempt to think. It's an odd-looking boulder, glowing teal. It's quiet for a good moment, the only noise being my own thoughts. A million voices all at once, accompanied by this distant humming, growing ever louder, ever-present. I'm trying with all my might to stop all the noise.

Nightshade starts gathering vines and twigs, so I, sheerly out of boredom, I stand beside her and help. She looks at me for a minute, her cheeks turning slightly purple for just a second. She holds out her hand to take what I'd collected, and our fingers slightly brush against each other as I press the twigs into her palm. Her hands are void of all warmth, and I quickly retract myself from her cold touch. She quietly apologizes, nodding. She moves away from me and sits down on a boulder, beginning to tie together the sticks and twigs, occasionally pulling at them to test the strength of her creation.

As I wait, I come across a sharp rock, and kneel down to pick it up. I take another glance at Nightshade, but she's almost scarily focused. There's a violent rustling of leaves, and the sudden snap of a twig. Startled and tensing, I clench the rock so tightly that blood begins to drip onto the lavender leaves beneath me. The pain is raw and stinging, and I hiss out, covering my mouth so that Nightshade won't hear me. Or, of course, any other possible threat in the distance, such as whatever just made a noise. Nothing seems to come, but I can see shadows out of the corner of my eye.

I look down to see my bloody hand shaking as it holds the rock, a trembling dagger in the other. I hit my dagger against the rock in an attempt to sharpen it, and to scare off potential harm. I am all too aware that I'm in a forest of nightmares, trapped with the girl of demons and death. The girl who seems so set on destroying me. My people. My kingdom, both kingdoms—in fact, perhaps peace as it's known all together. The rock and dagger click together. Click, clang, it goes, each noise a distraction from the wind, and the rustling, and the dripping blood thudding against the forest floor. After a few minutes... I just... *can't*.

Nightshade stands, her cloak blowing in the wind as she walks toward me, her eyes now covered in a black film. She slings her makeshift rope over her shoulder, as she quickly walks toward me. Will she kill me now? Is that rope really a noose? I throw my rock at her, and she easily dodges it with a slight tilt of her head. Still, her face conveys no emotion.

My breath shudders, and I'm seized entirely by pain and fear. I raise my dagger warningly. She stops in her tracks, then, in a blur, appears in front of me, the leaves near her feet propelled backwards in her wake. She stops right before the dagger, which I press against her throat, feeling my own tighten. A green fog surrounds the dagger, and it floats up, high, high, higher, until it's out of reach. Nightshade takes my bleeding hand between two of hers. Her eyes keep their black film, though glow red underneath where color should be. I launch my free hand to slap her across the face, to keep her away, but she simply drops one of my hands and catches my hand in her grip.

"I'm not what you should be frightened of now, darling, this forest smells blood," Nightshade says.

"So do you, you literally just did," I clarify, as deadpan as I possibly can, voice shaking and cutting out against my wishes. "And you're a blood-sucking vampire."

"I suppose you have me there."

She grabs the dagger out of the air, and I tense, slowly walking backward. Nightshade snatches my wrist and pulls me back, shaking her head. She grabs the bottom of her cloak, stepping on part of it, and slashing through it with her dagger. She takes the fabric, and ties it tightly around my hand, her fingers lingering for just slightly too long.

"Come now, darling," She says, dropping her hands. "The quicker we are to leave this forest, the quicker you'll be able to clean it before it gets infected."

She walks away and I follow, almost in a daze, blinded by a haze of confusion. I walk beside her, jumping at every noise. I stop at one point, closing my eyes. Nightshade puts her hands on my shoulder and assures me she wouldn't let the forest kill me before she gets the chance, and, upon my panic, reassures me she has a no-kill rule.

We continue to walk briskly, our hands occasionally brushing. Nightshade's laughing at me, I can tell. I can hear it in her breath, a breath she shouldn't even have. Every shift, every time I jump slightly at a noise. I can't stand her. I pause for a minute to catch my breath, for a moment, taking in the forest around us.

There's a fallen tree beside us, covered in moss and mushrooms, as nature grieves what it has lost, creating new life from the ashes of what once was. We sit beside each other on the tree, careful not to squish the mushrooms. Behind us stands a wisteria tree, the flowers blowing in the wind and some falling in Nightshade's hair.

"We're not far," I say, after a moment. "I'm not... afraid. I'm not stalling. I'm just tired."

"I'm sure it's called Fear Forest for a reason, darling," Nightshade says.

"Shut up, Nightshade," I sigh.

I stand up, and she follows suit. I think she's grinning, it's hard to tell with the mask, the hood, and the black eyes. Once again, there's screaming in the distance. Nightshade tenses, and stops herself before running in the direction of it. She's going to get herself killed one of these days. Not that I mind, of course. One less problem for me. For all of us, really.

Like I said, the tree isn't far.

It's the smell that hits first. It's overwhelming, to say the least. It's putrid, suffocating us with the scent of festering vegetation, or perhaps, something more sinister than that. The tree looms over us, glowing a near-blinding lime green. Protruding from the tree are a series of branches, bare of leaves, but rather, adorned in skulls. They glow a faint yellow, drowned out by the other colors surrounding them.

As Nightshade approaches the tree, I can't help but take a step back. The orange fog rolls in slightly after. It lifts, surrounding the area of the tree. It's a thin veil, of which I can see through. I attempt to walk through it, but it's quite literally walled me out.

"Well, darling, looks like I'll beat you to it. It's such a shame, I would've-" Nightshade begins.

"Well, well, well," says a familiar voice from the shadows.

It's Daman.

"You can't be here," Nightshade says darkly.

"As if you have any authority to tell me what I can and cannot do, little Lady Ligeia," Daman says.

Nightshade takes a step back. He takes a step closer. Green glows around her hands as she reaches for her bow and arrow...

Which turns to ash in her hands.

She doesn't know what I know. She doesn't know the legends. She doesn't know that the Senroom tree is the worst of all plants in this deadly forest. She doesn't know that the tree reveals a person's worst fear, and within the fog, the fears become almost real, as the tree begins to strike.

Daman steps out from behind the tree, several other figures in tow. Isolde, then Dietrich, then... me. My clone's braids are damp with blood, eyes glowing a bright pink. Blood slides down my neck, escaping impossibly deep bite marks. My doppelganger grins, black goop dripping from her lips. The rest of Nightshade's rebellion emerges beside her, effectively startling her. She steps back, and reaches for Aella's hand, only for Aella to step aside.

"What's wrong, are you afraid?" Daman quietly patronizes. "Figures. I always knew you were pathetic."

"And you're not?" Nightshade shoots back.

"Quit deflecting," Isolde chastises. "It's honestly quite unbecoming of you."

"I hope my actions make you squirm," Nightshade says. She makes a noise as if she's about to continue speaking, but before she can—

A faint caw echoes through the forest, and one of the rebellion members slowly walks away from Nightshade, trying to investigate the sound. Nightshade grabs them before they can walk any further. It begins with just one cawing sound, but each second, another caw arises from the forest, a garbled, dying sound that crescendos into an unhinged melody. Accompanying the shrieks above is the sudden eruption of the sound of hail overhead. The cawing grows louder, and louder, and louder, never seeming to stop.

It's a slow, agonizing descent of noise before I discover that there isn't a sudden change in weather. One by one, ravens drop to the ground, their corpses spasming on the forest floor. I feel bile begin to burn in my throat, and hold myself back from projecting my most recent meal over the carcass-ridden mud. One by one, the ravens begin to explode, their guts ricocheting into until everything within the fog was covered in guts, blood, and pus.

Beckett and Icylyn hide behind Aella, clinging to her. Nightshade, in turn, covers their eyes. Aella and the other three members of the rebellion simply watch, unexpressive. Daman begins to step toward Nightshade.

"Don't even think about taking another step," She warns.

"Or you'll what?" He asks, continuing to move toward her.

"I'll-" She starts, voice echoing.

He reaches a palm out to her and smiles softly. "It'll be over soon."

A raven swoops in, landing in his palm. Nightshade shakes her head. He grabs a dagger, a sickening grin overcoming him, laughing as he drives the dagger downwards. Nightshade stifles a scream, black tears rolling down her cheeks. The raven disappears completely, leaving a crazed Daman staring vacantly at a hysterical Nightshade. Green and black tendrils wrap around her hands, her fingers slowly turning black.

"Oh no, don't do that," Daman smiles. "We both know what happened the last time this happened."

Nightshade quickly turns to the members of the rebellion, all staring vacantly.

"You all need to get out of here. Now," She says, then turns to Daman, Dietrich, Isolde, and my clone. "The same goes for you."

No one moves.

"It's not real," I finally manage to yell. "Just grab the bark and get out of there!"

She doesn't hear me. Black vines slither out of the tree, wrapping around her ankles. She's too busy staring at her hands to notice. Daman presses a gun to her forehead, and a vine wraps around her throat. The tendrils surrounding Nightshade's hand twist and swirl, expanding and inserting themselves into the wound in Daman's hand.

"Wait- no- wait-" Nightshade chokes. "No, I didn't mean that. I didn't mean to do that. I didn't mean to do that. Wait-"

"We were right," Daman says as the wound in his hand turns black, the color in his skin quickly draining. He crumples to his knees, until he's nothing but ashes in the wind.

I have to remind myself it's not real. It's not. He's in Cazlamenta, he's perfectly fine.

The tendrils find their way to Isolde and Dietrich, and the same fate awaits them. Nightshade screams. It's indescribable. Guttural, and ghost-like, and completely inhuman. Nightshade falls to her knees, resting her head against the forest floor.

"Didn't think you'd actually do it," says one with green hair. They laugh, grabbing the ones with blue and white hair, and dragging them away.

"I didn't mean it," Nightshade says. "Come back, it's not safe here. I didn't mean it, I *swear*."

Vines continue to exit the tree, now also wrapping around her wrist. I begin to realize that there are spikes on the vines.

"Nightshade!" I yell, banging my fist against the fog. "Knock it off! It's *fake*."

"Nightshade~" My doppelganger says, kneeling in front of me. "Come on, look up. Having a breakdown is doing nothing for you. You look *pathetic*. It's honestly laughable."

My clone grabs a dagger, and puts it beneath Nightshade's chin, forcing her to sit up and look at her. She removes the hood from Nightshade's face. There's black tears rolling down her face, her hair somehow more a mess than ever, despite being pulled into a braid.

"Who are you fooling, Jinx?" My clone coos. "Look at you. You're weak. You can't even control yourself. Isolde was right. And that's why you're going to spend the rest of your miserable existence alone. You can't protect anyone. No one actually likes you. They're just... afraid. Afraid of a weak little porcelain doll."

Nightshade is held in place by the vines around her throat, which she's still oblivious to, despite the fact that they seem to be growing tighter. My clone quickly grabs Aella, slitting her throat. The tendrils quickly insert themselves into the wound.

"Aella!" Beckett and Icylyn shriek.

They both sprint for her, as her body hits the forest floor. Unlike the others, her body doesn't turn to dust and disappear. Nightshade's eyes turn bright red, and she tries to stand, tries to run to Aella, but can't.

"No," Nightshade sobs, then continues a constant alternation between screams and whispers, of which are all completely unintelligible.

"Jinx!" Beckett and Icylyn scream.

Their feet hover above the ground, bodies slowly lifting into the air.

"Just don't look down," Icylyn says, grabbing for Beckett's hand.

He grabs her hand, shutting his eyes tightly. A crazed laughter leads me to see the culprit. It's my clone. Her arms are slightly raised, fingers dancing. She seems to have telekinesis, and as her laughter grows louder and more unhinged, her eyes glow a deeper, brighter pink. Nightshade remains frozen.

"You're such a coward," the other me chuckles, her gaze seeming to burn through Nightshade.

Nightshade, shudders, her teeth gritted as she locks eyes with my doppelganger. Nightshade struggles against the vines, trying to stand. The vines only tighten and stiffen. My clone laughs in response.

"You... you won't hurt them," Nightshade says.

"Are you sure?" My other-self asks. "No. No, you're not."

"Leave them alone," Nightshade orders.

"If we die, Mamá's gonna be so pissed," Beckett says, turning to Icylyn.

"You're going to be fine, I'll get us out of this!" Nightshade yells.

"No you won't!" Icylyn screams, the temperature of the forest growing colder. "You killed everyone."

My doppelganger rolls her eyes. She hums to herself, aimlessly walking around. She looks at me and grins, putting a finger to her lips.

"We promised we were gonna be back," Beckett says, voice shaking. "Mamá's gonna be so upset."

"She won't be mad at us," Icylyn says. "Not *our* fault."

"Are we gonna die?" Beckett asks.

"I'll answer that," My doppelganger says, all too ecstatic.

Icylyn's eyes widen, and icicles spike out from the forest floor. She starts choking mid-air, trying in vain to remove non-existent hands from her neck. Beckett panics, and spins his finger around. The wind within the area picks up, and he tries to knock my doppelganger off of her feet, but all it does is whip her braids around. Beckett freezes in the air, and my clone shakes her head, clicking her tongue in disapproval.

"Alright, show's over," My doppelganger says.

There's the sound of snapping. Icylyn's neck bends in a way that necks should never bend. An arrow pierces through Beckett's throat.

"Now why'd you do that, Nightshade?" my doppleganger's voice rings out, deceptively sweet.

"Fuck. You," Nightshade says.

"You won't be able to bring them back, y'know," My clone grins. "Things are only going to get worse and it is all your-"

Blood begins to drip from my doppelganger's lips. A knife is lodged into the back of my doppelganger's neck. Her eyes fix on Nightshade, lips turning up, teeth slimed with red. There's a sharp squelch. My doppelganger falls to her knees, smile frozen on her face.

The knife plunges into the dirt. A cape trails over my doppelganger's corpse.

Nightshade grabs at the vines around her neck, everything but her arms covered completely in spiked vines. I'll never forget the look on her face. A look of terror and defeat. All the things that Nightshade is not.

NIGHTSHADE

The figure in front of Nightshade is faceless, jet black hair only falling down to her shoulders. Nightshade reaches her hand out, struggling. The figure makes no movement, simply stares down at her.

Nightshade gags, struggling, fingers not far from Daman's gun. The figure continues to just stare. Nightshade finally manages to grab the gun, and lifts it. There's something awfully calm about her. Awfully, *brutally* calm. The kind of calm more violent than any outburst, especially not when behind a canvas of blood and tears.

"You know who I am," The figure says.

Nightshade nods. She shoots.

The vines cease, and the fog dwindles. Nightshade sits, hands shaking.

"I tried to warn you," I say. "None of it's real."

"The forest shifts, right?" Nightshade asks, eyes blue, but distant.

She seems to sway. I nod.

"Get out before you miss your chance, then. It's not worth it," Nightshade says.

She promptly falls unconscious. I do as advised. I leave her there.

Chapter 8
Nightshade

I don't know how long I was lying there. For a long while, I pondered the fact that I might've been dying. By the time I woke up, sunlight was passing through the trees. I managed to slip into the shadows, but my wings burnt quickly. I was forced to venture deeper into the forest, staying in the shadows, until I found a small cave covered in chalk paintings. From there, I found the tunnel system to return to my own cave.

It takes nearly the entire day to walk back. I return my bow to the wall, hanging up my quiver, and then beside it, my hood. I pull the mask covering my face and neck up over my head, quickly tucking it into a drawer, along with my archer gloves. I stuff my long-sleeved overshirt in there, too.

Black blood soaks through the bandages of the shirt Rebecca gave me, having soaked the bandages. I'll bet I popped the stitches.

I slide a piece of the floor away, climbing down a small ladder into a small hidden room. I sit down on my bed, tucked into a crevice, and throw my shirt onto the bed beside me. I take a breath, pouring water over the wound. I did, in fact, pop the stitches. I stitch myself back together, biting down on my tongue so that I can't wince. I tuck my wings in, and put on another shirt, before carefully guiding my wings through the holes in my shirt. I hit snags, and bite down on my tongue until I taste blood. My wings are in worse shape than I'd hoped, covered in boils, and blisters, large holes protruding through them. I'll have to patch those up later. I toss my blood-soaked shirt off of the bed, and lie down.

Just for a moment, just for a moment, I only need a moment.

I lay there for a long time. Too long. I'm lethargic and restless and too many things all at once. I figure I'll probably wake myself up if I go get tea, then I can continue plans. I've already lost too much time. We have to keep the Two Kingdoms separate, I have to make sure the rest of the rebellion is okay, there's so much I have to do, I can't keep lying here.

Stars, do I want to.

It's sickening, how badly I want to lay here and never come out. Eventually, I force myself out of bed. I head to the kitchen, boiling water, and then sighing. I don't want to do this. I need to patch my wings.

I get to work, and avoid thinking about the fact that I failed. Avoid thinking about Fear Forest.

"I think we should bring theatre back when we take down the monarchy and resolidify the structure of the Two Kingdom's government," I say, flipping through the pages of Hamlet.

No one's around to hear, other than my dead pet Raven, Edgar. His ghost is on the table beside me. Edgar's always been a good listener. Even if it meant listening to me complain while I stitched up my wings. It's been a few days since Fear Forest. I'm perfectly fine.

The door to the cave starts whirring upwards, and Beckett and Icylyn run in. Beckett quickly pulls the lever behind him, and the two nearly collapse on the ground. I slam my book closed, and the mug I have floating in the air quickly falls onto the table. I stand up.

"What's wrong?" I ask, immediately.

Beckett and Icylyn start yelling over each other, before stopping, looking at each other, and taking a breath.

"They took Aella," They both say at once.

I take a breath, and hold onto the energy of the objects in the room, pulling my cloak, overshirt, hood, mask, bow and quiver to me at once, before quickly putting them all on. Thank the stars I didn't unbraid my hair. We're out the door quicker than they entered.

"Unus," Beckett says, kicking a pebble with his foot.

"Where?" Icylyn asks.

"Oh, that one's me!" Raven grins.

We'd collected Raven and Sage on our way to Couteau, knowing we'd need backup. Raven grabs a wanted poster with their face on it, folding it up and stuffing it in their mouth. Sage taps their shoulder, and signs, "Why?"

"I don't have pockets," Raven signs back, shrugging.

Sage grabs the poster out of their mouth, sticking it in her boots. Sage shakes her head, and Raven laughs.

"Duo!" Icylyn nearly shouts, beaming. She then clears her throat, and then a bit quieter, "Sorry. Duo- duo!"

"Nice catch," Beckett smiles, bumping into her shoulder. "Oh, boomshot, it's me!"

"Becca is gonna be *thrilled*," Icylyn says.

Beckett grabs the poster, having to jump up a bit to grab it, then gently tucks it into his satchel.

"Okay, wait, what's the point system again?" Raven asks.

"Group collectively gets one point for each wanted poster spotted," Beckett explains.

"And one deducted for anything 'royalty' related," Icylyn finishes it.

"Unfortunately, we're back down to Unus," I sigh, spotting a missing poster.

I haven't seen one of these in a while. I figured the missing posters would stop following Lila's funeral. Clearly, they haven't. I crumple the poster up, before turning it to ash between my fingers. I knew her, once. I like to think we were close. She's gone now, but she'd needed me. I just have to hope I haven't failed her yet.

"I'm sorry," Sage signs. "I know you were close."

I hesitate, tearing up the poster in my hands, then turning it to ash. I stick my now inky-black hands into my pocket, keeping my head down.

She's not... dead, I transmit to Sage. *She just doesn't want to be found.*

Chapter 9
Aella

"Your majesty," A guard says, out of breath.

"What?" Evsaphine asks sharply.

She's holding a small mirror in her hand. Blood is cracked and drying on my forehead. There's a syringe in her other hand, still stained with green. Not sedatives, no, I don't know what they injected in me. I never knew what they injected into me.

"We have reason to believe Nightshade is attacking the building. Come quick," The guard says, and turns to leave.

"Reste ici," Evsaphine says, squeezing my hand. *Stay here.*

She leaves with the other two guards in the room, each one on either side of her. Finally. I feel like I'm going to explode at this point, the chemicals in my veins feeling like metal, weighing me down. I'm pissed. I need to get out of here, before they can do anything else. Today they took my horns, and Evsaphine smiled at me as she set my horns down on a tray, one taken away to be discarded.

They said it again, they said they were going to 'fix me.' Yeah, totally. Obviously, that was working out so well for them. Their imaginary holy mission to fix their 'ill and ailing' daughter, so that she isn't a freak when she sits on a bloody throne she doesn't even want.

It's not like it hurts anymore. Well, emotionally. Physically, it hurts like a bitch. It's all just fucking fantastic. I love being told all of the responsibilities I'm going to have as queen once I'm "fixed." Yeah, like that shit's ever gonna happen. Sometimes it feels like I'm a ghost chained up, dying over and over again so that these assholes feel better about themselves, so they can pretend they're good people, good parents, trying to improve the one little hitch in their perfectly little royal line. No matter how far I run, they just come back. Veronica is right there, why not use her as their dumb little perfect princess? They know I'm not the kid I used to be when they could manipulate me, so why do they keep trying? Whatever. I'm gonna get out of this shithole anyway.

I take a deep breath, thinking harder and harder about everything that happened. About how mommy and daddy dearest couldn't give two shits about me. That I'm not supposed to exist, that other people aren't supposed to exist because of what assholes like Evsaphine and Lucius think. Of how they're stripping away every part of me they can. How my mom told me I looked beautiful once they took my horns.

Fuck.

This.

Shit.

I scream, too much to hold in, flames engulfing my body, melting the metal around my ankles and my arms. I grip tightly onto the chains, melting them to the point where I can pull myself off of the wall. I keep some of it. Could probably make some badass jewelry with Becca when I get back home.

Then little miss perfect decides it'd be a good time to step in. She stands there, just staring.

"You know they'll just find you again. Not that you bother to find new places to hide," Veronica says.

"That's because I have a home, princess," I spit. "It's a lot more than a hiding place."

"You really don't get it, do you?" Veronica says, laughing bitterly, and clicking her tongue, shaking her head. "Of course you don't. Why would you?"

"Shut up, you're going to get me caught," I say.

"Please, like they notice me anyway," Veronica scoffs. "You're the one they care about. You're the favorite. Do you know what it's been like, being second to you, my entire life? I spent my entire life alone because they always loved you more than me. "

I pause in the middle of picking the lock. I watch as my fingers flicker in and out of sight, flames reflecting on the walls around me. I let go before I can melt my only way of escape. I turn to look at her, closing my fists so tight that my nails dig into my palm.

"They didn't. They still don't," I say, thoughts I've been containing for far too long slipping off of my tongue. "They love the idea of who I was when they could control me. Lucius and Evsaphine hate me. Get that shit inside your head."

"No," Veronica says. "Unfortunately, they love you. They're *obsessed* with *you* and you've done *nothing* to deserve that. I hate you."

"I hate you too," I say.

And with that, I get out of that stupid room and leave that selfish brat behind.

Making noise is probably a shitty idea. Rookie mistake, I would know, I've escaped this shitthole enough times to learn that lesson. I couldn't give less of a damn. I scream all the french profanities I could think of, just to stick it to Evsaphine and Lucius, not caring if they hear me or not.

I freeze as two vines wrap around my wrists. They light on fire instantly, seeing as I lit myself on fire without thinking. I turn around to see the source. Sage gives me a very unimpressed wave.

"You are the worst," I sign, somewhat relieved.

"No. I do not appreciate the sarcasm right now. I will take a thank you," Sage signs, face completely deadpan.

"Fine. Thank you," I sign.

"You are welcome," She signs back. "Come on, Jinx is creating a distraction, the others are waiting."

I follow behind them as they walk. There's two guards outside, and it's clear both were easily taken down by Raven and Hazel, and Beckett and Icylyn. Beckett and Icylyn high five, practically screaming at each other. Both quickly turn their attention at the exact same time. They were always weirdly in sync like that.

"AELLA," Beckett shouts, face brightening.

The flames engulfing me quickly dwindle down as the two run at me, basically attacking me in a hug. Beckett, being far too tall for someone of the age of *thirteen*, nearly topples me over. Icylyn mumbles a quick 'ow,' then quickly switches sides with Beckett so that she isn't touching my skin. I tend to run warm.

"We were so worried about you," Icylyn says.

"There's no way they're taking me down that easy, ice storm," I say.

Hazel looks my way, and I notice her, stupidly wide eyed and looking far too hard at my forehead. I give her a look and shake my head.

Don't you dare mention it, I transmit to her.

She looks away, and I give Beckett and Icylyn one last big squeeze, then pat them both on the back and step away.

"So what's JJ doing anyway?" I ask.

Black and lime-green clouds rise from the entrance to the castle. Of course, she's being a dramatic shit. As always. There's a reason she's my best friend. I stretch out my wings and fly up to get a better look, perching at the very top of a weeping willow. I watch as she runs, laughing as she dodges each bullet. She snaps her hand with a flick of her wrist, and ten oncoming knights are immediately knocked unconscious. Boom. Out like a light. She sighs and fans herself.

"Is this truly the greatest you can do?" She teases the remaining guards.

One knight runs at her and she quickly grabs them by the shoulders, before pulling them close and delivering a kick to the crotch. She grabs them from under their arms, launching them to the side and knocking out a wave of knights.

Another assailant attempts to attack from behind. Jinx surveys the people she's knocked out, acting all nonchalant as she picks at a scab on her arm. Chuckling, she turns around, whipping her braid behind her as she makes her way to the gate, all the knights now on the ground, withering.

Nightshade runs and jumps, before climbing halfway up the gate. Once she reaches halfway up the gate, she lets go, holding on with only her right hand and foot. She looks at the wreckage, then to Veronica, who's standing at her balcony. Of course. Veronica can't stay away from drama. Jinx looks back at the knights.

"Oh you poor, mistrusting imbeciles. You can't take me alive if I never was!" Jinx yells.

She keeps going up the gate, and if any assholes try anything, she snaps and they fall back unconscious. She looks back at Veronica and waves.

"Enjoying the show, princess?" She shouts.

"Hardly!" Veronica shouts back, scoffing and rolling her eyes.

Nightshade makes a quick pouty-face before rolling her eyes. She turns back, climbing up the gate.

"JJ!" I yell, cupping my hands over my mouth.

She sees me and turns back to Veronica, blowing her a quick kiss with a wave. I cringe a bit, but it's worth it to see Veronica squirm. Jinx snaps again, the final knights falling. She climbs to the very very top of the gate, crossing her arms over her chest and falling backwards. Her wings spread, and she hurries in my direction. Wings growing more and more tired, and sore from chemicals and exertion, I fly down to the ground.

She flies straight at me, and like Icylyn and Beckett, nearly tackles me in her embrace.

"Oh my stars, I was so incredibly worried," She whispers into my ear, holding me tighter than I thought she could. "Are you alright?"

"No," I say, holding the fire back as much as I can. "We need to go."

"Agreed," She nods. "The Acosta's?"

"The Acosta cottage," Beckett smiles. "Or as it's commonly known, the Acottage."

"No one calls it that, nerd boy," I say, grabbing his hat and ruffling his hair, before stuffing his hat into his chest and leading the way. "Alright, let's get out of here."

It takes hours to get there, and everything hurts like *shit*. I know I can get there, I know I don't need help, I will be fine walking on my own. Still, it feels like I am *dying*. Oh my *stars,* am I going to get Evsaphine and Lucius for this one day. Well, one day, not today. As I open the door to the cottage, the ringing in my ears picks up, and I feel more dizzy than before. My legs give out beneath me, and everything goes black before I can even register hitting the floor.

I wake up in my bedroom in the cottage. There's clean clothes laid out on the bed, and water on the table. I sit up, looking at my hands, watching as they flicker in and out of view. It's time to stop sulking. My body seems to be fighting against me as I get out from under the covers, before tumbling back down on the floor. I take a glance at myself in the mirror. Smoke hovers around me, and I keep flickering in and out of sight. It looks like the blood has been washed off my face. I can't tell. If only my powers could stop tripping out for one star-forsaken second...

I grab the top off of the bed, pulling it carefully over my head, careful not to snag the shirt on my... horns. Right. I pull it over my head. It's weird without the resistance, I don't like it at all. I poke the tips of my wing through the holes in the back, spreading them out, then tucking them back in. I do the same with the jacket, then pull on the pair of pants laid out. I toss my dress across the room, then scream into my pillow. I light it on fire.

I hold it up and shrug the pillow out of the pillow case, dunking the pillowcase into the water on my bedside. It's dark out. Everyone's probably asleep. I'm starving.

I grab onto the side of my bed, hauling myself up. I nearly run into the wall, my legs still seeming to work against me. At least I don't have to vomit like I did the last time they stuck chemicals in me. Assholes. I stumble into the kitchen, holding onto the side of the countertop and setting my forehead against it. There's a strong energy in the room, something buzzing around me. It's overwhelming for a moment, and I feel almost light-headed. Rebecca's here.

"Thought you'd be in bed," I say.

"You thought wrong," Rebecca says, leaning on the countertop beside me.

"How long?" I ask.

"Two days," Rebecca says.

"You stayed up for *two* nights?" I ask. "Why would you do that?"

"You know why," Rebecca says, simply, moving about the kitchen. "Had to make sure you were okay."

I sit down, still flickering in and out of sight. My fingertips continuously relight, no matter how many times I blow them out. Rebecca looks at me questioningly, and I give up and nod. She nods back, and the humming in the room echoes in my mind. The pain quickly dulls, and my powers calm.

"You gonna give me the 'I'm a horrible influence for Beckett and Icylyn' speech?" I ask.

"Haven't done that before, so why would I do it now?" Rebecca asks.

"Just... yell at me and get it over with or some shit," I say, looking away from her.

I wait with anticipation. I have preset arguments in my head. It's taking her so long. She sits down next to me, and sets two bowls of food in front of us, with water. It smells good. It feels like a trap, she's going to get me into a spot where I can't argue back or leave, then she's gonna talk. But she doesn't.

"Do you *want* me to argue with you?" Rebecca asks.

"Just... do *something*," I say, stabbing my fork into the plate.

Rebecca takes a deep breath. She scoots closer, and takes my free hand into hers.

"You remind me a lot of myself," Rebecca starts. "Especially when I was your age. So I promise you, Aella, I get it. I haven't gone through what you have, and I curse the stars that you're going through all of that. And, look, you're nineteen. You're *supposed* to make mistakes, and you're supposed to be able to break rules, and sneak out, and learn for yourself what's right and what's wrong for yourself and the people you surround yourself with. You're at those beginning stages of those adult years, but had so much of your beginning stages stolen from you. Cut yourself some slack, you can learn new things."

I slip my hand out of her grip, and turn my head from her. We eat, nothing more than the sound of utensils scraping against plates. We finish, and Rebecca begins to clean up. Then and there, I want to tell her everything that happened. When they took me, what Evsaphine and Lucius did, the fight with Veronica, everything. But that feels like cowardice. She already has to deal with me, why burden her even more by listening to my stupid emotional issues?

"Did I ever tell you how I met Beckett's dad?" She asks, and when she gets no answer, "He was a pirate on the Red Revenge-"

"*The Red Revenge*?" I ask, startled. "You mean like... the *worst* ship? Like the one that keeps setting entire towns on fire *just because they can*? Those assholes?"

"Yes," Rebecca says, and the energy in the room becomes unbearable for a moment. "It was never his choice to be there. He was born into it, and spent his entire life trying to leave. But... the Red Revenge had kidnapped my girlfriend at the time. So, I snuck out. I was already secretly running a rebellion, and in deep shit with my parents. I was a stowaway on the Red Revenge for an entire voyage. It was my own anger that inevitably got me caught. Someone made some... bigoted remark, and I pulled out my sword. They sent Christopher to fight me... and I knocked him out immediately. Would've nearly tried to kill half the ship if Fenmore hadn't flown us out of there. So... I get it. You're allowed to be angry, and you're allowed to make mistakes. You're allowed to make *choices*."

"...what did you do after that?" I ask.

Rebecca smiles, and sits back down next to me, wrapping an arm around me.

"I didn't come back for a while. Captained a ship for a couple years, found Christopher again, beat the shit out of him in sword fights, came back, staged an attack on Cazlamenta with my crew and my rebellion... and it was unsuccessful. Shortly after that, I ran away again, back out to sea, got pregnant with Christine, and I settled down. In any case, it's getting late. I'm going to head to bed. I know you just got up, but you should continue to rest. Goodnight mi pólvora."

She gives me a tight hug, a kiss on my temple, then heads to bed without another word.

Chapter 10
Veronica

I'd been listening. Immature, like a child, my ears pressed against doors. Aella, Aella, Aella, Aella. Always Aella. Mostly in French. I can hear them shift around the room, and I quickly turn to leave. Sabine walks alongside me, silently.

"Veronica," my father says.

I stop in my tracks.

Shit, I think. *I've been caught. I'm going to be in so much trouble.*

I hesitate for a moment, then politely curtsey. Thank the stars it's a gut reaction, I can't fumble etiquette right now.

"Why don't you join us for lunch?" he offers.

It seems so foreign. I hesitate. My mom stares at me with cold, piercing, judgemental eyes. I raise my head. I nearly nod. But that would be disrespectful. They're expecting an answer, but the words are quickly fleeing my brain.

"Come," My mom sighs.

I follow close on their tracks.

The dining room is just as bright as the rest of the castle. The walls are a soft pink, carved and painted roses accenting the columns. Gold accents line the room, and the table is a white marble, flecks of pink, gold and baby blue. The plates and silverware are all rose gold, just like my mom's crown. Daylight spills in from the skylight and flower-shaped windows. These are the only windows in the castle not stained some shade of blue, purple or pink. It is so painfully, awkwardly quiet. So quiet that I tense every time my fork scrapes against my plate, a little bit terrified I'll be scolded. I finish, but I'm trapped in here.

"It's a shame," my father says, after a while. "We were making so much progress. Just a bit longer, and we would've been able to present Aella at the ball tomorrow."

"The what?" I ask, after a moment.

"You weren't spoken to," My mother murmurs.

"She never listens," my father shakes his head. "I wonder why the Woods haven't called off the marriage after spending time around her."

My gut sinks to my stomach.

"Selfish brat," My mom agrees.

"That's enough," my dad warns. "I didn't warrant you to speak."

My mom gives him a piercing glare, but says nothing else. I stare out the window, watching the vines tap against the window. Those will have to be cut. It's sunny out. It's been so foggy, for so long. It's nice to see the sun. I've spaced out again, haven't I? Shit. I'm stuck now. I'm going to get in trouble. They're speaking. Not to me. I can tell what they're saying, but I can't hear what they're saying. I'm stuck. I'm stuck, but I can't leave, and there's a part of me that doesn't want to, and-

"Wake up," My mother says.

I snap out of it, suddenly enraged. I wasn't *asleep,* she *knows* that.

"You should be listening," My father says.

"Right," I say, masking anger the best I can. "I apologize."

"There is a ball in Cazlamenta tomorrow, and we are to be attending. Stars, you were supposed to be practicing for that," my father says. "I expected better of you."

"I'm sorry," I say. "Are we sure this is the best time, though? Considering-"

"Yes," my mom says.

No concern about anyone's safety? Especially considering the... scumbags that call themself a 'rebellion' attacked the castle just this week? That's lovely. At least I'll be able to see the Woods again. It's been awhile.

"You appear to be done eating," my mother says.

I look down at my plate. Basically, yeah. I've been done for a while.

"You're excused, go make preparations," my dad says flippantly.

"Oh. Yes. Thank you," I say, standing, and exiting without another word.

I try not to feel disappointment bubble into my stomach.

"Look at you," Sabine smiles as I exit my room.

"Do I look okay?" I ask.

"You look beautiful," Sabine says. "He really doesn't deserve you, you know."

I pretend not to hear her, staring out the window. She doesn't push. She knows better than that. We walk down the hallway in silence. I catch my reflection in a golden mirror. I look good enough. I hope. I have this virtue at least. My mother's eyes, father's hair, father's skin, mother's face. Not tall enough, not symmetric enough, braids pulled perfectly, eyes gray when they should be brown, blue stars clutching too tightly to my skin.

I pass my mother in the hallway. I smile at her. She rolls her eyes. It looks so easy. Like she's done it unconsciously, without thinking. She loves me, I know she does. I'm too much like her. Too much, and not enough.

I can't stand the way she looks at me. Like the very thought of me is revolting.

It hits me in the gut. Tears aren't pretty. I hold them in, pulling my expression back into something poised. Can't ruin my makeup, not before the ball. Not before my mother.

My beautiful mother with golden hair. Golden hair, pale skin. My mother who fights. My mother who blames. My mother who survived men. My mother who grew up with an abusive father, a judgemental mother. My mother who married my father without a choice.

My mother who held my face after a night of too much mead. My mother and her golden hair and gray eyes, my mother who said she was proud of me. My mother who said I was beautiful. My mother who told me not to become a victim to my future.

My mother who only knew me as a failure. A disappointment. A bratty daughter who was never enough. Ugly and pretty. Too loud and too quiet.

Too stiff, and too clumsy. Too much, never enough. Her daughter. Her disappointment. Her replacement. Second choice.

She asks specifically not to ride with me in the carriage to Cazlamenta.

I can see it in my head. Over and over again. It shouldn't have affected me that much. Something about my mother rolling her eyes when I looked at her made something in my chest go cold. Even hours later, that's all I can think about. I make my way out of the ballroom, and was walk through the halls.

"Veronica," A voice says, almost delighted.

I turn to see Isolde there. I curtsey, and she offers a slight laugh as she crosses the distance between us. She puts her hands on my shoulders, then brushes the side of my temple with her thumb.

"Oh look at you," Isolde says. "You look beautiful."

"Really?" I ask. "I thought-"

"Of course, you always do," Isolde says. "Chin up, Veronica, remember that. You've been pulling out your hair, haven't you?"

I quickly put my hands behind my back, clasping them together and twisting the skin. She frowns, keeping one hand on my shoulder, the other running gently through my braids. Shame rushes through me. I can't pull my eyes from her gaze.

"You've been through quite a lot," Isolde says.

"Yes," I say.

"You're very strong, Veronica. So many would've crumbled by now. King Lucius was a fool to choose Aella as heir instead of you. No matter, I'm glad the stars sent you to us," Isolde smiles, then sours, eyes flickering to the side. "Noah, darling, quit lurking, it's unbecoming."

"Sor- Sorry Mother," Noah stumbles, quickly darting back into the ballroom.

"I don't know what I'm going to do with him," Isolde sighs, shaking her head. She turns back towards me. "My sons are going to have to learn a thing or two from you."

Isolde looks at me with pride. Like I have potential. She always told me that the stars had plans for me. She kisses the top of my head, and provides me with a warm smile. She has a reputation for being nothing but cold. She was never cold to me. She snaps, and a servant comes forth with a chalice. She takes a long sip.

"Go," She smiles. "Have fun."

"Yes ma'am," I say, curtsying. "Thank you."

She turns to leave. Daman steps into the room. I smile at him, and he smiles back. Warmth rushes through my body.

"There you are," He smiles. "I thought you were hiding again, but couldn't find you behind the curtains."

"You know me too well," I sigh, grinning. "You however neglected to consider-"

"Beneath the tables?" He asks, raising an eyebrow.

I laugh and nod. He takes my arm and leads me into the room. I giggle to myself and lean my head against his shoulder. To think, we could've been married already. Soon. Another young girl, somewhere around our age, approaches. Daman quickly pulls me into a dance, jerking his head to the side.

He was always so sweet like that. Protective.

My mother had the audacity to tell me he didn't really love me. That he was using me for my body, for my status, marrying me out of necessity. That he'd cheat on me, hurt me, discard me. I giggle again as he twirls me around, before moving to rest my head on his chest. I'm drawn to him, like a moth to the flame.

And then screams ripple through the crowd. Electricity crackles, and the windows shatter. Wind whips around the room, tossing people to the sides, knocking everything over. The flames in the room explode upwards, before disappearing completely.

"I'm going to kill her," Daman growls under his breath.

"I think we both know you can't do that," Nightshade's voice comes from behind him.

"Fuck!" He shouts.

He turns on his heels, pushing me out of the way. I stumble, sliding on the ice now covering the ballroom floor. I nearly hit the ice, when vines shoot out and stabilize me, but slam me against a column, holding me there.

"So improper," A familiar voice tsks at Daman. "What'll mommy and daddy do when they find out you have such a dirty mouth, huh princey-boy?"

Aella, as if things couldn't get any worse. Not far from her is Noah. He's staring at her, smiling with a fondness I've never seen from him, pushing his glasses up on his nose. He's leaned against a wall illuminated by a single candle, too focused on her to really notice anything else. He freezes and stiffens when he catches me looking, and gives a quick wave before diving out of the room.

"Someone go after Noah!" I scream, vines squeezing me tighter.

"Oh, don't worry, he's not part of this," says a warping voice.

The barefooted green-haired individual from Fear Forest. The vines part to reveal my hand and they grab it, slipping my ring off my finger, placing a firm hand on my mouth before I can scream in protest. I thrash, trying to escape. I pray to the stars that I have no open wounds, knowing all-too well the voice of a Shadow-Blood.

"Got it!" They grin, holding the ring up.

"Point Raven!" Beckett yells from somewhere in the room.

"Hey, Nerd-boy!" Aella shouts. "How many points for decking Daman in his stupid face?"

"Uhhh, dunno, ask the boss," Beckett yells. "Ice-storm and I've got a thing, I'll be right back!"

"Don't be stupid, Becca will kill me!" Aella yells after him. "So, JJ, what'll it be?"

"Twenty if he bleeds," Nightshade says.

The candles in the room all flicker on, everyone in the room being held by vines and ice. An elf with white hair stands in the middle of the room, veins glowing green and eyes seeming to flicker with flame. She changes her gaze at every moment, watching everything at once.

Aella pulls her arm back, punching Daman at full force. There's a disgusting cracking noise, and he hits the ground. A guard runs into the room and the ice seems to separate in their path. They bend over, breathing heavy.

"Everyone's down, your highness," the guard says to Daman. "The imports room, prisoner cells and... uh... the *other* room have been breached."

"Where are my parents?" Daman snaps, holding his nose.

Nightshade tilts her head back and laughs. It's terrifying. It's warped, and low, and sounds as though several other people are laughing with her.

"Oh! That was my idea! I helped with that idea!" Beckett yells.

"Beck!" Icylyn whines.

"Carriage! Right! Oh! Shit! I should not have said that! Byeeeee!" Beckett says, and Icylyn shakes her head.

She grabs him and quite literally flies out of the room. Beckett screams the second they're off the ground. Daman punches a hole into the wall he's closest to, digging his fingers through his golden hair.

"After them," He breathes, turning his attention to the guard.

"No," The shadow-blood shrugs, snapping.

The guard hits the floor, gently lowered by vines. The shadow-blood skips over to them, lifting them into their arm's bridal style. They smile.

"Mine now," the shadow-blood says.

They wink at the white-haired elf, before twirling around. They skip out of the room, leaving bloody footprints on the ballroom floor. Daman stands and hops on his toes, pushing Nightshade into the nearby wall at full force, hand gripped tightly around her throat. Aella yawns and grabs him by his hair, yanking him backwards hard enough that he hits the floor.

Something bubbles inside of me. The buzzing in my head returns

Louder

Louder

LOUDER

LOUDER LOUDER LOUDER LOUDER LOUDER LOUDER LOUDER LOUDER LOUDER

Until it's all I can hear. All I can feel. There's an energy exploding in me, dying to get out. The room feels charged with it. I'm hyper aware of it all. I can feel everything, everything in the room.

I'm going insane. I can hear people's thoughts.

People place their palms over their ears. People are screaming in pain. This has to be Nightshade's doing.

That doesn't explain why the sensation feels so familiar. That doesn't explain why I remember it.

Everyone's eyes glow a light pink. I'm angry and it hurts. Something in me feels wrong.

Aella places her hand into a tight fist and punches the side of her face as hard as she can. Over and over and over again. Suddenly the buzzing feels a little bit lighter. Something settles in my chest, something satisfactory. I feel a little less in control by the second. Something feels wrong, but better than anything I've ever felt. I don't want it to stop, and it's getting harder and harder to hold onto consciousness. My thoughts filter into something twisted, not in a way I'm used to.

Why are you hitting yourself, why are you hitting yourself, why are you hitting yourself? I think to myself, watching blow, after blow.

There's a beat to it. I can't recognize it. If only I'd paid attention in music class. That's all this is. Music. It feels like *music*. Something that turns sour as Nightshade tries to grab Aella's arms and hold them back. Nightshade's eyebrows are slightly furrowed, the way they are whenever she's in pain.

"Hey, what's taking so-" Beckett starts, running into the room.

His eyes, one brown, one green, turn pink. I remember him mentioning something about his goggles once, offhand. I watch as he slowly, lethargically, begins to untie the back of his goggles. It's like he's not in control of his movements.

Nightshade snaps and Daman falls unconscious. I yell and struggle, and Beckett throws his goggles to the ground, looking in Aella and Nightshade's direction. There's a blur across the room before his goggles hit the ground. Nightshade's sitting on the floor, holding Beckett, tying his goggles back on.

"¿Que me esta pasando?" Beckett breathes, sounding strangled. *What's happening to me?*

He puts his hands over his ears, trying to steady his breathing.

"Aella, Sage, and I will be fine, you take Icylyn and Raven and get out with the carriage," Nightshade says, smoothing his hair.

"But we want to help-" Beckett says.

"That wasn't a request," Nightshade says.

He looks like he's about to protest when green energy surrounds him, flinging the doors open and throwing him out. They slam closed.

"Everyone's out!" Nightshade yells, turning to Aella and Sage. "The tunnels are clear, we need to go."

She turns to me and winks.

"Too bad we didn't have time for a dance, darling."

They can't get out, I think to myself.

Sage's eyes glow a brighter pink and vines shoot out across the room, blocking any possible exits. Aella groans.

"I got it," Nightshade says. "Sweet dreams, everyone!"

And with a snap of her fingers-

"That's not fair!" Noah says, sounding so far away. "It was *your* fault-"

There's a crashing sound, followed by a snap.

"I told you to watch your tongue," Daman says.

"Did you just *break* my *glasses*?" Noah asks.

"I *told* you to *watch your tongue*," Daman says.

"... Look, dragging your unconscious girlfriend into *my* room and cleaning *your* blood with *my* bedsheets then blaming *me* for past shit and you being a bigot, and then you *pushing me into my bookshelf* is bad enough," Noah pauses to breathe. "But my *glasses*? *Really*? That's a *whole* new low. I could tell, you know."

"And I could tell mother and father you kissed a boy," Daman says.

"Oh come now," Noah says. "That was more than a year ago, I don't understand how you're still holding onto that."

I finally open my eyes, barely comprehending what's being said. Noah pauses, expression slowly going from timid and annoyed, to smug. He pushes his glasses up further on his face and straightens, crossing his arms.

"Are you *jealous*?" Noah asks.

"Hardly," Daman says. "How dare you even insinuate-"

"... Oh. Hi Veronica, you're awake now, that's nice" Noah says, snapping right back to being timid. He slips out of the room.

"What was all that about?" I ask.

"Don't worry about it," Daman sighs. "...come on, there's something I'm supposed to show you."

"What about last night?" I ask.

"It's related to last night," Daman says.

It's easier to stand than I thought it would be. Daman's already heading out the door. The second I'm outside the door, Noah sneaks back in to pick up his bookshelf and books.

"We managed to round up a few of the stray supernaturals who escaped," Daman explains. "About time you know what you're marrying into."

He leads me to a room that should never exist.

I don't want to describe it. This can't be happening. It can't be possible. It can't be real. But it is. It is real, and I watched it happen. I watched it happen. I didn't do anything. I didn't do anything. I couldn't do anything. It happened too quickly. Daman had his arms wrapped around my waist. The second I noticed the gun, it was already too late. I could hear the gunshots. I know that I'll still hear them for days... and days... and days... I'll hear them. I can still hear them.

Kids. Starving kids. Scales cut off on the floor. Elves handing their own ears over to a dragon to package. A guard gave them the guns.

They killed each other out of *mercy*.

I can still hear the gunshots.

I can see the blood splattering on the walls, on the floor. It's like paint. It's like splatters of paint. Why couldn't it have been paint? They were just kids. They had to be around the same age as Beckett. Some of them were my age.

That could have been me.

No, no, it couldn't have been. I'm human.

It could've been.

"You see," Daman says, still holding me tightly, as my knees give out. "This... is how we solve our problems."

They were just kids. They were supernaturals, but they had come for help. We're supposed to fix them, not kill them. Every part of me is shaking. I can't speak. I can't breathe. I tug at my hair, unable to move my gaze from the litter of bodies scattered across the floor. And Daman is smiling. He's smiling, as if it's all a show. Part of me wonders if it is. Part of me starts to wonder if it's all just some horrible, horrid prank. Part of me starts to hope that maybe... maybe that all of these blood-stained kids will open their eyes, and admit that the wounds were all fake. I hope. Stars, I hope, foolishly, deep in my bones, set in my illusions, that it's fake. But it isn't. It isn't fake. I can still hear the gunshots.

I run out the room. I can still hear the gunshots. I don't remember how I got out of Daman's grasp. I remember his breath on my neck, his head on my shoulder. So close, too close. *Always* so close, *too* close. He isn't distraught. He isn't distraught. There are bodies on the floor and he is unphased.

I run out of the room. I can still hear the gunshots. Daman chases me. He says he doesn't understand why I am "behaving so erratically." I can't breathe. I pull at my hair, still sprinting. There's got to be an escape somewhere. There's got to be-

The staircase.

Like the idiot I am, I decide the staircase is my best option. Daman yells at me to stop, and without thinking, I do. I always do what he tells me. My mother always does as my father tells her. She hates me because I'm so similar, too different. I pause, and slowly turn around, to where he was still standing on the ground.

"Come back down here," he says, in that voice that always made me tremble.

"No."

"Veronica... you're not being very smart right now."

His eyes are cold.

"You lied to me," I yell, slamming my hand against the railing.

The thud reverberates around the room, seemingly running down the railing. Bits of my blood trail from my knuckles, onto the railing, eventually dripping toward the floor. I hit my fist again. And again. And again, and again. I can still hear the gunshots.

I scream, squeezing my eyes tight.

"It's a lie!" I yell. "All of it, all of it's a lie."

"You don't want to keep talking," He warns, slowly making his way up the stairs.

Shut up, he'll always yell, pushing me into the wall, launching a fist to my face.

Pulling my hair, pressing his palm into my lips.

Kissing my forehead with his hands to my throat.

And I called that love?

Still lost in my thoughts, in the now all too quickly occurring realizations, I try to step backwards, but find myself moving forward, my fists both tightly curled. It is now no longer just me shaking. It's everything. Things fly off of shelves. Tables slide across the ground. Windows shatter. Something vibrates in me. Some insane mix of fear, anger, despair and betrayal. There's something more, something else. It lay dormant until now, something familiar yet foreign. The same thing I felt last night.

"I should've known," He mumbles to himself, grabbing a pistol from a holster. "I should've killed you in that forest months ago, when I had the chance. If it weren't for those rats and your excuse of a guard. It's high time I remedy that mistake, isn't it, my love?"

I slowly shift my gaze toward the pistol, the energy continuing to buzz and bubble over. I want the pistol gone. It's the only thing I can think.

I want it gone.

The pistol shakes in his hand, eventually flying across the room. Daman continues getting closer, and closer. I back up a bit, and he starts to run. I turn to run, but he grabs my dress, pulling me down. He starts hitting me, and I try to squirm away, kicking. I kick up my leg, going straight between his legs. He screams out in pain, something horrid, and I bite back the urge to apologize. I take the opportunity to get up, jumping to my feet and running. I nearly stumble over the railing.

"Get back here," He threatens.

Daman is on the ground for a few minutes, immobilized, before slowly standing up, limping slightly. He lunges at me, wrapping his arms around my throat and pulling us backwards, sending us both falling against the wall. We both slam down on the floor, tumbling down the stairs. As we slide down those few steps, he adjusts, putting one arm around my neck, his elbow just inches away from my chin. He bites something, and there's a slight popping noise, followed by a spitting noise, and a cork bouncing down the stairs.

"Stay still," He grumbles, his lips brushing against my ear.

I feel cold anxiety in my stomach, my body moving far too slow, and reach up, trying to remove his arm from around me. He repeatedly orders me to stop, and wraps his free leg around my arms, using the other to keep himself steady as I thrash around. I hold my lips as close together as I can, biting the tips of them from within my mouth. I won't let him. I don't know how I'll avoid it, but I won't let him pour that down my throat. I can't. Not after what I know now. After what I'd seen.

The weird energy returns, all but seeming to consume me, and the bottle explodes, shards of glass going everywhere, some hitting him and narrowly avoiding me. Daman hisses in pain, his hand now covered in blood and glass, both seeming to leak from his palm as he opens his grip. My relief is short-lived. Within a few seconds, a sharp stinging hits my neck. I let out a half-breath, half-scream, finally pushing him off of me, and bolting up. My mind is already foggy, and my movements are sluggish.

I stumble backward, hitting the railing and almost flipping off of it. I quickly catch myself, grabbing onto the railing for stability. I run down the stairs, trying my best not to fall, trying to evaluate an actual exit, rather than just somewhere to hide it out.

He runs in front of me, launching his bloody fist into my eye, knocking me down. I pull him down with me the best I can, kicking from behind his legs, just like Sabine taught me. He falls and I grab his hair. I attempt to hit his head against the wall.

I'm far too uncoordinated for that. Instead, he just manages to grab me. I punch him in the stomach, as hard as I possibly can. He lets go of me, taking a second to breathe, and I quite literally start rolling down the stairs, imagining flashes of myself hitting the bottom and snapping my neck. I grab a baluster once I'm close to the ground, hoisting myself up and leaping over the railing. I hit the ground with a snap, and suck in a breath.

He's gonna come for me soon, I gotta go. I'm so tired.

If I could just... stay down for a moment.

My thoughts blur as my eyes grow heavy. It's getting harder by the second to keep them open. I peel off my heels and keep running, my ankle screaming at me. Everything's fuzzy. The humming in me starts to dull. I can barely see where I am, can barely remember where I am. I don't know where to go. I can't go home. I'd get sent back here. I have nowhere to go. All I know is:

I have to... I

Can't think.

PERCY CADAVER

I have to get out of here.

I barely make it out of the courtyard before my feet fall out from beneath me. The world stops turning. It all slips into nothingness.

Part Two

Chapter 11
Nightshade

"Check," Beckett mumbles.

I take a long sip of my now cold tea. I'd been so focused, I'd forgotten about it until now. I'm stiff, but alert, tugging and retying my shoelaces, before undoing them and doing them again. Beckett takes a watch out of his pocket, clicking it open and closed, open and closed, leg bouncing up and down beneath the table.

You should have been using that to time, Sage transmits. *Probably could have been done hours ago.*

Not this one, Beckett transmits. *Doesn't work.*

I look back at the board. Beckett seems to study me, looking down the second he notices I've caught on. I smile and make my move. He mumbles something under his breath, something sounding like Spanish. He takes his turn. I had been hoping he would make that move. I can tell by the look in his eyes, and the way he'd previously been fiddling with my chess piece between his fingers, that he is aware the move he took was a major risk, and probably not the best idea.

"Checkmate," I say.

"Finally," Aella groans.

"Good game," Beckett smiles.

"Indeed," I say.

The two of us begin to pack up the chessboard. Aella and Sage are sitting on the ground, facing each other. A flame lights in Sage's hand, then Aella's. They try on their own to put it out, and when they can't and the flame gets too big, they put out the other's.

Icylyn's sitting on the floor with a large basket and several smaller ones. She's sorting the berries, and from then, sorting by color, texture, and size. She keeps switching the baskets around, frowning as she does.

Raven, quite literally, is hanging from the ceiling. They're upside down, twisting flowers around into flower crowns. They're singing something off-key and haunting in a whisper.

Hazel's been gone for a while, Sage transmits once again to the group. *I thought she'd be here by now.*

It might've been a low-staff day, so they couldn't switch her out as fast, Icylyn suggests.

Staffing shortages are never a problem there, especially guard-wise, believe me, I transmit with far more venom than intended.

"Oh," Icylyn mutters, staring down at the floor.

Beckett's next to her instantly. The temperature drops just as quickly, and I soon realize I've probably made a mistake. Beckett adjusts so that his knee hits against hers, offering his hand. She takes it, squeezing it tightly and resting her head on his shoulder. He has to lean down a little bit.

Before anything else happens, Hazel's coming down the stairs, still in armor, something slung over her shoulder.

I uh, Hazel transmits to the group. *Picked up... uh- ...Veronica.*

Oh my stars, unpick her up, Aella transmits, image flashing in and out of view.

Hazel looks at Aella, completely deadpan, and gently sets Veronica down on the stairs, stepping over her. She hangs up her helmet and armor, stretching. She looks back at Veronica, frowns, and sets her down somewhere else.

Well. This is nothing if not a curveball. It's an interesting one, to say the least. As much as this could be a potential setback, I can't help but marvel at the sudden turn of events. What can I say? Karma may be a vixen, but I find danger and fate often linger around similar establishments. Danger and Fate are more than vixens, however, more than mistresses. Danger and Fate are sweet, dear lovers. And my Nightshade persona is nothing if not a flirt.

In any case, Veronica would prove herself useful yet. Well, that is if she were to join us. It'd be foolish of her to return home, not with the rumors that have reached her kingdom about her. I may as well be getting ahead of myself, though. I don't entirely know the context.

Hazel, I transmit to the group. *An explanation, if you please?*

Hazel doesn't hesitate. *I was finishing my shift, said bye to Noah, then stuff started flying around the castle. There was a whole lot of screaming, and I could hear Daman yelling back at her. The next thing I know, Veronica's running out the door and unconscious seconds later.*

So why didn't you just toss her off the cliff? Aella transmits.

Beckett's hand shoots to his face and his eyes blow wide. He chokes out a laugh, then widens his eyes, slapping another hand over his mouth. Aella shoots him a quick glance, eyebrows turned up in judgment, then crosses her arms and leans back in her seat. Raven giggles, giggles soon turning into a burst of loud laughter, to which Beckett, Icylyn, and Hazel quickly turn to shush them. Raven swings back and forth, losing their hold on the chandelier. They proclaim a loud, "oop!" and then find themself surrounded by green mist, gently lowering themself down onto the table.

Either Veronica is an incredibly heavy sleeper, or the sedative is very, very strong. I don't know as much as I should about that, that's a question better suited for Beckett or Icylyn. In any case, whatever is keeping her unconscious longer is working in our favor.

To be quite frank, I've never particularly *disliked* Veronica. I dislike the way she treats people. Then again, she doesn't like us very much. For good reason, I suppose. In any case, once we'd had her on our side, it'd be a turning point.

After all... it's not bad to have a tele-controller on your side.

So... none of us are dragging her to Couteau, what're we gonna do with her? Beckett transmits.

Sage and I could always take her! Raven offers.

All due respect, dearest, you don't have a house, Hazel puts a hand on their shoulder.

Yeah but we have a bitching mausoleum that no one's using, Raven transmits. *House enough.*

I think if she woke up in a mausoleum it would send the wrong message, Icylyn points out.

Whatever we do is going to send the wrong message, but no, not our place, Sage says.

She's not coming back with us, Aella's eyes go fiery. *No chance. Maybe we should just stick her on a pirate ship, make her* their *problem. She might come out less spoiled.*

I weigh the options. They're all thinking about this entirely incorrectly. They see Veronica as an inconvenience. What they don't realize is that she's a turning point for us. We'd have to go about this carefully. She isn't aware she's one of us and will need to change her entire mindset. Not to mention the fact that we've ruined her marriage, attacked, and kidnapped her.

Manipulation. Most people make the mistake of hating the negative traits they've received from their parents. There's a power in embracing them. Veronica is easy, malleable. I hate myself for thinking it, but it's true. While it's true that Isolde and Daman could easily manipulate even the strongest of minds and wills, Veronica isn't exactly... well...

For the most part, she's strong-willed. I'll give her that.

"What're you thinking this time, JJ?" Aella asks, signing as she speaks. "That face always means trouble. Stars, I hope it's trouble."

"Give me a moment, I need to compile my thoughts," I respond.

So you don't actually have a plan? Aella transmits to me directly.

Was I really that obvious?

I have an excellent plan, thank you very much, I transmit back.

It better involve doing something questionable.

I feel like that's unavoidable at this point. I know for sure I can't take her back to my cave. First of all, that's just wrong. Given the boundaries of our relationship, I cannot take her to my house while she's unconscious. Second of all, that is my house. My house is my house, and I don't like people in it, or knowing where it is. Aella, Beckett and Icylyn are the only exceptions to that, and even at times they're on thin ice for that. We can't put her with the Acostas. I don't trust Rebecca, regardless of the fact that she's Beckett, Icylyn and Aella's mother. It would also be rude to just drop Veronica there, both to Rebecca and to Aella, who's already clearly laid that as a boundary. I have trust and respect for Hazel, Sage and Raven, but I don't think this is a responsibility they would be able to take on.

It would likely be easier and more merciful to simply kill her at this point. Unfortunately for everyone involved, I don't kill. Killing would send the wrong message. It would prove the royals correct about me.

I'm not exaggerating when I say I'd rather swallow a silver sword than prove the royals correct.

Morally, murder is just incorrect. As dangerous as it is, I can't help but be a sucker for second chances. Everyone has a chance to grow beyond their past, or their past mistakes. Death is an ending for many. Who am I to end a story that can yet be rewritten? That's my purpose, isn't it? To rewrite the story handed to me and many others? If the royals can write their history, so can I. Though, it's seeming as though I haven't loosened my grip on the quill since the age of ten. I don't mind.

Murder also seems a bit redundant to me, seeing as I speak with the dead.

Murdering Veronica is entirely off the table. I know the story she's telling. I know it doesn't belong to her. She's simply repeating the one fabricated to her by the royals, the golden lies spun of blood and bones. She lays there, a pawn I'm not sure where to place on the board. Her blood is laid out on the manuscript.

Is it her move? Is it mine?

Where do either of us stand in this twist of fate?

Maybe that's it. Maybe I won't return home for a while. Maybe I'll stay in the base. Maybe I'll teach her how to grip her own pen.

Stay with her until she gets her bearings, then let her choose where to stay from there.

I place a hand on my thigh, to keep myself from bouncing my legs, noticing not only have I been doing that, but I've been biting down on my knuckle, spinning a strand of my hair around a free finger, pulling apart my braids. I'm suddenly back in the room, all too aware. The mask I wear on the lower half of my face is now slightly damp. I'm instantly disgusted, and find my way to a bookshelf without another word. I feel along the tops, careful to make sure each one is touched. There has to be an equal amount of wear on each book, an even amount of dust. I pull down on one, and the shelf slides away. I step into the room. I quickly slide the entrance closed, and take a breath, lighting the candles in the room. It's quiet here.

I lower my hood, and grab the cloth that connects from my neck to my nose, pulling it over my head and throwing it into a basket, piled with dirt, mud, blood, and sweat covered garments. I find a matching mask, and put it on, before re-braiding my hair, and lowering my hood on my face. I re-enter the room, clearing my throat. Raven nudges Sage's shoulder to get her attention. Everyone's eyes are back on me.

"For the meanwhile, I'm compromising this hideout," I say, continuing to speak over the protest, signing as I speak. "We'll need to locate a new one. Beckett, Hazel, I expect the two of you on that as soon as possible. I'd ask that we don't involve Rebecca Acosta-"

"Wait, JJ-" Aella starts

I put a finger up to her, continuing before I can lose track of my thoughts.

"I will be remaining here with Veronica until it is safe to relocate her," I say. "Hazel, reassess the old hideouts, see if they're still safe to use. Beckett, I need you to consult your mother without giving her information. Meeting adjourned."

"Can we vote on it?" Hazel asks.

"No," I say.

My voice warps, as a warning, and green fog wraps in tendrils around my arms. Sage rolls her eyes and grabs Hazel's forearm, dragging her out of the hideout. Raven perks up, twirling as they follow the two out.

"You said you had a *good* plan," Aella crosses her arms.

"No," I say. "I said I had an *excellent* plan. And I do."

"It sounds like a shitty plan, but I trust you!" Beckett grins, then turns and whines. "Okay, Aella, meeting's done, can we go home now? I'm hungry."

"Me too," Icylyn murmurs, staring at her feet.

"...fine," Aella huffs, then turns to me. "Don't be stupid."

The three of them are gone in a swirl of flame.

I sit down, leaning against a wall and taking a breath. My eyes slide closed, and I move to pull down my mask. I can hear Veronica's heartbeat all too loud. I'm in over my head here, but when am I not? There's a shift in Veronica's heartbeat, and then it's faster and faster.

"You're safe here," I say, not bothering to open my eyes. "You passed out trying to run from Cazlamenta and one of the members of the rebellion brought you here. I'm not going to harm you."

Something taps my throat.

"It's a wonder you haven't choked on your lies," Veronica's voice is rough.

"That sounds like projection, darling," I say, sliding my eyes open.

Veronica has one hand against the wall to steady herself, the other shaking, holding a dagger against my throat. Her eyes are bloodshot, sliding from gray, to pink, to gray again, unfocused. Her gaze shifts about the room, eyebrows furrowed. She stumbles, her dagger falling to my chest, poking it. I grab it out of her hand before it can harm me. She leans with her back to the wall, holding her forehead and whining.

"I'm gonna vomit," Veronica moans.

I kick a bucket over to her. She looks at it with disgust.

"I'd rather not clean your vomit out of the floor, darling," I say.

"There were kids-" She begins, then coughs.

She grabs onto the side of the bucket, and leans her head forward. I carefully gather her braids and hold them back, unable to find a ribbon to tie them back with. It goes on for quite a while, and honestly sounds quite painful. She eventually sits up, draws a breath, and wipes her lips with a handkerchief, which she stuffs into the bucket. Tears continue to roll down her face. She smacks my hand away, and I drop her braids.

"Don't look at me," she orders.

She turns away from me, and tucks her knees to her chest, wincing as she does. She grabs at her ankle, shaking. Her breath hiccups, and she's deadly silent for a moment. She coughs, hand reading for the bucket every time she does. She chokes out another breath, then grabs at her hair, yanking at it, beginning to hyperventilate.

"*Fuck*," She shakes.

And then she starts screaming. It's shrill, and horrid, and sounds painful. She screams, her entire body shaking. She rests her forehead on her knees, punching the floor with one hand, pulling at her braids with the other. It takes a good few minutes before the screams dissolve into sobbing.

"*Fuck*," She whispers. She picks up her head, and says, "Fuck. Fuck. *Fuck*. FUCK."

She hits her head against the back of the wall, hands practically vibrating as she lifts them up and presses them against her face. Her sobs turn into whines, then back to hyperventilating. She grabs the bucket and holds it against her chest, lowering her head into it.

"If you touch me I'll-" She starts, then begins retching.

It's safe to say I got the picture.

"You can't keep me here forever," Veronica rasps. "People will come for me. Sab- my guard will realize I'm gone. She'll come for me. My father will send out troops... Daman will... Daman will *ruin you*."

I hand her another piece of cloth and stand, stretching. She tenses the second I move, and I consciously stay away from her area as I move about.

"I didn't kidnap you, Veronica."

She wipes her face and looks up at me. She presses her lips in a thin line, squinting and scrunching her eyebrows. Her head tosses slightly to the side, her braids with it. She looks slowly around the room, then back at me.

"Well, it sure looks like you did," She says, wiping her cheeks.

A breath of amusement escapes me before I have the chance to stop it. I sit down in front of her. I know I'm making a stupid decision, but she's already seen the top half of my face. The last thing she needs right now is more of a threat. I unclip my cloak, leaving my face mask on. I carefully fold it beside me so that it won't wrinkle, willing my eyes to be blue rather than black or red.

"You're welcome to leave," I say. "Though, I wouldn't recommend it."

"I can't walk, my ankle's all messed up... bitch," She says, struggling to find an insult.

"Did I not say I wouldn't recommend it?"

Veronica huffs and crosses her arms. Then she pouts, and her shoulders start shaking, eyes pointing upwards. She's crying again.

"Your ankle will heal in time," I say. "You'd be more than welcome to leave when it does, but again, I don't think that's in your best interest."

"Sabine's going to worry," Veronica says, eyes wide. "Daman-"

She cuts off, and recognition flashes across her face. Recognition... and *terror*. Her breathing slows and shakes, and she freezes completely. Her eyes glaze over pink, and the energy in the room becomes unbearable. She starts hyperventilating, eyes drifting around, holding one hand against her chest.

"Do you know how to count?" I ask.

"I'm-" She breathes. "I learned- of course, I'm not *stu-*"

She breaks off, seemingly unable to breathe.

"Hey," I say, as softly as I can.

I start breathing, emphasizing and making it slow.

"Count backwards from 100, skip every four numbers. You can do it in latin, if it's easier."

"Stupid," She says, eyes rolling backward.

"It's not. Try it," I say.

She glares, but does as told. It takes her a few minutes. She stumbles, and her counting isn't perfect, but the important thing is that she's keeping herself distracted. I allow myself to stop breathing when I notice her breath stabilizes. She's getting closer.

"I hate you," She murmurs, once she's calmer.

"I know," I can't help but smile.

She makes a sound that sounds almost like it could be a laugh. She shakes her head, rolling her eyes and groaning. She rests her forehead on her knees, pushing her braids back with the palms of her hands.

"They lied," Veronica whispers. "They're not helping fix supernaturals, they're... they're torturing and killing them and- and I-"

"They're horrible people, Veronica."

"They loved me."

"You felt loved. They kept you on a string. There's a difference."

Veronica looks at me, a mix of disbelief, anger, shock, and pain all at once. Yet, all the same... I can tell she knows what I'm saying is the truth. The humming in the room dies down, and her eyes shift back to gray.

"I can't go home," She whispers. "They'll send me back to him. I can't lose him. I can't go back. I love them. I don't want to die. Oh my stars, Isolde, my mother, my father, Sabine, I can't *lose* them but what if- I- they'll find me. What if I'm found to be worthless? I should've reacted differently, I-"

"It is possible to escape The Woods," I say.

I regret the words once they leave my mouth. My connection with the "lost" princess was to remain a secret. I clear my throat, and look away, hoping that in her panic, she didn't catch on. Unfortunately for me, this seemed to be the one moment she decided not to be oblivious. Veronica stares at me a moment, then rolls her eyes again and looks away, beginning to cry again.

"I want to go home," Veronica murmurs.

I remember it all too clearly. Lila sitting beside me. We were both ten at the time. I was braiding my hair, and Edgar tried to pluck the strands out. Lila was crying. She was crying and crying, and couldn't look at anything but the castle. She wouldn't stop. She couldn't stop. She was afraid. Of what had happened, of what was to come... most of all, of herself.

"I want to go home," She'd sobbed.

The Woods had broken her far beyond what should be possible.

I explained to her that it was never a home. It was a dollhouse. A beautiful dollhouse, but something false all the same. Something with a beautiful facade, filled with nothing but thorns where there should be roses. I promised her I'd burn it to nothing but ashes, that the people who abandoned her, hated her, all of them, all of them would see ashes, know nothing but ashes. Vengeance was always something that ran through my veins, even as a child.

That was the night I became Nightshade. It all started with an attempt to protect Lila.

I stand, not thinking to give Veronica a look. I walk into the other room.

"Where are you going?" She asks, sharp, voice shaking.

"Just a moment, darling."

By the time I enter with a cup of water, she's sobbing again. I figure there's probably going to be quite a bit of this for the duration of my time with her. I carefully set the glass down in front of her, then step back.

"Is this poisoned?" She murmurs, voice raw and empty.

"No," I say simply. "I won't be offended if you double-check, I'll let my blocks down."

Veronica just stares at me. It's like there isn't a single thought behind her expression. There's no way she could actually be that dense... is there? She opens her mouth, then furrows her brow and pierces her lips. She seems to bite down on her top teeth, then her tongue. She looks down at the water and stares at it for a moment. She puts her nose down in the cup and then sniffs. She shrugs, then takes a long sip.

"You could've just..." I trail off.

"What?" She snaps. "I could've what?"

"Oh. Nothing, nothing at all."

She rolls her eyes yet again, scoffing into the cup. Perhaps she *is* really that dense. I watch as she cradles the cup between her palms. She holds the cup against her lips, drinking it while staring into nothingness, tears dripping down her cheeks once again.

"I thought... I thought they were fixing supernaturals," Veronica says into the glass.

"We don't need to be fixed," I say. "We simply are. We're like the land. We're magic. We love as the land does, hate as the land does, and draw strength and weakness as it does. We are not better or worse than any other person. To believe the stars could hate any being for how we were created is a narrow concept spun by those grappling for whatever control they can. I suspect you're beginning to see that."

"They were *kids*," She whispers.

I move to sit down beside her, and she flinches when I do. I consciously return all of the death energy within me deep into its origin place within me so that there's no chance of it leaking out. Then I extend my hand. She stares at it for a moment. Confusion is the first expression to pass her face. Then disgust. Then embarrassment. She tosses her head to the side, away from me.

"I don't want your pity," She spits.

But then her hand is in mine.

"They *promised*, they said the stars had a plan," She whispers. "How could they do that? They were supposed to be helping. They were supposed to *save* the supernaturals not... not... how could they *do* that?"

"There are very few things I don't know," I respond. "And that... is one of them."

She takes her free hand and begins tugging at her braids again. Her breathing grows fast again. I give her hand a quick squeeze, and she responds by squeezing as tightly as she can. It's almost as if she were at the edge of the cliff, and my hand was the only thing preventing her from falling. I can feel my heart begin to beat, and I'm not quite sure I like it. That's far from relevant at the moment. She looks back at me for a moment, almost pleadingly.

"Those who weren't shot... or given a gun to shoot themself with...they begged the others to shoot them," Veronica whispers, face blank, voice staggering with rising anger. "That's how bad it is. That's how bad it is, and I actively supported it. And I idolized them. Isolde was more of a mother to me than my own could ever dream of being... and I wanted to be like her. *Stars*."

"Isolde is a manipulator. Nothing more," I say.

This doesn't seem to help. She gasps for breath, and I squeeze her hand tighter. She blinks her eyes shut as tightly as she can and tilts her head all the way backward. She just whispers the word "okay" over and over.

I realize that no matter what, she's going to be like this for a while.

"Can you take any more earth-shattering discoveries that I can only assume you were terrifyingly oblivious to?" I ask.

"Hit me," She says.

"I'm not going to harm you," I say.

She looks at me like I've said the dumbest thing she's ever heard. Then I realized what she meant.

"Were you aware that you're a supernatural?"

Veronica is slow to accept things. It's understandable, considering what she's been through, but also quite tedious. She's been with me for two weeks now. I realize soon after that I'll need to take her outside. She'll need fresh air from time to time and eventually should be out in daylight hours. I think the latter is a dangerous request, but apparently, it is essential for most beings to be exposed to sunlight.

She often thinks I'm asleep during the day. I sometimes am, but rarely have I slept with her here. There are too many risk factors. That being said... I hear her. I hear her all of the time. Her cries sound painful. I hear whenever her sobs get a little too close to screams, when she has to muffle herself with her pillow. When she's choking on her tears. I pressed my ear to the wall once, to the floor she was standing on.

I heard something shatter in her.

"No one's coming for me," She'd said.

She's silent now, her warm brown skin seeming to glow softly in the moonlight. My mind wanders a moment. How someone could look so pretty in all lighting, in all situations, is beyond me. That's not at all what I should be thinking about right now.

She seems to be changing. For the better, it seems. I'd helped her climb the tree earlier, making sure to teach her how. For all her obliviousness, she's a quick learner. She climbs next to me, but keeps her distance. It's considerably less distance than before. After a moment, she scoots closer. She picks off a leaf, one I told her was safe to eat, and chews on it.

"Are you hungry?" I ask her.

She shakes her head. Clearly, she's lying.

"I'll get us food," I promise, but before I can continue, she rolls her eyes and looks away.

I just lean back on my hands, holding loosely to the branch. She keeps her eyes down and away, gently kicking her legs. She pulls at her eyebrows, then eyelashes, then hugs her arms around her torso. She whispers "okay" to herself a few times, then gazes up at the moon. Her eyes seem to dart away when they fall on the stars, and she looks at the ground once more.

"You only want me because you think I have magic," She murmurs after a while.

There are many things to think about that. I'm not quite sure which is the most solid. Whether I should be amused, whether I think she's clever for considering that. Another thought is whether or not I should consider if what she's saying is true. There's a part of me that can't help but feel bad for her, that she's discovered people seem to only value her for her uses.

"I *know* you have magic," I say.

Shit. That was incredibly smooth of me. What can I say? I'm better suited for escalating situations, rather than the alternative. She scoffs and rolls her eyes.

Veronica winces as she hops down from the tree, continuing to walk with a limp. I hop down in front of her, and she stiffens, shaking a bit, and yelling. I quietly apologize.

"What's wrong?" I ask. "Why are you limping?"

"My ankle's still bugging me," She murmurs.

"I think you have the potential to grow as a person," I blurt, offering my arm. "That's why I want you around. You are an asset because of your powers, and because of your connections within the royals, but that's not the only reason you are of value. You're of value because you're loyal and witty, and clearly willing to see a change. You've got a little bit of a moral backbone."

"Late recovery there, sweet-talker," She says.

"I'm being honest," I say.

She's quiet and slinks down. I look at her ankle. It's in horrid condition. How did I not notice? She tugs a few braids out, making a face and then setting them down. She puts her head in her hands.

"You don't even have to join the rebellion. Your safety is our concern as of now. My concern."

"Are you gonna sweet-talk me then kill me like you killed Lila?" Veronica asks. "Just to get to them? Because it won't work. Obviously."

"I did not kill Lila. She's very much alive," I say, putting a finger up when Veronica's expression whips to shock and disbelief. "We were close. She's in hiding now, but I became Nightshade to protect her."

"Wow," Veronica laughs. "That is *such* a lie!"

"I can assure you it isn't," I say.

"Yeah, okay Nightshade."

"Jinx."

"What?"

"Jinx."

"Nightshade."

Chapter 12
Aella

It's all just been a bunch of horseshit lately. I can't even go to my best friend because she decided to keep Veronica around. Veronica, of all people. Whatever. That's not even all that important. It's... not a great time in the Acosta household right now.

A few years before I got adopted, the Red Revenge attacked the Acostas. Christopher, Rebecca's husband, was killed. So were her daughters, Christine and Chrystal. Their graves sat in front of the cottage. Rebecca and Icylyn woke up early, picked fresh flowers, laid them on the graves, the whole thing.

I stayed with Beckett. Stress and grief doesn't exactly mix with his epilepsy. He had a seizure this morning. Spends most of the day rambling. Isn't quite sure who he is. Isn't quite sure who I am.

Noah once stole a book on medical disorders and sat with me on top of Jinx's cave, reading the contents aloud. I wasn't listening to most of it, aside from just enjoying the sound of his voice. It wasn't until he started reading about postictal psychosis that I had any interest. The symptoms sounded exactly like things Beckett experienced.

Rocking back and forth on his bed, Beckett kept rambling. He was completely out of it. He so earnestly believed he was a shadow-blood. He so earnestly believed he could see his dad and sisters in his room. No other thoughts seemed to be coherent.

It's going to be like this for a little bit. A week, probably, if fate is kind. But fate's a whore. I stayed with him most of the day, then Rebecca swapped me. I don't know. Probably a shitty move, but I had to leave.

So I'm sitting at the tavern in neutral territory. The river and surrounding land, not too far from where the Acosta cottage is in Mortem Venenum. Maybe a ten-minute walk at most. It's free territory until after sunset, then it becomes river siren territory. Well, all of it except for the tavern, otherwise called The Sparkling Maiden. I figure a couple of drinks, a couple of hours of flirting with strangers, then I'll crash back home and be ready to deal with all the bullshit in the morning. This whole older sister thing is hard, but I signed up for it. Besides, despite what I say... I really do have a soft spot for Beck and Ice. They can't know that, though.

The Tavern's a cute place. It's a small building with a thatched roof and stain-glass windows. The door's covered in moss, and the rest of the building in vines. They surround the walkway, the arch to the doorway, and even the tiny heart-shaped faded chimney that blows out wisps of smoke. The door knocker is made of gold, not silver, and is gargoyle shaped. You gotta knock six times, then wait for Orrin to make sure you're not a serial killer or a bigot or some shit like that. Supernaturals don't get many safe spaces anyway.

Orrin's the guy who runs the joint. He's a grump, and kind of an asshole. I love him. I think he's great. He hates me a little, but I'll grow on him sooner or later. He's a shadow-blood with creepily pale skin and long white hair always tied back. Apparently, he has ties with Rebecca, he was in a rebellion with her.

There's a couple of booths in here, and a bar, where I'm seated, swishing on the barstool, knee bouncing at what seems to be supersonic speed. Since there's no sunlight to stream through the windows, the lighting is dim. Everything's lit up by candlelight. There are not many people here tonight.

Sitting on the countertop of the bar is Dorian. He's about fourteen, real close with Beckett and Icylyn. Beckett's got a big crush on the guy. He's got black hair with a stupid middle part, and red eyes outlined by eyeliner. He's a walking vampire stereotype. He's missing his wings, though.

"Dorian, what do you have?" Orrin asks, arms crossed.

"It's only blood," Dorian waves him off, voice thick with an Irish accent.

"Are you scaring people off again?" Orrin asks.

"Wouldn't dream of it, love!" Dorian says, hopping off the counter. "I'd really better be heading off."

He gives me a nod and a wink and dives behind the counter. The kid's ballsy, I'll give him that. I'm about to flag down Dela, the bartender on duty, when the bell at the door of the tavern chimes. I turn on instinct. Noah and Hazel walk in, both in casual clothing for once. I'm more excited than I'd like to admit.

"Would you look at who finally got out of the castle?" I grin.

"Aella," Noah beams, pulling me into a hug. "I'm so relieved you got back out."

"Aww," I pout when we finally pull away. "Were you worried?"

"Of course I was," He stammers, turning red and avoiding my gaze.

I smile in spite of myself, and lean down slightly, resting my forearm on his head. His face seems to color more. I laugh, and turn my attention to Hazel.

"Hey, Haze. Night out?"

"Yes ma'am," Hazel smiles. "Phineas and I switch shifts this weekend, so I figured I'd get Noah out. You could keep him out of danger for a bit? Maybe I could...?"

"Go," I grin, pushing her.

"Thanks, Harley," She smiles.

Her gold eyes crackle with electricity and she spins around, grabbing something out of her bag. Something she stole from the Wood's tech room, where they'd gotten modern imports from other countries. Apparently they were called "headphones." She tosses them on and bolts out the door without another word.

Noah attempts to wave, but she's out the door before he's really registered what's happening. He sits down at the bar, picking at his nails. I slide onto the barstool next to him, resting my elbow on the bar, my cheek on my fist. He pushes his glasses up on his face, eyes looking anywhere but at me, biting his nails.

"Awww, what's wrong?" I tease. "You seem nervous."

"I- uh- don't-don't get out much."

Stars, I'm a little bit fucked. I realistically could take home anyone in this bar, yet my heart's doing flip-flops for the anxious royal boy who's a little bit of a loser. A little bit of a loser and can't leave his castle. He's sweet. He's pretty. His leg is bouncing under the table, matching mine. I can't help but grin.

"You want anything?" I ask. "My treat."

"No- no, thank you," He smiles, picking at his bottom lip with his teeth. "That was nice of you, though."

"Don't say that so loud," I say, gently punching him in the shoulder. "I got a reputation to keep."

"Right," He laughs softly. "I could tell. So why'd Hazel call you Harley?"

I snort. That one's a fun memory.

I'd gone out for drinks one night with Sage and Hazel. I'd been sitting on top of one of the tables, some girl's tongue down my throat. I don't remember her name. Some creep whistled. I pulled away from the girl, and she looked at me for a moment, confused. I looked at this disgusting, surly old man, and stuck my thumb in my mouth. I lit a flame behind my eyes and bit down hard *on my knuckle. A simple, clear 'fuck you.' My favorite gesture. It hurt every time, but felt so good to see their reactions. I laughed, feeling something deep inside me, my hands warming up. I turned my head back to the girl and leaned forward, putting my lips on hers as she held onto my horns.*

"Harlot," the man had growled.

I laughed into her lips.

"Just a moment," I'd said, my lips still on hers.

She raised an eyebrow, but looked down at my arms, which were completely in flame. She rolled off of me, and I leaned my palms against the table. Fire-resistant. It was a good call on Orrin's part. I crossed my legs and raised my eyebrows, trying to look as unassuming as possible.

"Harlot? That's really close, how'd you know my middle name, mister?"

"I- what?" He asked.

"Does your mommy know you're kissing girls?" His friend patronized.

I laughed. I spread out my wings, feeling the tingle of heat as fire spread over my body.

"Everyone out," Orrin had sighed. "I don't see this ending well."

I didn't wait for everyone to get out before I slid off of the table. I leaned my head to either side, ending in a satisfying crack on both sides.

"My mommy doesn't know I kiss anyone. *My mommy's too busy being a tyrant."*

One of his other friends paled. *"You said your middle name was close to harlot?"*

"You from Couteau?" I crossed my arms and grinned at him, nodding.

"I don't feel like getting involved," He'd said, turning around and shaking his head.

The creep grabbed him by his collar, *"Where do you think you're going?"*

"That's Princess *Aella Lola* Harley *Belladonna,"* the other explained, not even turning back to look at him.

The creep looked back at me. I grinned and waggled my eyebrows, waving.

"One thing wrong there baby, it's Harlow, actually but Harley's cute. I like it better than the whole princess title. Someone write that down, is anyone here literate?"

I felt the flames entirely engulf my skin. Something was burning inside of me, something outside of me. Something that was me. The creep's friends went scattering. I bared my teeth, vibrating with excitement.

"Princess, huh?" he asked, backing up. *"I mean... oh come on now. Relax. I just wanted a turn."*

I ran up to him, throwing him up against the wall. I kneed him in his dick, then raised him up by his throat. I tilted my head to the side, grinning again. I licked the bottom of my teeth, the top row razor sharp.

"Say please," I said.

"I- please," He said.

I dropped him and kicked him as hard as I could.

"You really thought?" I asked. *"Come on, creep. I'm 19, and you look like you're rotting at this point. You're gonna leave young girls, or people in general, alone. They'll tell me, or they'll tell Nightshade. And we* will *come for you. Got it?"*

"Got it," the creep rasped.

"Handled the trash Orrin," I smiled and winked.

Orrin rolled his eyes. *"Get out, I gotta run damage control."*

I gave him a half-hearted salute and headed out of the tavern, leaving the creep on the ground where he belonged. Hazel ran over to the counter and left a pouch of coins. Sage shook her head, smiled, and the two followed me out.

"Harley," Hazel repeats, laughing as she signs.

"Inside joke with Haze and Sage ended up spreading to the rest of the rebellion," I say.

"I'd love to hear it sometime," He says.

"What's your type again?" I ask.

He sputters. So it seems his type isn't limited to men. Had to triple-check.

"Maybe I'll tell you the story on a date," I continue as he chokes on his water. "I bet I could sneak us to a beach without us being spotted by pirates or the cove sirens. I'm not a restaurant kind of girl, I'm not fancy like that. Fortnight, midday? I know a tunnel connects to Lila's old room, I'll meet you there."

Noah looks like he's going to pass out at this point. Oh, this poor, sweet little prince boy. I'm going to break him if I'm not careful. But I also get the sense that he could be my first real heartbreak. I've had feelings for many people before, but there was something different with him. More than wanting to be with him, or thinking he was hot, more than wanting him in my bed. There's a stupid part of me that wants to laugh with him, hold his hand. Stupid cheesy shit.

"Actually?" Noah asks.

"Yeah," I say. "Might be a fun thing, me and you."

"I just- I- uhhh," he trails off, burying his face in his hands. "Okay- sorry, I need a moment to collect myself. Wow. *Wow.*"

"Is that a yes?" I ask.

"Yeah- yeah, it is," He smiles, nodding quickly and readjusting his glasses.

"Good, you'd better show up then," I say, gently punching him again. He laughs. "Come on *your highness*, let's go find your guard so I can go home. I don't want Becca up late and worried."

I'm not used to feeling stupid and ditzy like this. I don't exactly hate it. Besides, it's a welcome distraction. It keeps my thoughts light back on the way to the cottage. That is until I realize I'm being followed. I hear too loud of a rustle from the trees, and light myself on fire. Probably a poor response, considering the sirens are out. I couldn't give less of a shit about the sirens, though. They can choke on my fist. I look up to see two glowing red eyes staring down at me. Dorian jumps down from the tree and begins walking alongside me.

"Hi, creep," I say.

"Hello love," He grins. He quickly sobers. "How are they?"

I know better than to sugarcoat with Dorian. The kid's seen enough shit. I'm not good at sugarcoating anyway. I just shake my head at him, and he nods.

"And Beckett's... is he?" Dorian asks.

"Yeah," I nod. "Bad. Might want to give it a week."

Dorian nods and walks away, not another word. It's a good few minutes of silence before I reach the cottage. Beckett's sitting on the porch, murmuring to himself, nonsensically, switching languages. He barely acknowledges me as I sit beside him. His eyes are puffy, like he's been crying. He's switching between Latin and Spanish faster than I can pick up, but I can make out the phrases "you never stick around," "no one believes me," and " I don't believe myself."

"Come on," I say. "Let's go inside, you shouldn't be out here."

He looks pained. He looks between me and something in the distance, then he slowly runs his hand through his curls. There's fog stains on his goggles, and I realize not only are his eyes puffy, but there's dark circles beneath them. He looks just over my shoulder, and mumbles something in Spanish, too quiet and jumbled for me to make out.

"Te querrían dentro, donde es seguro," I tell him. *They would want you inside, where it's safe.*

"Scio suus ' mea culpa." *I know it's my fault.*

Latin is a staple language in the two kingdoms. Everyone is brought up with expected education in their home. A primary home language, then English for basic communication, followed by Latin for heavy emotional conversations, and sign language for basic communication once again. If you're a stuffy rich person or noble in Couteau, you also get French lumped in near the beginning. If you're a nerd, other languages come after that. Beckett knew a lot of languages, and he tended to jumble them when he was like this. Any stable sentences came out in Spanish or Latin.

"¿Ellos te dijeron eso?" I ask. *Did they tell you that?*

He's silent. He runs his hand through his curls again and squeezes his eyes tight. He puts two hands firmly over his ears and cries. I put an arm around him and pull him close, kissing the top of his head. I wrap both my arms tightly around him, and he seems to sink, pulling up his goggles to wipe at his face.

"Mi culpa mi culpa mi culpa mi culpa mi culpa mi culpa," he weeps, body shaking. *My fault my fault my fault my fault my fault my fault my fault.*

Even if I try to say anything, he won't hear it, won't believe it. I want to tell him he's being stupid, and he's wrong. But I can't do that, can I?

"Era yo, quería jugar en el faro. Seguí corriendo hacia la cala. Estábamos jugando..." he whispers. *It was me, I wanted to play in the lighthouse. I continued running towards the cove. We were playing...*

I open my mouth to speak, but the singing in the distance becomes louder, clearer. It's beautiful. I want to hear more. I get the urge to run into the water, to play in it, to sleep in it. I don't know why I'm so tired. At this point, it might just be easier to throw Beckett in. He'd have less to worry about.

Sirens. I'd love to shove my mace down their throats one of these days.

I scoop Beckett up, grabbing from beneath his knees. I hold his back with one wing as I unlock the door and make my way inside. All previous thoughts or enchantment wear off. I find my way into his and Icylyn's room. Icylyn's balled up in the corner of her bed, her bunched covers at the edge of the bed, solidly passed out. All of Beckett's many clocks are ripped off of his wall. His side of the room is just...a mess in general. I set him down on his bed, then grab his pillows off the floor and set them down.

"Are they still here?" I ask, sitting down on the bed next to him.

He nods. I ruffle his hair.

"Alright, nerd boy, here's what we're gonna do. You're gonna tell them if they still need to talk to you, they can do it in the morning, because I know you haven't been sleeping. They'd want you to rest, whether or not you think their death is on you. Got it?"

He looks at me and grumbles something under his breath, whining. I stand up, grabbing the blankets off of his floor and covering him up. I begin to untie his goggles, which forces him to shut his eyes, and gently press his shoulder so he'll lie down. I set his goggles down on his bedside table, before shutting his window and locking it. I'm silent as I exit the room. I head to my room, only to lie awake for hours.

Sometimes his psychosis lasts for a while after seizures. I think the longest one lasted a month. It doesn't last as long this time. I'm sitting on the porch with Rebecca, watching Beckett and Icylyn run around. The buds on some bushes have finally turned to fruit. We didn't think it would happen, even though Icylyn had refused to let the flowers freeze this year. It's good to hear them both laughing. Genuinely laughing, not the way Beckett does when he's upset.

"Don't you have somewhere to be?" Rebecca asks.

"I don't- *shit*," I say.

I jump to my feet, fixing my blue curls in the reflection of the window, before I quickly unlace and loosen my shirt. I turn to Rebecca.

She smiles gingerly and steps forward, fixing a piece of my hair. She adjusts my shirt, and gives me a nod.

"Go," Rebecca laughs.

"Yeah, yeah, I'll be back... at some point," I say.

I close my eyes, letting the feeling of magic seep through and take over my skin, yet feeling a grounding control of it. I dissolve into the power. I am the power, I've always *been* the power. I open my eyes, now standing in the tunnels, skin still aflame. My flames light up the cave. I look to the side and see the tunnel walls licked by orange light, from a fire that is not my own.

Noah's standing there, hair tied back in a soft, messy, low-bun. He's got a loose grip on a mirror, and on the other hand, he's got something near his mouth. He's filing his teeth. He's filing his teeth and there's fire on his skin. He's beautiful in the orange glow, eyes crackling with fire. It's certainly a turn of events, but I'm not complaining. I'm not complaining at all. I cross my arms, leaning my shoulder against the tunnel wall. I can't help but grin, holding the tip of my tongue against my sharp teeth.

His eyes catch me and he jumps, yelping and dropping the mirror. It breaks the second it hits the floor, shards of glass littering the ground like sparkling snow. I watch as the flames on his skin grow, then completely disappear. He flickers in and out of view, then stabilizes.

"You got hotter," I say, whistling.

"Was that a joke?" Noah asks, a little bit of a smile surfacing.

"I've been spending too much time around the nerd duo," I groan, deflaming.

He laughs, the sound is soft, like music. Shit, this boy's got me sappy. He pushes his glasses up, then looks at me, then away, then back at me. I watch his expression go from nervous, to a visible 'fuck it.' He lights a finger aflame and crouches down, trying to pick up the pieces of the mirror. He winces. I shake my head and crouch down beside him, lighting my forearm aflame and sweeping shards onto my hand. I don't stop until I get every piece, then I dust my hands off over the mirror. Flame surrounds the mirror, and then it disappears.

Never once did I think about teleporting like that. He's cute and smart, I'll give him that.

He looks at me with lips parted, eyes widening, and quite literally lighting up. Like I've done something incredible. I can't fight a laugh. My hands are bleeding, but it's worth it. It doesn't really hurt anyway. I offer him my arm and he looks confused for a moment but takes it.

I know where I'm going, so after a while of walking, I stop looking at the path, and instead, look at him. He brightens when we get to the rocks leading to the cove. The cove sirens seem to be away for the time being, and no pirate ships are docked. We pass the hidden cove, cross the docks, and find a spot beneath the hill to Cazlamenta. It's covered in sand and connected to the beach. I don't think I've ever seen Noah look this excited. It's cute. He's cute. I'm ruined. He takes off his shoes, sets them on a rock, and digs his feet into the sand. He grins at me.

"I imagined it would be soft, but never this soft," He says.

He sits down, digging his feet into the sand and laughing to himself. I've had feelings for too many people at this point, but none as long as him. And none quite like the ones I have for him. I take off my coat, toss it behind me, and spread out my wings. The sunlight feels good on them. The warmth of it feels like it's holding them, holding them like something that's supposed to be there. I dig my feet down into the sand, matching Noah. His gaze is locked, almost entranced, on the wide expanse of ocean ahead of him.

"Noah," I say after a moment.

His head snaps to me, all soft expressions and big blue eyes.

"Yes?" He asks.

"Do you still have your wings?"

He nods.

"Can I see?" I ask.

"Yeah, I can- is it okay if I take off my shirt?"

"Yes," I laugh.

He continues picking at his bottom lip with his teeth as he unbuttons his shirt. It takes him a moment, and a few layers, but eventually he's able to unfold two blood-red wings. They're big and undamaged, and beautiful. I let out a low-whistle and he smiles again, flapping them around a bit. It's likely he hasn't let them out for far too long. He leans over and gently hits the side of my wings with his. I laugh and hit back, causing him to fall onto the sand, laughing with his entire stomach. His torso has splotches of red scales, as does his neck. Over his skin, there are orange scars flowering over him. Electrical scars.

"Can I ask?" I ask once it's almost awkwardly quiet again.

"Ask what?" He asks, pushing up his glasses.

"The scars."

"Oh," He mumbles, then shrugs. "Electric chair."

Heat surges through my body as the anger builds in my stomach. It hits me all at once, and my hands begin to shake.

"It's not that bad though," He says. "It's not as much now, it looks worse than it is."

"How do you have the scars?" I ask, genuinely confused. "You shouldn't be able to burn-"

"Electricity and fire burn differently," He explains. "At least for us."

"And they knew?" I ask.

"That it hurt and it burned? That was the point," he says simply. "It's how we learned. They- uh- they *don't* know that I'm... um. You know, *not* human. You're the only one who does. I got pretty good at keeping secrets after a while. Runs in the family, I guess."

"Screw them," I say. "We'll get them one of these days."

"Yeah?" He asks, looking away.

"Yeah," I say, flames still on my body.

I've heard Rebecca yell at Icylyn and Beckett far too many times, warning them not to turn their back on the ocean. To keep their eyes on it. I couldn't keep my eyes off Noah, and it was too late before the water came surging at both of us. My flames were quickly doused. Noah yelped, then laughed, causing me to break and laugh just as loud.

He takes my hand and attempts to pull me up. I shake my head and stand, but he's too focused on what's ahead of us. He starts running into the water, still laughing. He's still running when he's waist-deep. I lean down, keeping an eyebrow raised, eyes locked on his. His eyes focus and widen, and his cheeks seem to color. I sink into the water, scooping it in my hand.

And then I splash him.

His shocked laugh sounds like a melody. Like a birdsong. It sounds stupid, I know, but sometimes he reminds me of a trapped bird. Small, somewhat frail. Beautiful. Smart, but probably is a bastard somewhere deep, *deep* down.

"Stars," he says. "I believe I'm stuck on a rock or something. I cannot move."

"Well, that'll make it harder for the tide to drag you out to sea," I tease.

"Would that truly be so bad?" He asks.

I fight a laugh, then bend over, offering him my hand. He grabs my forearm, then grins. He tries to pull me down. It's a little bit pathetic because he can't. He opens his mouth to speak when a larger wave comes charging in our direction, hitting him in the face and sweeping me off my feet. The waves start to drag us out. I grab Noah with one arm and stick my hand in the sand with the other. I scoop him up in my arm, and walk onto the shore, his arms dragging on the ground. He hangs limp, shaking his entire body when he laughs. I drop him onto the sand, then lie down beside him. He's laughing still, and I can't help but do the same. It's contagious, I swear.

There's sand on my eyelashes, daring to spill into my burning eyes, salt staining my throat. My ribs hurt, lungs desperate for me to stop laughing. The pain is nothing compared to the thunderous crashing of the waves, the sun burning my skin oh so gently, and Noah's wings brushing against mine. I could hold onto this forever.

I find myself thinking the stupidest, sappiest shit. I'm not willing to share all of it. I know for certain that it wouldn't be all that bad to have him around, to bring him places with me. That's as much as I'll say.

I turn towards him, to see his gaze locked on me.

"Oh don't tell me you want to kiss," I tease.

He overdramatically frowns and puts a hand on his forehead. He looks away and lays back down, chewing off a piece of his nail. I sit up and stretch, noticing how the sun has dried the droplets of seawater previously covering my skin. I scoot closer to him and clear my throat.

"Sit up," I tell him.

He sits up, folding in his wings. I grab his chin and prop it up, grinning at him. His eyes widen as he blinks rapidly. I watch as his blue eyes spark, the reflection of flame glinting in them. My gaze shifts to his soft lips, and I lean in.

"Is this okay?" I ask.

"I-" He says. "This won't completely ruin us, right? I care a lot about you and- what if we upset-"

"Shhh," I say. "We're already ruining the friendship. What's one kiss? And I'm sure people will just... deal with it if this goes any further."

"Would you- am I- should- can I kiss you?" He asks.

I laugh.

"I'll lead this time, loverboy."

I pull him closer, sand scraping against my skin as I scoot nearer to him. He's soft, and I'm sharp. He tastes like saltwater and escape, like lives I can't have. I let my eyes slide closed, letting my hands find their way to his hair. His hair is usually soft, and silky, but now all my fingers find are tangles and saltwater. My fingers find a rough sea where there is often a shallow river. We are fire, we are water, we are the unforgiving winds connected to both.

For once, I see a wildness in him. I feel a calm in me I long since thought died. I'm kissing him, and he's holding me. I am smoke in the wind. I am the storm. He is the hurricane, he is the eye. He's the burning leaf the forest made the mistake of doubting.

The water hits our legs, the bubbling of the tide coupled with the hissing of our flames. His lips unlock from mine, and his forehead presses against mine. I can hear the solid shake of his breath against the whistle of the wind.

"I never thought you'd taste so sweet," he murmurs.

"Because I talk so mean?" I grin. "You know, I've heard that my tongue-"

He simply presses his lips against mine, and I laugh against them. My fingers bury themselves in his hair, finding his bun and unraveling it. My hands get lost. So do my thoughts. We turn, lying, alight, water crashing against us. Us. An idea. A new bright flame. Unlikely to be doused, despite the wind, the rain, the tribulations. Probably a horrible idea, but stars am I a slut for a bad idea.

I'm pressed against a rock wall, Noah's head resting on my shoulder, still damp hair on my scales. It starts to hit me, this situation that we're in. Catching feelings, igniting the spark, that's one thing. If it were to get out, stars, if we were to get anywhere further than just having 'feelings' for one another...

Have you ever tried to throw sticks into an open flame, only to watch it turn into a wildfire? I'll bet you haven't. I'll bet you haven't, because that's stupid. That's something you should never do. Yet here Noah and I are, ripping branches off the nearest trees to fan the flame of two dry lit leaves we found on the ground. What am I even saying? I don't talk like this, this is disgusting. I don't know if I'm getting all poetic because I'm getting sappy, or if JJ's rubbing off on me. Both options are awful.

His scarred arm is across my lap, and his head tilts back and forth, eyes sliding open and closed.

You know, I want to tell her. I would if I could. I don't think I can. I don't think I want to.

"I should probably..." Noah yawns. "I've got to cover my tracks before dinner."

"I had fun," I tell him. I mean it. He's fun to be around.

He sits up. A shadow sweeps across his face, the rest of it painted in sunlight. His skin and scales seem to glow with it. He sweeps his hair back into a bun, eyes tilting down and lips twitching upward. He stands and offers me a hand. I damn well can get up on my own, but I take it anyway.

"I did as well," He says, pulling me up.

He looks away from me, rocking on his heels, and picking at his fingers. I watch as his head moves back and forth. His ocean eyes finally settle on me, and he jumps on his heels, pressing his lips against my cheek.

I open my mouth to make a remark, but he's disappeared by then.

I guess I better disappear too.

Chapter 13
Veronica

"We've been walking for so long," I can't help but whine.

Nightshade was impatient for my ankle to heal, and now I see why. She wanted to drag me somewhere *else* to kill me. I don't know why she couldn't have just done it already. And what's worse, she said she was going to take me to a cave. She is going to kill me in a gross cave that probably has... gross grimy things in it.

"Would you rather I grab you and fly us there, darling?" Nightshade asks. "Or rather, we could see how your body reacts to my enhanced speed?"

"Why don't you just kill me faster?"

"And here I was starting to believe you were on your way to trusting me."

"Don't push your luck."

She exhales a semblance of a laugh through her nose, and her eyes crinkle a bit. She turns and keeps walking. I think we're starting to grow on each other.

I don't know how to feel about it.

I don't think my life will ever go back to the way it was. I don't want it to. There are things that I miss. As much as I hate to say it, I miss my mom. I miss Isolde and Dietrich. I miss Daman. And of course, I miss Sabine.

Thankfully, we've stayed on the grass the entire time. The minuscule, sapphire blades brush the bottom of my feet, dewdrops clinging to my bare ankles with every step. Scandalous, I know, but it's not as if I could return to my castle to steal clothing items. Needless to say, the cold is embracing my arms in ways I surely didn't agree to. The air is damp, and heavy with fog.

Most of Couteau is for a majority of the year, save for when it begins to clear closer to Caeara. Fear Forest, however, was never an exception.

The fog and general lack of color, save for the occasional lilac tree, or the vast plains of dark blue grass, left Couteau seeming bleak and lifeless. I suppose that's why my kingdom has the reputation it does.

"Why are we in Couteau?" I ask.

"I thought you might want a last glimpse of home."

"It still sounds like you're going to kill me."

Nightshade ignores me. "That and there's more grassy terrain on this side of the Two Kingdoms. I didn't want to hear you complaining about walking on sticks."

"How kind of you," I say.

We continue going north but remain quiet for a while. My legs continue to burn, and my ankle begins to throb. After a while of this, Nightshade turns abruptly, heading west. She continues to keep her mouth shut, so I follow suit. In the distance, frogs can be heard screaming, and birds singing more gentle tunes. The further west we go, the more trees diversify, and more have leaves. The fog begins to dissipate, and the sound of rushing water grows ever nearer.

I always found Couteau more beautiful than Mortem Venenum. Though I suppose I have a bias.

We cross into neutral territories, passing small cottages far more richly decorated than the cottages nearby on the outskirts of Couteau and Mortem Venenum. I've heard tales of the river sirens, but I'd hoped it was nothing more than a tall tale made by rebels, or mothers afraid of their children drowning in the river at night. Perhaps some nobleman.

But it seems once again, everything I'd thought was wrong. I was blind to the truth. There were noblemen who'd gotten too close to finding out the dirty secrets of The Woods. And those noblemen were killed, their bodies dumped into the river.

My thoughts of disgust are quickly interrupted by the deafening sound of the river, more massive than I ever imagined. I look down, seeing myself screaming as the river swallows me whole, grabbing my hair, and pulling down my dress. Holding me against the sharp rocks at the bottom as it drags me, suffocating, toward the sea.

"Come on, we don't have much longer before we lose the cloud coverage," Nightshade says. "I have faith in this cloak, but not that much faith."

"I'm sorry, you expect us to cross this?" I ask.

"Yes," She says.

I take a deep inhale, then look her dead in the eyes.

"Not all of us can *fly* Nightshade."

"You can levitate, and the last I checked, your legs are fully functional once again. Unless you'd prefer I leave you here? I'm sure the sirens would adore your company tonight."

"Once again, I'm sorry to disappoint, but I'm human. Second of all, you don't seriously expect that we can withstand the force of the river?"

"I can," She says, then she squints, and the small bit her visible eyebrows seem to knit from beneath her hood. "I'd be more than willing to hold your hand as we cross if you're so frightened, darling."

Stars, sometimes she just makes me want to stab myself! Or her! Though that'd just be a waste of a perfectly good dagger. Oh, how I miss my dagger collection. In any case, that's not the point right now. Even though that very much should be the point right now. I had the pointiest dagger once, I actually got it–

Now's not the time.

I glare at her with the full weight of my rage... well, mostly annoyance– and turn my attention back to the river. Fine. I'll cross it. But I'm not going to like it. I turn towards the river and raise my chin. This river doesn't look so scary. I'll cross it, I'll cross it and I'll show her–

Goosebumps rise on my skin as a hand– cold as death– seizes my arm. I stop in my tracks, instinctively reaching for my dagger holster. When I find it empty, I round on my assailant, fist closed. But it's just Nightshade, who grabs my fist easily. She's laughing. When she laughs it warps and echos, her shadow-blood voice filtering through her mask. When she laughs it sounds as though another, deeper voice is laughing with her, though through her. Her head is tossed backwards, her hood nearly flying off. Her choppy, messy ginger side-bangs pop out, almost shocking against her all-black attire. She continues to hold my fist but lets go of my arm to pull her hood back down.

She doesn't stop laughing. There's not even a slight pause for breath, though I assume she doesn't need that.

She's insufferable. If only the sound of her cocky, stupid laughter had reflected that.

"I admire your boldness, darling," She sighs, still laughing. "But we weren't ever going to cross the river. I wanted to see how long it would take you to—"

"I hate you," I say.

"You don't seem so sure about that," She says.

"Shut up," I murmur, my stomach dropping. "So, what's the plan then?"

She kneels and starts digging. I hope she isn't entirely insane to the point of believing she can dig us a path. She's quick, her hands moving at an impossible speed, blurring before my eyes. Beneath a layer of dirt is a wooden square, which Nightshade pulls up. She crawls forward, then sits, dangling her feet. She looks at me, crinkles her eyes, then falls.

At this point, I think theatrics sustain her more than blood does.

I grab the rusty rungs of the ladder and hesitantly make my way down. I'm slow, cringing as the ladder groans. It's a short, albeit agonizing climb to the bottom. Nightshade's at the bottom, mock yawning.

"Well, darling," She says. "That sure took you long enough."

I open my mouth to speak but decide against it as green, fog-like tendrils surround her wrists. She flicks her wrists and the opening to the tunnels snaps closed, leaving us in darkness. I stumble, carefully walking to the side with my arms out.

"Nightshade," I hiss.

"What is it?" She asks.

"I can't *see*, idiot."

"Right. My apologies, I'm used to making this journey alone. I was lying before, the only way to get to the cave from the base undetected is through this entry point. I forgot that— would you like me to lead you?"

"Like I have another choice," I say, extending my hand.

Among the many things Nightshade suffers from, she seems to be ailed by chronic cold hands. They're dry, too. Dry, cracked, and cold. But there's a part of me that doesn't mind holding her hand all that much. I don't know.

Maybe I'm just scared in this tunnel and she's just familiar. Maybe I'm losing it.

We're silent. I try my best to match her pace, even though my legs feel as though they'll stretch out and melt into the ground. She begins to slow, her touch slowly becoming more and more bearable.

I'm not sure which I hated more growing up. Which I feared more, I suppose, the dark, or silence. Not much has changed, I suppose. I try to find comfort in the sound of our footfalls, though all I can hear is the sound of my breathing. Too loud, too frantic. It doesn't match Nightshade's. Of course, it doesn't, Nightshade's breath is perpetually slow. It's not like she needs to breathe anyway. What if I'd suddenly stopped breathing? How would I know if the wall started closing? Did the tunnel system even have an exit? I feel like it'd be very easy to suffocate down here.

I grasp for one of my braids, taking comfort in the pain of pulling at my hair.

My chest feels tight and heavy, and my head seems to sway. I can barely hear our footsteps. I can barely hear anything except my loud, disgustingly somehow incorrect, impossible breath.

And then Nightshade's humming. Something lighthearted, yet almost melancholy. It steps between cheerful and somber, something I can't quite place. Whatever she's humming, it's in the minor chord, I'd wager. For once her voice doesn't warp, and it almost feels weird not to have her voice come out in melody, backed in a repeated echo, almost like a round in a song.

For all the things that are so rough and brash about her...

I'll have to admit. Her voice is somewhat lovely.

I mean– I suppose. It keeps me distracted for a while, at the very least. I can feel her fingers sliding over mine, at least until,

"Why do you still wear your engagement ring?" She asks. "You don't have to answer."

"Isn't it important for your plan or something?" I ask.

"No," Nightshade says. "We just needed yet another way to delay your marriage. But that's not the real reason you keep it, is there?"

"I miss him."

I confess it all too easily. The words flow out before I even think of them like the words are a breath I've been starving myself of. I do miss him. I miss him every day. I think of him every day. I hate him, but part of me still loves him. Part of me aches to run to his arms, for him to change. But I don't want to go back.

"That seems to be a dreadful predicament," She murmurs, sounding almost heavy.

"It is," I say, something catching in my throat.

She squeezes my hand. I never expected any attempt at consultation from Nightshade. I suppose there are a lot of things that have happened this month that I would never expect.

"Are we almost there?" I ask.

"Nearly," her voice warps, and there seems to be a hint of excitement to her tone.

She finds her way towards a wall, still keeping her hand in mine. She pulls a lever, and there's a loud creaking sound as light pours into the tunnel. A ladder descends with a deafening crash. It's just as dreadful as the previous ladder. She steps back, extending an arm, offering for me to go first. I frantically shake my head. She hums and turns back to the ladder, ascending in a blur. I don't think I'll ever get used to that. Perhaps I need to surround myself with more vampires.

The ladder leads to an empty forest. There are scattered trees, and a stack of logs nearby. In each tree, there are hung targets, each with varying sizes and styles of arrows lodged deep inside them. Nightshade quickly closes the entrance to the tunnel behind me, burying it in the mix of dirt, leaves, and pine below our feet. Before I can register what's happening, she takes my hand, leading me quickly towards the entrance to a cave, blocked by a large wall. She digs into her boot and finds a key. She turns the key to unlock yet another lever, which she flips down, and relocks.

The wall to the cave begins to rise. I jump at first, and she laughs, voice warping. She steps inside, beckoning me to follow her. I do, albeit a little reluctantly. She pulls yet another lever on the other side of the door, and the wall closes, assorted candles lighting up the cave. I've been here before, the day my wedding was interrupted, but I hadn't taken the time to actually look at it.

There's a long table in the center, and several chairs surrounding it. Not too far left of the table, near the crevice of a wall, is a blanket. It's surrounded by several pillows, and a small side table with an open book lying face down. On the back wall of the cave are several different bows, ranging in size and craftsmanship. Several quivers hang, along with several other places to hang things. On the floor of the back wall is a large map of The Two Kingdoms, which I can only assume fell.

On the wall closest to the blankets, pillows, and table, posters have been hung delicately in the crevices. Upon further inspection, I realize that they are all wanted posters and news clippings.

The first one I see is of the shadow-blood with green hair. They're all but bearing their teeth in a grin, one eye closed, the other entirely black. There's blood dripping down their forehead, and splatters of crimson appear in the white flowers in their hair. Below their portrait reads, "Raven Ash. Shadow-Blood. Wanted for crimes of trespassing, theft, murder, resisting arrest, supernatural identity, homosexuality, association with Nightshade."

Beside their poster is one of the white-haired elf, though at a much younger age, flames sketched in the background. It reads, "Sage Hemlock. Elf. Wanted for crimes of arson, manslaughter, theft, resisting arrest, many accounts of killing law enforcement, vandalism, supernatural identity, homosexuality, association with Nightshade."

To the far right of their posters are a collection of mathematical equations and blueprints. Among these are two more posters. On one is Beckett, beaming in the sketch of him. "Beckett Acosta. Elf. Wanted for theft, trespassing, vandalism, property damage, scientific misconduct, supernatural identity, association with Nightshade." Beside his poster is another, in which the subject's eyes are sketched wide with fear, but an otherwise blank expression. "Icylyn Summers-Acosta. Dragon? Elf? Wanted for theft, destruction of property, murder of law enforcement, supernatural identity, association with Nightshade."

Several news clippings also line the walls.

"Lost Princess Proclaimed Dead."

"Crown Princess Escapes Again."

"Execution Halted By Explosion."

And many others.

Behind the table, closer to the wall hanging Nightshade's weapons, a square is outlined on the floor. It's similar to the entrances to the cave, and there is an identical outline at the entrance to the cave.

Books lay everywhere. There are several stacks that reach the top of the cave roof, several lying open on the blanket, or on the table. Almost as common as the books, or perhaps even dust, are the tea accessories. Several teacups and saucers are placed on each surface.

Nightshade hangs her cloak up alongside her weapons. She then pulls her mask down, grabbing at the fabric from her neck and pulling it over her head, dropping it on the ground. She removes a long-sleeved shirt to reveal a black, sleeveless tunic. There are holes cut in the back, allowing her bat-like wings to poke through. She stretches out her wings as she stretches her arms. She's more scarred than I was expecting, far too many burns and blemishes dotting her skin, as well as nics from swords and electrical scars. There are holes in her wings, patched with old fabric. She unbraids her hair in a blur of motion, matted and layered tangled waves of ginger falling to the bottom of her back. She turns, eyes blue. It's odd to see her face. She looks softer, vulnerable even. Her eyes light up, pressing her lips tightly together as she smiles.

"Oh my lovely boy," She coos softly, staring at the table. "I was wondering where it was that you were wandering off to."

She whistles and holds out an arm. She softens, scratching at the air with her finger. I blink, wondering what on earth she's doing this time.

"Can I ask?" I ask.

"My raven," She says, not looking at me. "His name is Edgar. He died when I was young and tends to make appearances from time to time. He's a sweet boy, and the loveliest of company."

"Oh," I say.

"Whatever insult you want to say won't affect me, you can go ahead and say it," Nightshade says, attention still trained on Edgar.

"The stars would disapprove," I say, gesturing to her 'living space.'

"If any being claiming to deify themself stepped within these walls, they'd find an arrow lodged through them before they got the chance to consider disapproval."

"That's a loaded sentence."

"I've broken faces for far less."

It's quiet for a while, awkwardly so. At that time I, for whatever reason, decided to make it worse.

"Is Edgar the reason why there were all those ravens in Fear Forest?"

"That wasn't real," Nightshade mumbles, seeming a bit dazed.

Her chest stops rising, and her eyes shift from blue to red. She sways where she's standing, twisting a piece of her hair around her fingers. She blinks hard, shaking her head, seeming to snap out of it. Her eyes slowly morph back to blue, but she doesn't begin to breathe again. She turns her attention to Edgar, a melancholy smile painting her expression as she strokes the air.

"I wasn't aware you could see any of that," she says.

"I could," I say. "The tree works like that."

"Oh," she says.

It seems clear that she's not going to answer my initial question. She extends her arm once more, then drops it to her side. Without another word, she walks down a staircase on the left side of the cave. I'm not sure why I follow her. She reaches the bottom of the stairs, opening a door. She steps into what appears to be a kitchen, adorned with white walls and shockingly yellow cabinets and countertops, and utensils hanging down from the ceiling.

When she's cloaked, her movements are sporadic, precise, and quick. Here in the cave, they weren't so much. She is slower, more delicate. She seems almost graceful, dancing, twirling about the kitchen. She easily reaches something from the top shelf, when I realize she has a cabinet full of jars of assorted teas. On the same shelf seem to be different add-ins, including jars with red, thick liquid. She grabs one of those jars, as well as a jar of tea, and begins to heat water.

I don't know what possessed me to say it. What possessed me to think it.

"You're incredibly human."

She looks at me, studying me for a moment. Her expression softens a slow shift from puzzled to bittersweet. She purses her lips together as she offers a sad smile, keeping her fangs hidden as she speaks. She pours the red liquid into one teacup, eyes trained on the task.

"There's nothing human about me, darling."

NIGHTSHADE

Chapter 14
Nightshade

I think there's venom in me. I dream about it every night.

The venom runs through my veins, twisting with everything dirty and wrong with me.

I never should've stepped foot in that star-forsaken forest.

I dream about it every night. I wake up convinced I'm drenched in the blood of hundreds of corvids. I can hear screaming in all directions. I watch my world collapse. I watch the people, the ones I love, the people I've sworn to protect, the people who have pieces of my soul...

And I watch as they die by my hand. I watch as Veronica falls to ruin, as The Woods die. I'm powerless to stop it. I'm falling, and my wings are clipped. I can't fix it.

I've been avoiding sleep for this very reason. I awake with a start.

There's a clatter, and I spring to my feet. Before I know what I'm doing, I'm in the kitchen. When I enter the kitchen, it's sort of a disaster. Various knives are in the walls, fruit is splattered on the ceiling. Veronica is sitting on the floor, with a pot on her head, and several pots, and pans lying beside her. Her breath is shaky, and I watch as several glasses fly across the room. I catch them in one fell swoop, setting them back down on the counter. I kneel in front of Veronica and remove the pot from her head. She looks almost like a wounded animal, breath rising and falling unnaturally, scared and confused. The gray in her eyes is now replaced by pink.

"This shouldn't be happening," She whispers, voice succumbing to a vibrato.

"Well, I'd hate to say I told you so," I mumble. "Though, I suppose some of your opposition was an act. How long have you known you're a supernatural?"

"I'm... I'm not," Veronica mutters.

I just look at her for a moment and wait. She's stubborn.

"Veronica," I say. "That won't work on me, darling."

Her eyes shift away from me. She brings her knees up against her chest and holds them tightly. As she hugs her knees, she taps her fists on top of each other. I just sit and wait. It's quiet for an uncomfortably long time. Nevertheless, I leave the silence to torture us both, if I push her too far, she'll completely shut down. So here we sit, on the floor of the kitchen, in complete and awkward silence.

"I'm not a supernatural," Veronica mumbles.

"So you've known for a while, then, and you're just in denial," I put together.

"Okay, fine," She relents. "I thought... I thought if I pretended, if I prayed enough, if I was good enough, it would all just go away. I couldn't... *wouldn't* believe it."

She squeezes her legs tighter into her chest, and it seems like she's going to dig her nails deep into her hand with how tightly she's balling her fist. She presses her forehead against her knees, taking a breath.

"The more you ignore your powers, the harder they'll be to control in the long run," I say. "I know it's terrifying, believe me, but it's not something to be ashamed of."

"I just wanted just some part of me to be normal," she mutters. "Part of me thought that if I was, then maybe -just maybe - people would like me."

"Normality is painfully overrated, darling," I gently nudge her with my shoulder. "Besides, it's generally a good sign if you're on bad terms with Lucius, Evsaphine, Isodle, Dietrich, and Daman. Means you're not a horrible person. Which, as far as I'm concerned, you aren't."

"I'm not?" Veronica asks, looking up.

"Your morals were a bit skewed, previously, but then again it's because you're easily susceptible to the lies that have been forced down your throat. Which is perfectly understandable. What is impressive has been your ability to move with the changes. But even before you knew the truth, you didn't let them kill me. While it is true, you can be somewhat bitchy at times, that comes with its own charm. Personally, I'm glad you're here."

Veronica is completely silent for a few minutes. She scoots a bit closer and rests her head on my shoulder. The back of her hand brushes against mine. I slowly touch my palm against hers, looking at her expression. She nods, and I hold her hand. It's quiet for a while. She's trying to process it all.

"I have telekinesis as well," I say after a while. "I can teach you that bit. You're going to have to learn mind control on your own if you choose to."

"... mind-control," She breathes, horrified.

I pat her head.

"You don't have to learn it if you don't want to. But, as of now, your telekinesis is triggered easily, and I'm assuming it's a fear response. So... I'll try to be a little *less*, and I can help you work on your telekinesis if you want me to."

"I think I'd like that," She says, after a while.

I squeeze her hand, before standing up. I walk over to the wall and begin to tug out the knives, before sending them back to their drawer.

"Sorry," Veronica mumbles sheepishly, rocking on her tiptoes.

"It's no fault of yours," I say.

"Except the part where it is," she murmurs.

"You were having a panic attack, weren't you?" I ask.

"Shut up and let me help you clean," she murmurs.

She begins picking up pots and pans from the floor and setting them down on the counter. She readjusts the light-blue bow that is holding her braids in a low ponytail behind her head. The one that matches her dress exactly. She lifts her chin just slightly, before squatting down and grabbing more pots, standing and setting them down with a little twirl. I walk up the wall and begin wiping down the ceiling. It isn't long until the kitchen looks somewhat decent again. Well, as decent as a cave kitchen with yellow cabinets could look. I drop down from the ceiling, and she startles a bit.

"My apologies," I say.

She waves me off, movements rigid, face still twisted in awkwardly hidden fear. We stand there for a moment in a suffocating silence. She sways back and forth, bouncing up and down on her toes. I hop onto the counter and sit down. I look away, fiddling with my hair. Veronica leans her back

138

against the counter I'm sitting on, and just stands there for a minute. I say nothing.

"Fine," Veronica says. "Teach me."

"Well," I chuckle. "You accepted the offer much quicker than I expected, darling. Are you sure you're ready?"

"Yes, stop patronizing me," She rolls her eyes.

"Had to be sure," I grin, hopping off the counter and offering my hand. "Shall we?"

Together we're sitting on the floor of a room that we completely emptied, aside from a few pillows. We sit across from each other, criss-cross. I'm somewhat nervous myself. She's gently tapping her fists on top of each other, but she looks a lot calmer than I'd expect her to. Part of me thinks this is too soon, but if she really, truly feels ready, there's no way I'm going to stop her.

"To do this, I'm going to be inside of your head, which means you need to trust me," I tell her.

"You're going to *what*?" Veronica squeaks.

"I promise, I won't peek. If you're not quite ready yet, I completely understand, and we could-" I begin.

"No, no," She shakes her head. She looks up at me with the full force of her fiery determination. "I'm ready."

I'm unable to protest. Even without her powers, I know she could get what she wanted with her determination alone.

"It might help if you close your eyes and try to concentrate," I tell her.

She nods. She takes a deep breath, squeezing her eyes shut. Her leg bounces a bit, but otherwise, she's still. I wait for a bit. For some people, it's harder to concentrate than others. Painfully, impossibly harder to focus on the task at hand. I suspect that Veronica was one of those people. I am also one of those people.

"I'm going to enter, now," I tell her, "I'll give you a countdown. Three... two... one."

If there's one word I could use to describe her mind, it would be that it's *loud*. A lot louder than I would've expected. A thousand thoughts are seeming to jumble in an overstimulating cacophony of chaos in the confinement of her mind. The vibration of her mental imagery was intense, to say the least.

"Holy shit," Veronica says. "I can *feel* you in there. That's so strange."

"It is a bit strange at first," I say. "You'll eventually get used to it, darling."

"I don't know how you could," She says.

"Are you aware of the vibrations within your mental energy?" I ask her.

"The buzzing? Yeah."

"Perfect. So, first, you're going to want to send that energy out into the room, can you do that for me?"

"Mhm," She mutters.

Her mind quiets out a bit. The energy of the air becomes static very quickly. I open my eyes, and I can see the pillows vibrating on the floor. She's catching on a lot faster than either of us thought she would. It's quite impressive, but then again, most things about her seemed to be.

"Woah," She whispers. "I can feel the objects in the room."

"Can you picture them in your mind?" I ask.

Veronica nods. I ask her if she can try to lift them. She shrugs, tipping her head to the side just slightly. She says she'll try. She takes a breath in and out, before squeezing her eyes tighter. The pillows begin lifting slightly off the ground. With every exhale she takes, they lift just a bit higher, until they're at least five feet off the ground.

"I don't think anything's happening," She says.

"Open your eyes, darling," I say.

She does, though she seems reluctant. Her mouth opens slightly, and she lets out a slight gasp of disbelief. She cups her hands over her mouth, and her eyes seem to sparkle a bit. She sways back and forth a bit, laughing in awe. My heart jumps into my throat. The pillows start slowly lowering and then rising back up.

"You're doing it," I smile.

"I'm doing it!" She nearly squeals.

The energy shifts quicker than I expected it to.

Veronica looks up at me, still smiling, but there's something vacant and sinister about it. My gut sinks as I fly across the room, hitting the wall. I'm blocked from Veronica's mind almost instantly. She laughs. It sounds uncontrollable and almost painful, with a heavy sense of twisted glee. She wasn't quite prepared. We should've taken it in baby steps.

But stars, as terrifying as the scene was... her laugh. Stars, her laugh could end the world.

She laughs nearly breathlessly, pillows rising and circling her at an impossible speed.

"Darling?" I ask.

She finds her way up, and I'm slammed against the wall once again. I'm in front of her in a blur, careful to avoid the whirlwind of pillows. I take her hands, hoping to dull her connection to her surroundings temporarily and snap her out of it.

"Veronica," I say, carefully.

Her eyes lift, looking just past me. The pink dulls, just slightly, the gray in her eyes peeking out.

"I don't know what's happening," She breathes. "I don't know why I feel like this, how to control it-"

Her eyes snap back to pink, and she wraps one hand around my throat, grinning. I grab her wrist, squeezing it until she lets go, then I simply step backward. Pain flashes behind my eyes, searing into my head, seeming to split it apart.

"Forgive me," I say, not sure my voice can even be heard. All I can hear is humming, threatening to crack through my skull, digging its nails into my brain, ravishing me.

I snap, and her body hits the floor.

I try not to think about the fact that her head is leaning against my chest. I try not to think about the fact that I am bringing Veronica uninvited. I try not to think about the fact that Aella may hate me for this.

And I try with all my star-forsaken soul not to think about the fact that I do not at all trust Rebecca Acosta.

I approach the cottage, thankful that I haven't heard the song of sirens throughout the entire excursion. The lights are still on inside, and sweet smells emerge from the chimney. There's the sound of laughter, chaos, and the irreplaceable, unmistakable feeling of magic. I step up the three steps to the porch, then carefully kick the door three times with my foot.

Of course, with my luck, Aella is the one to open the door. Any joy in her face drains, and a fire lights in her eyes, on her skin, as she fades in and out of sight. Her lips twitch, showing gritted, razor-sharp teeth. I'm not sure how I'm going to explain or come back from this one, but I can only hope things resolve.

"This *better* have a reason," She says through gritted teeth.

"I wouldn't have brought her near you if it didn't," I say.

"I kissed Noah," She says.

"You *what*?" I ask.

She gestures at Veronica.

"I don't feel bad about kissing him now. Deal with it. Get inside before those," she stops, clears her throat, and then shouts, "Weak, wimpy trust-fund babies drown you. Stars know they can't just get a life!"

I step inside, and Aella slams the door behind me.

"Did you really have to do that?" Icylyn asks.

Aella yells and then storms down the hall, entirely on fire. Beckett exits the same hall. He looks back at her, all curiosity and amusement. He jumps onto the couch next to Icylyn, leaning on her, surveying the scene. Seeming all too used to his antics, Icylyn doesn't react even slightly.

"Hi Jinx!" He says. "Why is Veronica unconscious?"

"Long story, I'll explain later," I respond. "Is your mother home?"

"Yeah? It'd be kinda weird if she wasn't."

As if on cue, Rebecca walks into the room. I'd forgotten how incredibly potent the feeling of magic was around her. She looks at Veronica, eyes squinting slightly, eyebrows creased, lips pinched. She just stares for a minute. She leans against the wall, then crosses her arms, positioning herself. Her gaze turns to me, and panic gathers in my stomach. I want to turn and run.

"Do you want to explain what happened?" Rebecca asks, carefully.

I let go of my breath. I take a moment to compose myself, and then I nod. She shifts her weight and gestures towards me, pursing her lips.

"Veronica's..." I hesitate.

"Like me," Rebecca nods. "I know. I feel it."

"I was trying to help her learn to control it," I explain. "I started with telekinesis, was planning on just doing that–"

"And she surrendered to the magic," Rebecca reasons. "I understand. I think I can help. You were right to bring her here."

"Aella would disagree," Icylyn chimes in.

Rebecca signs, seeming to deflate. She nods slightly, eyes trained on the ground. She looks down the hall and makes a face, before clapping her hands together and moving toward the couch. Rebecca studies Veronica for a moment, then looks me over quickly.

"Beckett, Icylyn," Rebecca says.

"Sí, Mamá, nos vamos," Beckett nods, taking Icylyn's hand and leading her out. *Yes, Mamá, we're leaving.*

"Jinx," She says, once they're gone.

I shouldn't have come here. I shouldn't have brought Veronica. I can only see Rebecca harming us in this situation. She's too nice, there has to be something wrong with her. My heart is beginning to pound in my chest. I steel myself and wait for whatever's next.

"Are you alright?" she asks. "You look like you've been wearing yourself far too thin."

"I'm perfectly fine," I say. "It's Veronica I'm worried about."

Rebecca nods. She looks back at me, and her eyes look tired. She ages, yet seems so young all at once. She offers me a smile, it's almost melancholic. She stands up and leaves the room. She returns, holding two glasses of water. I can't help but stare at it desperately.

I can't help but flinch when she approaches. It's embarrassing, and a direct, clear show of weakness. She doesn't react, just sits back down on the couch. She sets down the other glass and looks back at me. The overwhelming presence of magic slowly becomes more bearable.

"Would you go talk to Aella?" She asks. "I'll explain everything to Veronica, but I'm going to need time with her, and can't be with both of them at the same time."

"Yes," I say, quickly turning to leave the room.

"And Jinx?" She says.

"Yes?" I respond without turning back.

"What you're doing is incredible, and you should be very proud of yourself," She says, then pauses, carefully choosing her words. "Just... remember not to lose yourself entirely in the process. You should care for yourself, and be cared for. Sometimes the best revenge is for your oppressors– or the people who hurt you– to see you thriving."

"I'll consider your opinion," I say, and continue down the hall.

There are four rooms in the hall. I put my ear up against the first door, to hear complete silence. I can only assume that it isn't Aella's. I repeat the action for the second door. There's the sound of many, many clocks ticking, which is quickly overpowered by the sounds of Beckett and Icylyn talking over one another. I approach the third door, hesitating before I grab the handle. I turn it, preparing to see Aella inflamed and enraged.

Instead, she's nowhere to be seen.

I shut the door behind me, carefully crossing the distance to her bed. I look for the specific folds and dents in the sheet and figure out where she's sitting. I sit beside her, giving her some space.

"Fuck you," Aella says.

I nod.

"She better have- tried to kill you or something, I don't know, there better have been a reason-"

"She did," I say.

"You should understand what a horrible person she is," Aella says through her teeth, appearing momentarily, all flames from the waist up.

"I understand where you're coming from-"

Aella leaps up off the bed, all fire, all rage. Her face bears an expression that could declare wars, turn armies to stone, and set fire to any corner of the earth. I've seen that look hundreds of times before, but very rarely at me. Her wings extend, and she leans forward, her deep voice unusually shrill when she yells.

"No, you don't! You don't understand! And I'm not going to just sit here and..." She stammers for a moment, then grabs a pillow, tossing it as hard as she can at the wall. "Fuck!"

The temperature in the room becomes unbearable. It's painful, seeming to infiltrate every nook and cranny of my being. I feel starved for breath, though I'm aware I don't need it. My eyelids grow heavy, and my vision blurs.

"I'm sorry," I murmur, barely able to see straight. "She's trying- I wouldn't have brought her... if it wasn't important. My intention wasn't to hurt you, I swear of it. You can get me back for this."

"Fuck, JJ," She whispers, sitting down and putting her head in her hands.

It's hard to keep my head up. I fight the urge to vomit. All I can think about is that I feel like I am dying, and yet, Aella is so distraught. I reach out to touch her, hoping to do something to help. She flinches, grabbing my wrist. She sighs and grumbles under her breath, deflaming. She scoots closer, linking my arm around hers, and resting her head on my forehead.

"I'm sure you had a reason," Aella says. "I hate Veronica, and I'm pissed, but I trust you."

"Good," I say, barely able to form a coherent thought. "I trust you as well. And you should know my trust belongs to a very select few."

I wrap my wing around her, the room spinning around me.

I pass out.

It's so cold when I come to, that I can only reason that it is my conscience compensating for my body's desperate need for it to be so. Conscience forsaken, I can't help but just lie there, appreciating the drastic change from the melting, overwhelming heat. I'm leaning on someone– Aella, I can feel her scales on my cheek. Frost layers the room like a delicate, freshly spun web.

"Oh, good, you're alive," Aella says, half-heartedly.

"Was that even a doubt?" I mumble, sitting up.

"Nah," Aella says, tucking in her wings and knocking our shoulders together. "I forgot you vamps overheat so easily. Usually, I can keep it down, but..."

"Can you, now?" I tease. "I could see why that would be difficult in my presence–"

"Shut up," Aella rolls her eyes, laughing.

"Aella," I mock gasp. "You know better than that."

"Because you're physically incapable of shutting up?"

"Precisely."

I lay down on the bed and take a breath. Aella stays seated but stretches. I think about asking if I missed anything important but decide against it. Aella seems to have calmed down, and there's no screaming. Which makes me begin to question if Aella killed Veronica. But then again, I don't think Rebecca would've allowed that.

Then again, maybe she would've. But I doubt Icylyn or Beckett would've let that happen. Probably. It's probably best that I go check. I stand, though pain sears through my body, in every part I've refused to let heal, to let rest. Nevertheless, I push on.

I'm immediately taken aback by the sweet smells coming from the kitchen, and the even sweeter sounds of Veronica's laugh. It was lyrical, always, as the songs of morning birds I'd never see. The kind of sound you could listen to for hours.

"You're not bad," I hear Beckett say. "For a beginner."

"What's that supposed to mean?" Veronica asks. Rebecca chuckles.

"You might be good at cooking with my Mamá, but your pie skills still have a way to go," Beckett says.

"He has an ego when it comes to mechanics and pies," Icylyn supplies.

"Me? An ego? What?" Beckett asks.

"You've been spending too much time with Dorian," Icylyn says.

"No!" Beckett's voice squeals. "I... need to go fix one of my clocks, I can hear it ticking wrong, bye Ronnie!"

Beckett speeds to his room faster than I'd ever seen him run. I can't help but laugh as I find my way to the kitchen. Aella laughs as well and runs after Beckett to tease him. As I enter the kitchen, I watch as Veronica scrambles to help clean whatever's in her vicinity. Veronica looks clueless, but she's quick, precise, and determined.

She turns abruptly and seems a little surprised when she sees me in the room.

"Oh!" She says. "You're in here. Hi, Jinx."

It's the first time I've ever heard her say my name. She's never addressed me as anything other than Nightshade. I can't explain how it feels. Validating isn't quite the word.

"Are you- are you doing alright now? I'm sorry, this is the first place I thought about taking y-"

Before I can finish, her arms are around my waist. I falter for a moment, looking at Rebecca, trying to figure out what she's done with Veronica. Rebecca shrugs and smiles, taking a long sip of water and exiting the kitchen. Veronica quickly drops her arm, stepping away from me and looking at the floor. She tugs on a braid, breathing a little heavier.

"Sorry," She stammers. "I-"

I step forward and wrap my arms around her, squeezing her tightly. I can feel her shift as she stands on her toes.

"I'm sorry I tried to hurt you," She says.

"I don't blame you," I say. "You were simply responding to the nature of magic. It's wild and dangerous, believe me, I know."

"Right," Veronica says. "Still."

"We've probably overstayed our welcome," I say, after an uncomfortably long silence.

I drop my arms, holding them behind my back, and take a step backward.

"Right," Veronica says. "Um, okay, I'm going to say my goodbyes to everyone."

"Everyone?" I ask.

"Yes," Veronica says.

"Am I dead? Hallucinating?"

Veronica rolls her eyes and turns.

We move under the motherly embrace of the cover of night. We're swift, silent, far enough from the river that the sirens' song is nothing but a cry lost to the wind. Veronica's breath is steady, nearly consistent with the sound of her heartbeat, the sound of fabrics hitting against each other, twigs cracking under our feet. The trees have paid us mercy tonight, it seems. Even outside of Fear Forest, it can be a gamble.

My mask is now damp with my breath. My body aches for my bed. It's hard to think of anything other than my desire to return home. My home. *My* home.

"So," I say after an eternity. "It seems you and Aella... discussed."

"We've agreed to be somewhat amicable. For the time being, at least."

"So you still-"

"Hate each other's guts? Yeah. Oh, also, when you bite someone's neck-"

"That was quite a turn," I say.

"Shut up, hold on," She says, waving both her hands. "When you're sucking blood, do you like, suck through your fangs? Or do you just make the hole and *then* suck?"

"The latter," I answer.

Veronica hums, satisfied. She goes quiet again, simply looking around. Sometimes it's as if I'm watching her brain leave her body. I've often felt the same. I expect Beckett has also. I stare up at the moon and wonder why, when we worship the stars, we disregard her. She who pulls our tides, and holds our planet from destruction. She who bathes the night in light and its beauty.

If Orion, why not Artemis? Why not Hekate, why not Selene?

I know how our religion was formed. We were told the stories of the constellations, and oral history passed down by the early Woods. And yet, chock-full of lies. Names, faces, and narratives were erased. Something sacred quickly became nothing more than a tool of manipulation.

And here I seem to find myself, head out of my body. My body is moving on its own, swaying in the direction it knows, it yearns for. I snap back and look over at Veronica, who looks as if she's mentally weighing out different options.

"You can ask whatever it is you want to ask," I say.

"I want to know more about Lila," she says.

I stop abruptly. My brain seems to completely stall out for just a moment.

"Yes, I suppose I'd be curious as well," I say, after a moment. "Give me just a moment, I need to reason what I can say without betraying too much of her information."

It takes me all too long, but I've got it. I take a breath, digging deep into the recesses of my memories.

"We were both kicked out of our homes at the same time, at the age of ten," I begin. "I was... performing a heist..."

I stop, shut my eyes, and sigh.

"... I was robbing the bookshop," I admit. "I saw her running. She tripped over an uneven piece of the ground, and hit the ground, hyperventilating. I still remember the way she was sobbing, pressing a hand against her mouth to smother the noise. She was bruised quite terribly. It's fuzzy, but I'd gotten her to the cave, where she explained what happened. I promised to protect her. A couple of months later, the Woods had a funeral for her. To cover up what they did. To cover up the fact that they threatened to kill her if she ever returned. They found out she was a Shadow-Blood. No one had ever seen Dietrich cry before the funeral. Isolde was stone cold, and Daman looked terrified. Noah... that's when I met Noah. He'd run away from the funeral, and I followed him. He was sobbing, holding missing posters and–"

My voice cuts out. I can see it so clearly. His dirty blond hair was so much lighter. He was only eleven, and it would darken soon. Yet, he never did. Despite everything, he always stayed so bright.

His pale skin was rubbed raw, stained with tears. His cries sounded beyond painful. I'd watched as he went to hang a poster, but instead, fell to his knees. He stared at the picture and held it to his chest. I'd sped to him, not caring anymore who saw me speeding through, and pulled him with me into the shadows.

He looked at me as if I were death Himself.

"So I reunited him with Lila," I say. "I couldn't... not. Not with how he-um-"

"Are you crying?" Veronica asks.

"No, of course, not I have something in my throat," I say.

"Anyway," I say. "They still talk sometimes, according to him. He probably has more contact with her than I do."

I wholeheartedly believe it.

"But why did The Woods..." Veronica trails out.

"I'm afraid Lila wouldn't want me to answer that one," I say.

Veronica nods. We leave it at that.

Chapter 15
Nightshade

Veronica filtered into the group quicker than I imagined she would. Still, she was barely anything more than acquaintanced with the group. That is, shockingly, except for Beckett. We'd assembled the entire rebellion for a routine graffiti and poster removal day in the Mortem Venenum town square. Raven, Beckett, and Icylyn were all but shouting over each other, trying to explain the 'poster game' to Veronica.

As we walked further into town, I found their banter quickly drifting to the background, noticing the growing sound of chatter in the distance. I put a hand out, signaling to the group to stay close, stay hidden, and stay quiet. Time seems to slow around me as I run to the nearest building, quickly climbing up to the roof to get a better vantage point. I tug on my quiver, readjusting my cloak so that I don't burn, and crouch down.

My heart quite literally stops when I see them. It always does. Panic catches in my chest, and everything feels fake. The Woods are standing in the center of the town square. Noah keeps his eyes down, Hazel standing close by his side.

It's showtime, I suppose.

I speed closer, jumping between buildings and settling back down into a crouch, hiding behind a conveniently placed tree. My eyeballs roll without my permission the second I see Daman open his mouth.

"As the kingdom of Couteau has neglected to report, too concerned with their wasted energies on the crown princess Aella," Daman says. "Princess Veronica has been missing for the past month. The love of my life has been taken from me."

He pauses, sucking in his cheek, stone-cold face wearing a soft, pained expression. Wolf in sheep's clothing.

"I am lost without her," He says. "And I can only imagine how lost she must be without me, without us. How scared and alone she must feel. And yet, this so-called *rebellion* of star-forsaken monsters and terrorists has taken my fianceé, the woman who was to stand beside me during my future rule. They have taken what isn't theirs. I can only imagine what horrible danger she is facing, what mind-games they're subjecting her to."

His voice cracks at the last bit. He rarely goes with the sensitive appeal, given all his preaching about masculinity, and how it's 'weakness' and 'vulnerability' to show sadness. I have to admire the change in tactics, especially given how consistent he typically is with his methods.

"I just want my girl back," He says, and then, the cruel, merciless tyrant-in-training steps back out. "And to you miserable gutter rats, if you're listening, you'll regret stealing the precious thing that will *never* belong to you."

I roll to the side, still crouching on the roof, but making myself visible. I cup my hands around my mouth.

"Actually," I shout. "I'd rather prefer the name your *ex*-fianceé gave us. I believe that The Scumbag Rebellion fits us more accurately than 'The Miserable Gutter Rats,' but I'm willing to listen to further critiques. In any case, Veronica doesn't belong to *anyone* other than herself."

We have limited time, so pay attention, I transmit to Veronica and the rest of the rebellion. *Hazel, continue to keep Noah safe but stay as backup as needed. Raven, Sage, your assignment hasn't changed. Get close enough to Cazlamenta to do whatever damage to the courtyard you can. As we know, they're obsessed with cosmetics, and that will keep them at least somewhat occupied while we plan further attacks. Icylyn, you're on poster and general defacement duty, but be aware in case things go entirely off-plan and we need you to freeze the situation. Beckett, get Veronica to the hideout, quickly and without a show. Aella, are you prepared to finally attempt Operation Firestarter?*

Finally, Aella transmits.

I turn to Veronica, who looks agonized, and I watch as her eyes slowly shift into pink. Beckett notices, and takes her forearm, gesturing in the other direction. Veronica sighs and nods, looking defeated. He starts running, and she runs after him. I lock eyes with Icylyn, who nods at me, and then promptly disappears from sight. Hazel puts a hand on Noah's shoulder and leads him to the nearest castle. Raven and Sage give each other a look, and head to the same carriage, sneaking inside among the now chaotic crowd.

"Are we seriously doing this right now?" Aella shouts to me. "I mean, honestly who cares?"

"For star's sake, Aella," I respond.

"No, honestly, let them take her, why should we care?" Aella yells back. "I mean, it's a shitty enough thing to do as a friend, but as a leader?"

That felt personal, I transmit.

I'm over it, Aella transmits.

Swear? I transmit.

Swear. Now hurry up and hit me back.

"I highly doubt you could lead any better," I say.

"Do you mind?" Daman shouts.

I hop down, closer, and Aella begins to storm in my direction. Isolde murmurs something, crossing her arms with her palms out.

"I want all troops on the two of them. Bring them to me *alive,*" Dietrich commands.

"Are we sure we want Nightshade *alive,* darling?" Isolde asks.

"Your input is irrelevant, my queen," Dietrich says. "Do not go against my commands."

Isolde scoffs. She uncrosses her arms, then rests a hand on his shoulder, her index finger sliding against his neck, sharp nails no doubt digging into his skin. She leans closer to him, whispering something into his ear. While lip reading isn't part of my repertoire, I know exactly what she's saying.

"You're going to regret that."

It's enough to send a shiver through my spine. As much as I hate to admit it, Isolde terrifies me. I don't have time to think about it. Aella's quickly approaching from behind. She grabs my braid from beneath my hood and tugs as hard as she can. I stumble backward with the force of it, quickly knocking me out of my head before I have the chance to think upon my past experiences with Isolde.

"Not the time, Aella," I protest, swatting her away.

"No, this is *exactly* the time," Aella says.

"Do you really want to do this?" I ask, raising an eyebrow.

I watch Dietrich signal the guards. Right on time.

"You have no idea," Aella says.

Ready? I transmit.

Please, how *many times did we practice this one?*

I grab onto her shoulders as she yanks my braid out of my hood, using the leverage to knock me to the ground. I grab her before I can register the pain, and throw her backward, flipping her onto the ground with me. I can hear her breathing heavily beside me.

My apologies, I transmit.

Think we got their attention? Aella transmits.

I look up at the oncoming hordes of guards. Then I lay back down.

I'd assume so, I respond. *Injure, don't kill. We want them down, but-*

Yeah yeah, I know the drill, Aella transmits.

I stand up, and Aella follows suit. We look at each other and grin. I stretch out my arms and yawn. Aella laughs and stretches out her wings, balling her hands into fists that quickly light aflame. I look over to Icylyn, who's down an alleyway, ripping up a poster and stuffing it into her satchel. She gives me a firm nod, then disappears from view.

I look over at Dietrich. I'm not quite sure if he can see me, but I wink anyway.

The guards are too close before he can call them off.

I flick my wrist, snapping, and I've got the nearest ones unconscious. It takes me a moment to recover from the overuse of power, but Aella's still raring to go. She grins, all veneers, eyes lighting aflame, wings alight, looking like a burning star in the flesh. She lunges, extending her arms backward, wings fully spread. She grabs her mace from its holding place on her leg and sprints forward, running on top of the unconscious guards. She doesn't stop, simply holds onto her mace and aims for the legs as she runs by.

If it weren't for all the armor, I'd almost feel bad for them.

Aella stops running and grins, taking a breath. A guard holds her in a chokehold, and her eyes widen and flash to me. She grins even wider and sticks her tongue out, before completely flaming. The guard screams, stumbling backward.

"Aella," I say.

"What?" She asks, looking down at the guard. "Are you dead?"

The guard groans.

Aella gestures to the guard, and rests her mace on her shoulders. Another guard catches up behind her, raising their sword.

Behind you, I warn.

Aella spins the handle of her mace a few times, then turns and swings, stopping the sword before it hits her. She turns and kicks the guard as hard as she can, then swings at them in the direction they start falling. She keeps hitting until they hit the ground with no possibility of coming up soon. She sticks her mace into the ground, grabbing the end of the handle tightly, and leaning down, breathing hard. She's laughing to herself, wiping the sweat off her forehead.

More guards start coming at her, but I watch as ice catches them by the ankles, slowly spanning upwards. I look for Icylyn, but she's hidden herself fairly well. I speed over to Aella, and then tap on her shoulder.

"My turn," I say.

I speed up to the roof, trying to get a better vantage point.

"Hello Icylyn," I say.

"Hi," she says, then disappears once more.

I quickly assess the open spots in the guard's armor, then catalog them in my mind. I grab my bow and quickly start loading it. I crouch down, getting into position, tilting my bow just slightly. Time slows around me as I let go of the string, reload, let go, reload, watching as guards react within milliseconds of one another. Aella begins collecting arrows, grabbing them out of, collarbones, stomachs, arms, and legs, and grabbing them in her free hand.

Hazel, start making sure the carriages head out. But first- I begin to transmit, looking towards.

Yes ma'am, Hazel responds, sounding distracted.

"Aella, move!" I shout.

Aella looks up at me, and then at the sky. Her eyes widen, and the first strike of lightning hits far too close to her. Why hasn't she moved already?

Lightning hits again, and again, breaking the ground, narrowly missing nearby shops. Aella goes up in flames, quite literally, and disappears. There's the sound of crackling flames behind me, and Aella appears, breathing heavily.

"That was fun," Aella says, breathlessly.

"Is there any chance they'll come after us?" I ask.

Aella looks down. "Well, especially after that last attack, I think they'll be down for at least a week. So we've got time to figure out what we're doing with Veronica, and our next plans."

"Good," I say.

Icylyn, I transmit.

A pillar of ice rises on the roof, and Icylyn appears inside of it.

"Thank you," I tell her. "Do you think you have enough energy to pick up Sage and Raven and bring them to the base?"

"Yes," Icylyn says, disappearing in a case of ice.

Aella sticks the handle of her mace back onto her leg, dropping a handful of my arrows into my quiver. She puts an arm around me, pressing a hand against her side. The heat becomes nearly unbearable, and the scene around us changes. The flames drop, and we're no longer in the town square, but rather, the base. A wall of ice drops, and with it, Icylyn, Sage, and Raven appear.

Beckett and Veronica are both seated at the table, sketching.

Aella's breath falters, and she falls fully against me. I quickly catch her.

"*Fuck,*" she groans.

I remove her hand from her side and stare at her palm. It's covered in blood. I could've prevented this. How could I have been so stupid? How could I not have noticed?

It's impossible to block the scent out. I can't remember the last time I ate. I'm *starving.* I'd give anything for just the tiniest taste–

No. I got her hurt. I'm not even going to think about this right now. Even if the sight and scent are nauseating. Veronica stands, grabbing her notebook, and walks to the other side of the room. I lead Aella to the table, sitting her down on top of it.

"Beckett, would you hand me my needles and threads?" I ask.

Beckett pales but nods. He jumps up from his seat and then returns, handing me both. Raven has ointment and a rag in my other hand almost instantly. I quickly douse the rag in the ointment, handing the jar back to Raven.

"I barely even feel it," Aella says.

I press the rag firmly against the wound and she winces.

"You're a real sadist sometimes, JJ, you know that?" Aella hisses.

"Just proving a point," I say, beginning to clean the wound.

It's relatively quiet for the next few minutes. I try to distract myself from the fact that I'm cleaning blood, and instead, that Aella got hurt. Aella got stabbed, and it was undoubtedly my fault. I keep getting distracted. I freeze, unable to keep moving. A hand sits gently on my shoulder. I turn to see Sage, looking blankly sympathetic.

"Do you want me to take over?" She signs.

I carefully set down my supplies.

"I am perfectly capable of doing it," I sign back.

"Your eyes are red," She signs. "Glowing, and red. You look distracted. I will do this, go eat."

Edgar flies in, landing on my other shoulder. He begins pecking at the side of my head. I try to shoo him away, but he doesn't stop. The hunger becomes almost overwhelming, and Edgar simply just grabs at my hair with his beak, tugging.

"Alright," I sign, then put my hands up in mock surrender.

I take one last look at Veronica, Aella, and the others.

My rebellion. The people I was constantly putting in danger, simply because Lila and I had a vendetta to carry out.

I speed out.

Chapter 16
Veronica

I started to wonder if I was the only one genuinely concerned about the fact that Aella got *stabbed*. I guess things like this are normal to them, which I find absolutely unthinkable. Maybe I was just zeroing in on that. Maybe I was just trying to ignore everything that just happened.

My chest has been aching lately. I've been aching. Not just the normal pains of anxiety, but also an insatiable yearning. Something in me has been crying out, yearning to go home. I don't know what home is anymore, and I can't help but miss Daman, Sabine, and The Woods.

I'm ashamed to say it. Seeing Daman, hearing him talk about me...

I wanted to run to him. I wanted to wrap my arms around him and apologize for leaving. I miss him so much.

But, stars, I hate him. He hurt me, ruined me. All he ever did was belittle me. I've done so much growing without him since then. It's ridiculous for me to feel this way now. So why can't I help but miss him? I never want to go back to him, but I yearn for him all the same.

By the time I zone back in, Jinx is zooming back into the room.

"Aella?" She asks.

"All good, JJ," Aella says.

Jinx nods. "Well then, while we're all together, are there any other matters we need to address?"

"Hazel said the Americans just shipped in more imports," Raven chimes in, pausing to sign.

"I am all for being against the Woods, but isn't that a good thing?" I sign. "I thought we liked progress."

"If you ignore what we trade to get those exports," Sage signs.

"You'll learn soon enough," Icylyn says, signing. "We all do."

"Think reeeeeeeeaaally hard about it," Beckett says, then quickly signs. "I mean, I don't think it's true, but..."

I rack my brain to think of whatever they could be talking about. It takes too long, but when it finally does come, I want to scrub my brain free of it. I can hear the gunshots again.

"No," I shake my head. "They don't."

"Yes, they do~" Raven sing-songs, simultaneously signing.

"It's a theory. And even if it is true, it won't happen again any time soon, and hopefully, won't ever again," Jinx says. "They'll be scrambling. Between trying to form a bond with... Couteau... and the fact that we've recently cleaned out their dungeon, and now that they're courtyard has been attacked– we've been given more time to tear them down from the inside out. Previously, it's simply been showing the public that we won't back down, no significant damage."

Nightshade pauses, grabbing her teacup and taking a long sip, before continuing.

"However, it seems fate, for once, has been working in our favor. Before, our efforts were mostly focused on taking shipments of new imports, sometimes stealing from the royals and giving to the destitute, cliche as it might be, but mainly... causing trouble where we can. Now we can help our communities in whatever ways we can, but can truly focus on tearing down larger, more detrimental plots. Which is why we're having this meeting."

"If there's anything those royals *hate*," Raven says, laying on Sage. "It's unpredictability. Gotta keep 'em on their toes if we're going to successfully piss 'em off."

"That's true," Beckett nods, snapping and pointing at her.

There are murmurs of agreement, and Jinx sits down on top of the counter. She never took off her mask or hood when the entire group was there. I guess it's easier to stay Nightshade that way, or something. She's less vulnerable.

I don't know. She's been different lately. Especially when it's just the two of us. I don't mind it. It's not a bad change, not in the slightest. It does make me question more than I'd like to, though. I've been questioning more and more about myself lately.

"We should take Couteau," I blurt before the thought even finishes forming in my brain.

"...What?" Jinx asks, seemingly caught off guard.

"We're too focused on Mortem– *you're* too focused on Mortem Venenum– sorry– While it is the kingdom with more power and influence, it is not the *only* kingdom. Couteau is in shambles, incredibly weak, which is why they were relying so much on my marriage to Daman. The people are sick, hungry, and dying, supernatural bodies finding their way into the bog with many others. It's why the bog siren population is so incredibly high in Couteau. The conditions are so bad that men go to work and don't come back. No one can afford to spend at any shops, and the economic state is in shambles–"

"I'm only hearing negatives," Aella says, watching as Raven translates everything for Sage.

"I'm not done," I say. "With enough work, Couteau could yet be saved, however, m– the king and queen are far more focused on locating... and torturing... their own daughter. And their younger daughter was too caught up in being obsessed with obtaining their attention that she didn't even realize."

I look over at Aella, who sits up straighter. She narrows her eyes at me and crosses her arms.

I continue, "In any case, it may be a weak kingdom, but it's a kingdom nonetheless. And its weakness will make it all the more easy to overtake. They've fatally understaffed their guards, and in any case, the king and queen are idiots. I'd like to propose that Aella and I take Couteau in the name of the rebellion."

Jinx's face seems to have turned a bit purple, and she sucks in a deep breath. Aella leans her shoe against the table, tilting her chair back, and clapping slowly. She grins, baring her teeth.

"I'm in," She says, signing.

"It won't be easy," Jinx says.

I feel a laugh bubble at the edge of my lips. "Please. They'll be powerless to stop us."

"If you would excuse me a moment?" Jinx says, and in a blur, she's left the base.

Almost immediately follows the sound of Beckett laughing. Raven grins and puts out their hand. Sage rolls her eyes and stuffs a few coins into Raven's palm.

"Does someone want to explain what's going on?" I ask.

"No one tell her," Aella shouts, laughing, signing fast. "This is *priceless.*"

"Not priceless, I lost a bet," Sage signs.

"But they're so clueless," Beckett whines.

"Exactly," Aella grins. "It's funny."

"So no one's going to tell me?" I ask, signing.

"Sorry, princess," Sage signs as Raven laughs and shakes their head.

"Icylyn?" I ask.

"I'm just as lost as you are," Icylyn says.

Beckett looks over at her, and she looks mildly confused for a moment. It takes me a moment to realize they're having an entirely telepathic conversation. I drum my nails against the table, annoyed. Icylyn puts a hand over her mouth and giggles, causing Beckett to do the same.

I rest my chin in my hand and shake my head, still drumming my fingers. Aella chuckles. Jinx speeds back into the room, seeming to have sobered considerably.

But there's something in the way she looks at me. All foreign, all comfortably familiar.

"If we put this plan into motion," Jinx says, "There's no going back."

I smile.

"Good."

Part Three

Chapter 17
Nightshade

A month. Well, even longer now. A month, two weeks, and three days, but truly, who was keeping count? A month, two weeks, and three days since Veronica learned the truth. Well, at least since she'd learned some of it. A month, two weeks, and three days since she'd started living in the cave with me. A month, two weeks, and three days of learning to trust each other. Far longer than that, far too long of feeling things for her that I never should.

I tried. I really did. I never wanted to develop these feelings for Veronica, but here I am, absolutely smitten. As if it isn't hard enough for me to sleep normally, it is especially tonight, failing to muffle out the guilt-ridden thoughts of Veronica. Being nocturnal and an insomniac doesn't bode well for trying to sleep during the night, or at all. Though not nocturnal, Veronica was often the same, especially toward the beginning when she hadn't much trust in me.

We've gotten to a level of trust where we can sleep in the same room. Separate beds of course, or rather, divots in the walls covered in leaves and whatever scraps of fabric I could find. I bookmark my page and shut what I'm reading, staring at the warm glass of tea I've left on the floor. I focus, feeling the energy of it, and watching as it slowly floats in my direction. I grab it out of the air and take a sip, allowing myself a glance at Veronica.

She's rarely at peace. Yet, she lays there, so still, the only movement being the rise and fall of her breath. I smile to myself. I take a long sip of tea, content in the warmth and the sweet, familiar taste, never mind the familiar twinge of blood. I finish the cup and lower it back down onto the ground. I lay on my side, struggling to get comfortable, when I hear a pounding on the cave door.

There is not a bone in my body that wants to get up and answer it, but I drag myself out of bed nonetheless. I climb the ladder of the room and push up the floor panel, crawling to the main floor of the cave. The knocking starts again, so I speed to answer, lest the knocker wake Veronica. I pull the lever and watch as the cave opens upwards.

Seeing him feels like whiplash. I freeze, my heart jumping in my throat, blood-rushing cold. I quickly shut the cave behind me.

"Give her back," Daman says.

His blond hair is disheveled, and matted down with grease and sweat. His eyes are bloodshot and dark-rimmed. It would almost be satisfying to see him like this...

Just not here. I should've known he'd come back.

"She came here of her own volition, seeking refuge from *you* in particular," I say.

Edgar flies in. I stiffen, raising my arm as a post. He lands on my arm, and I make clicking noises at him to calm him down. I listen as he screams at Daman, and shush him, stroking his head with my finger.

"I've come to collect what's mine, and you know it," He spits, pulling out his pistol.

Edgar's wings expand and he begins flapping them wildly, smacking against my head. He doesn't cease screaming at Daman. I don't make any attempt to stop him. It's not like Daman can see him.

"Stars, your views of women haven't gotten any less disgusting–" I start.

"Nor have yours," He says.

"Yes, well, there's a reason women flock to me and not you, now isn't there?" I say. "And in any case, she doesn't belong to you. She doesn't belong to anyone. Her decisions are hers to make, and not yours."

"She's my betrothed, just because you've tainted her–"

Whatever he was about to say is droned out by the whirring of the cave door lifting off the ground. There stands Veronica, seemingly still half asleep. There she stands, seemingly glowing in her light blue nightgown, braids tied back in a matching blue ribbon, rubbing the sleep out of her eyes.

"Hi Daman," She murmurs, sleep still in her voice. "Please kindly vacate the premises before I make you."

"I'm here to bring you back–"

"Nice pistol," She says. "Is this one new?"

"Don't interrupt. Listen, Veronica–"

"Is he seriously still talking?" Veronica groaned, rolling her eyes, before grinning at me.

"Bite your tongue before I have to shut you up myself," He grits.

"Mmm, you see, I'm not really into you anymore, so the flirting isn't going to work, sweetheart," She says, snapping her fingers and shooting him a finger gun.

I don't think much of the action and neither does he. He doesn't notice that as he continues to drone on, belittling her, insulting her, trying to scare her into submission, is that her eyes slowly begin to turn pink. She slowly begins to lift her arm, and he doesn't realize that he is mindlessly mirroring her actions. She points her finger-gun at her shoulder, and he does the same, too caught up in his speech to notice.

"Pew," She says, softly.

Daman screams in pain, having shot himself in the shoulder. Veronica yawns, rubbing her eyes again, slowly inching closer to me. Daman doesn't have any words, he just keeps looking at his hand, then the gun, then the wound, in stunned silence, and occasional whimper in pain.

"Bye Daman," She says.

"But–" He begins.

"Bye Daman," She repeats, as he begins to walk away.

He slowly turns around and begins to walk away as she spins her finger around and points. We watch and wait until he's far beyond our view. She then turns to me and blinks, her eyes turning gray once she opens them.

"I thought you didn't know how–" I start.

"I'm a quick learner," She murmurs.

She stumbles a bit closer to me, yawning. Not only is she already not very awake, but using powers like hers often are very draining to the user. They are especially draining to those who haven't practiced much, like her.

I can hear her quietly mutter something about being tired. She looks as though she's going to collapse, here and now.

"Do you want me to carry–" I start.

"Mhm," She nods.

I bend down just slightly, and she wraps her arms around my neck. She jumps up a bit, wrapping her legs around my waist. I walk into the cave, leaning back so she won't fall as I pull the lever to close the door to the cave. Within a few minutes of walking through the cave, her grip begins to loosen, her breath begins to slow, and her head lulls against my neck.

Before I'd met her, I'd never known what it was like to feel my heart beating in my chest. I'd never known the feeling of blood rushing to my face. Cupid seemed to have me backed up against a corner, tipping my chin towards Veronica with the end of his poison-tipped arrow. It is a cruel game. But here she is, and here we are. We find ourselves backed into a corner, dancing to a symphony of outcomes I never would've ever imagined. Funny how time is capricious like that.

Oddly enough, I'd fallen asleep that night, a rare occurrence. Due to my immortality, I didn't have to sleep often and often didn't. Every so often though, my body would reach a limit, and I'd either be forced to rest or I'd collapse. Now, is that healthy? Next question.

However, that is how I found myself this morning, and how Veronica had stumbled upon me. When Veronica had made her way into the main space of the cave, I'd been passed out on the table, head against the chessboard, blanketed by scraps of maps and unusable plans.

When I awake, she is walking about, practically waltzing as she softly hums to herself. She promptly plops down on the floor. When my eyes meet her, she gives me a slight smile and a polite wave. I blink myself awake, and sit up, leaning back with the palm of my hand placed behind me on the table. I stretch out my wings a bit and her gaze shifts. She sits down beside me on the table and hands me a cup of tea, still warm, steam rising from the top of it. She takes a sip of her own and sets it down on the table beside her.

"It's not poisoned," Veronica says softly. "Swear to the stars."

"... is it?" I ask, the teacup reaching my lips, amused.

"No. I didn't tamper with it at all," She says. "I just thought you should know."

The cup is warm against my cold hands as I take a sip. She relaxes a bit. She then twirls one of her braids around her finger, seeming anxious once more.

"You aren't," She pauses, fumbling for the correct word. "Afraid of me, are you?"

"Where would you get that idea, darling?" I ask.

"When we were in the forest, the, um–" She starts, gently tapping one fist over the other. "That, of course, and the fact that you sometimes seem almost nervous around me."

"Oh," I say.

"Yeah," She looks down at her feet.

"Well, I believe I'd mentioned it before, but I'll mention it again," I say. "I don't hate you, nor do I fear you, and I rather like you. What you saw... I wasn't afraid of your powers, and certainly not of you. I just didn't want them to have control over you. And believe me, you don't make me nervous."

"Do you swear on it?" I ask.

"I swear on the night that bore me and the forests that raised me," I say. "If it eases you, you can read my mind, I'll lower my barriers."

"I believe you," She says, though I notice the doubt lingering in her tone.

I hover my hand above hers, looking at her. She looks confused for a moment, then utters a quick, "Oh," and nods. I take her hand in mine. Her hands are almost as warm as the teacup sitting between us. Her gaze meets mine, and my eyes can't help but wander towards her lips.

I feel shame rise, forbidden and as penetrating as the sun. Not the time for me to be thinking of things like that. Not the time at all. Likely, it will never be the time. I mean, we are simply night and day, not meant to coexist, simply testing fate by being beside one another at this table. We hover there, leaning towards each other like magnets until she leans backward. She doesn't remove her hand from mine though.

Maybe that's all we're meant to do. Coexist.

I can only hope that I'll learn to accept that.

Chapter 18
Veronica

If you'd asked me a month, two weeks, and three days ago if I'd ever see myself comfortable around Nightshade, Aella or Beckett, I would've thought you mad. Yet, here I am, living in Jinx's cave, laughing at something Beckett said. He and Aella are visiting. Aside from Icylyn, who's spending time with her friend Dorian, they're the only ones who know the location of the cave.

"Okay wait," I say after a while. "So, what's the deal with the goggles?"

"Oh, these?" Beckett had responded, tapping on his goggles. "Yeah, so my powers kicked into gear early after the Red Revenge crew... um– not important, you just need to know they just kicked in earlier than they should've. The problem is, most elves have laser beams that shoot out of our eyes, and I never learned how to control that, because there was so much going on when they kicked in. I made these so I wouldn't, y'know, destroy everything and everyone I looked at! Plus, they look pretty neat."

"Get out of the kitchen, JJ," Aella yells, saving me from having to come up with a response.

To which, Jinx shouts, "I am currently in the process of making tea!"

"Can– can I have some?" Beckett asks, without shouting.

"Absolutely," Jinx yells from the kitchen.

"Thank you!" He smiles.

For a while, it surprised me how they interacted with each other. They're a lot less hostile towards each other than I would have imagined months ago. I'm not going to lie, they are a whole lot dorkier than I would've *ever* imagined. Aella is often involving people in some sort of prank, Beckett is usually ready to go on science rants to whoever would listen, and Jinx spends a fair amount of time reading and drinking tea. Sometimes Beckett and Jinx will play chess and have each other at a stalemate for literal hours. I'd thought they'd spend most of their time scheming, but that isn't often the case. Jinx tends to plot things out once she's alone.

Then again, that's been changing ever since we began plotting to take Couteau.

Jinx walks into the room and sets tea in front of Beckett, who beams and thanks her. She sits down on the floor near us, and Aella plops down next to her. Beckett slides a few papers over to Jinx with a proud grin on his face. Aella starts tossing around Jinx's hair as she begins to inspect the papers. Jinx doesn't seem to mind, let alone notice.

"And you're sure you can make these?" Jinx asks.

"Please," Beckett scoffs, before winking at me. "It's simple industrial mechanics!"

"Simple because it'll explode, right?" Aella teases.

"Not this," Beckett says. "This will capture flashes of light into portraits, and thus we'll be able to have traceable evidence! ... However, I will be needing gunpowder. The trap I'm currently working on... yeah that *miiiiiiight* have a higher chance of exploding but Ice and I are planning on running tests until we're absolutely *sure* it'll work, I promise."

"If you think this is possible then I absolutely support it," Jinx says, sliding the papers back to Beckett, who pumps his fist in victory.

"Another win for the twig," Aella says.

"Yeah, whatever," Beckett says.

Jinx stares off into the distance, becoming increasingly vacant. Beckett flips through the pages of his notebook, scratching something into the margins, posture becoming almost sickening to look at as he hovers his face closer to the paper. Aella leans over, lazily tracing her eyes over the paper.

It's almost painfully silent for a moment. Something suddenly feels off. I look over at Jinx, whose features are twisted up in concern. Her eyes turn black, and her voice begins to warp as she speaks.

"We need to go. Now."

The four of us are standing on a rooftop, Beckett slowly backing up and grasping Aella's arm as he looks down. Jinx's cape flies in the wind, her hood flying backward and releasing two dark ginger Dutch braids. Her eyes are pitch black at the moment, and reflected in them is a burning house. That house was definitely not burning a few minutes ago. Yet, here we were, smoke clouding the air with black ash that filled the air, with it the suffocating smells and screams. It's a dark and twisted song, the shrieks crescendoing against the harmonious tune of the softer crackling. Jinx immediately starts sprinting across the roof, making it to the end and turning back just before she jumps and spreads her wings, falling backward and spinning into a swoop.

"She's such a dramatic bitch," Aella laughs and shakes her head, before hitting her heels together.

Wheels pop out from under her shoes, and she slides down the side of the roof, opening her wings the second her feet leave the roof. Beckett shudders and takes a breath. He squeezes his eyes tightly and shakes out his hands, before offering me his hand. I take it.

"Okay, so we're going to run off the side... of the roof. With my ability to control the wind – and your telekinesis– there's a 90 percent chance we won't die," He says.

"And that other ten percent?" I ask.

"We'll burn that bridge when we get to it. Okay, let's go!"

The two of us take off, sprinting off the roof, both of us screaming. I feel the energy buzzing and humming in my head, before surrounding my body and keeping me in the air. I hold on tightly to Beckett's arm so he doesn't fall, as he quickly spins his fingers around, summoning wind around him.

"Holy shit," I whisper as he lets go of me, completely shocked by my ability to remain in the air.

"I hate heights," Beckett says, looking down, blinking, and shaking his head.

By the time Beckett and I get there, Jinx and Aella are already inside the burning building. Beckett has a lot less hesitation running into the building than he did running off the roof. Then again, it is strange for a kid his age to be so used to thrusting himself into constant danger. I charge in after him.

Inside, Jinx is carrying a coughing little girl on her hip. Upon seeing Beckett and I, Jinx sets down the little girl, and kneels to her height, taking the little girl's hands in hers.

"Okay, Ardeth, do you see that boy right there? The one with the curly hair and the goggles? Good, he's going to take you outside, alright? He's going to take you outside while I locate the rest of your family, okay?"

"And my doll?" Ardeth asks.

"Of course," Jinx smiles. "I won't forget about Meadow. Now, run along, it's not safe here."

I don't know if it was the adrenaline rush of flying off a building and running into a burning building, but something, right here and now, is making my heart beat faster than I'd previously thought possible. There she is, her pale skin seeming to glow in the light of the flames as she gives Ardeth an encouraging smiles, and stands, before running back into the flames. This is... new. This fluttery feeling in my stomach. Foreign and familiar.

I didn't think I'd feel this after...

It doesn't matter. Whatever I'm thinking will have to wait, burning building and all.

"Hey, V, a little help?" Aella says.

As we walk over to each other, she places a kid's hand in mine. She then lifts the other one up and over her back, placing him on the ground. She nods at the back door, before turning around and following wherever Jinx had gone.

And if I'm being perfectly honest, my mind is not at all where it is supposed to be. Even when the children and I make our way out of the flaming house, my brain is stuck inside it.

Okay, fine, yes, I *may* be thinking about Jinx. There is just something about these feelings that seems so unbelievably wrong, yet so undeniably right. Sabine used to say that I am essentially the personification of denial. But that's not relevant.

After all, this is an upsurgence story, not a love story. Never mind that thus far I've only ever been attracted to men, I'm not attracted to women, least of all *Nightshade* of all possible candidates. I will give her points in that she's a much, much better person than my ex on all accounts. But again, Jinx and I are just very good friends. Stars, we're *friends* now.

Snap out of it, I think to myself

I do as I tell myself and snap out of it, burying that internal dialogue deep *deep* down, reasoning that will be the safest and healthiest way to deal with my feelings.

At the same moment, Beckett is pulling little devices out of his gear-covered brown satchel, and setting them on the ground, the three kids circling the devices. As the kids giggle, little toy-like creatures crawl on the ground, and onto their shoulders.

Fog rolls in from the woods. Aella and Jinx run out with a good few more people, as the foundation of the house begins to crack and sway.

Jinx runs back in.

As the building is crumbling, Jinx runs back in. Then the building collapses.

"Jinx!" I scream.

"She's okay," Aella says, putting a hand on my shoulder.

Sure enough, from the rubble, she rises. She is ashen, and one of her wings is literally on fire, as is her cloak, but otherwise, she looks generally unphased. I let out an impossibly heavy sigh of relief. Jinx stomps on her cloak, putting out the fire, wincing at her wing. She walks towards us, and Ardeth runs to her. Jinx kneels to her height and pulls something from behind her back.

"Meadow! You got her," The little girl smiles.

"Of course," Jinx smiles gently at her. "I promised, didn't I?"

Sometimes I want to go back in time just to tell myself that Jinx really isn't all that bad. However... that fog. That fog is most certainly going to be a problem. The fog, and, of course, the now-collapsed house. Or the fact that Jinx is, quite literally, on fire. Jinx is giving the adults a rundown of the situation, while Beckett is keeping the kids distracted.

"Orrin should be able to find a place to house you for the meanwhile, while we figure this out. And if he gives you any trouble, tell him Jinx sent you, alright?" Jinx says.

"That is some thick fog," Aella says, crossing her arms and facing the forest.

"Indeed," Jinx says, stepping towards us once the family is out of sight.

"It's not fog," Beckett says, tone darkening. "That's gunpowder. Listen."

Sure enough, there's the crackle and boom of firing guns. This means that this likely isn't an attack by The Woods. Although, from Beckett's reaction alone, I could easily guess that it isn't. He's giggling now, holding on tightly to Aella's arm, paralyzed. She puts an arm around him, and for once, her expression is soft, worried. It's only for a split second, before her eyebrows knit and her eyes light ablaze, holding Beckett tighter.

"JJ?" Aella asks.

"The Victory's Bastard Crew doesn't attack sporadically like this, not for the most part," Jinx shakes her head. "From what I know of The Golden Fury and The Nox Lilium crews, this would be an entirely uncharacteristic attack. Which likely means for the next month or so I'll be dealing with The Red Revenge and Company."

Beckett's squeezing Aella to a point that looks painful, laughing now uncontrollably. He looks furious and terrified in a way I've never seen from him. He lets go of Aella and starts walking forward, beginning to untie his goggles. Aella catches him by the back of his vest and drags him back on his heels.

"What? She can't do it on her own! Let me at them. I can get a couple of them. Just let me-" He says, squirming.

Aella picks him up and tosses him over her shoulder.

"They've made it to their ship by now, Beckett," Jinx says. "Going after them is-"

"Suicide," Beckett says bitterly. "Yeah. Trust me. I know."

We went straight to Rebecca's house straight after, at Aella's request. It takes a good while to get everyone calmed down, but it does happen, and soon enough, Aella and Beckett are joking and teasing each other.

"Anyway, saving all those people from that building?" Aella grins, "We totally kicked ass."

Jinx sits cross-legged on the couch, and she bumps fists with Aella without the two even looking at each other. I sit beside Jinx, though careful to give her space. Beckett takes a look around, and then just lays down on the floor. I feel it deep within my soul. I think all of us do.

"You okay, twig?" Aella teases.

"Never," Beckett says, as dramatically as he can, exhaustedly sprawled on the floor.

"Y'know what, fair," Aella says.

Icylyn walks into the room, looks at us, then looks at Beckett. She promptly lays down next to him, almost scarily mirroring him. No one pays her any mind.

Rebecca isn't home, so Jinx seems a whole lot more comfortable. She had enough time previously to speed out and grab one of the books she'd had a hard time putting down lately, and was seemingly consuming every line, eyes glued to the page, fingers running across the pages. Jinx laughs, the kind of laugh that would send a chill down any spine, and it doesn't help that at that moment her voice decided to slip apart, distort and echo. Something about it was hauntingly beautiful. Her laugh is like a piano touched only by time. The keys of laughter may be worn down and distorted, yet they still bounce off the walls of any room as if they were nothing more, nothing less than the comfort of a faded memory.

Not only that but– for the first time I've seen, she doesn't cover her smile with her hand, or keep her lips tightly closed. My stars, it's beautiful. Part of me couldn't help but stare at her fangs, though with interest rather than fear. After a minute she notices, and covers her mouth.

"My apologies," She says.

"No," I say, a bit too frantically, then cough. "I mean, no, no, um, I wasn't- you're very pretty-um, *they're* pretty- pretty neat, um, your fangs are pretty cool, they're cool."

Nailed it.

I make the mistake of glancing over at Aella, who's grinning wickedly. She chuckles to herself, shaking her head.

"You're so useless, just tell her you like her already," Aella says.

Jinx spits tea all over and then starts choking. Icylyn leaves and returns with a towel to clean up any droplets. I give Aella a look, and Aella just laughs. I can feel the energy buzzing in my head, and hold on to it, slowly raising my arm, watching as Aella's does the same. She smacks her hand across her face. She looks at me, rubbing her face, before going back to cackling. It's a horrid, infuriating, grating sound.

Okay, yes, fine, I admit that I may have the slightest of feelings for Jinx. Whatever! It's just a slow-passing thing. No need to make a scene. It is fine. It will be fine. She doesn't have to know. She will not need to know.

This certainly won't come to bite me in the ass later.

Chapter 19
Veronica

I did not think this through. I *definitely* didn't think this through. Like, at all. What was I supposed to do? The guards were after Aella, and Daman was not only after me, but he was *hell-bent* on killing Jinx. Though it probably would never happen– I couldn't let it. So I didn't. Or, at least tried to prevent what I could.

Unfortunately for me, I don't know quite enough about my powers and how they worked– or their limits, especially since I was weaker in my ability. I've all but drained them for the time being. So, when I went against the guards and couldn't make them attack each other, or knock them all down in one go... well... to put it nicely, I was doomed from the start.

It wasn't quite sunset yet, but Jinx had escorted Aella, Beckett, and Icylyn home post-rebellion meeting just in case. During the meeting, Hazel ran over with news that my parents had sent out yet another "search and rescue" for Aella. I was certainly not bitter about that. Not in the slightest. Okay. Fine. Maybe a little bitter about it, it would've been somewhat nice to have my absence acknowledged, by my parents and kingdom. That's not relevant. We'll be taking their kingdom anyway. What's relevant is that I'd opted to stay at the cave. But, I didn't actually stay.

I ventured to the area, not far from the cave, mind you, of which Hazel had seen the royal guards of Couteau. What I wasn't expecting was the royal guards of Mortem Venenum and much less Daman at the head of the troops... He reared his horse around to face the guards.

"And if any of you see Nightshade, she's to be apprehended, dead or alive. Preferably dead."

That was not going to fly with me. But did I think of a plan first? Absolutely not, no. I just leaped out of the bushes I was hiding in, scratching myself and tearing at my clothing as I did so. That definitely caught some attention.

"You couldn't kill her if you tried," I say. "And if you want to try, you're going to have to go through me first."

And– well– they did in fact beat me. Really quickly, actually. Like, like *really* quickly.

Okay, yeah, maybe that isn't that surprising, in retrospect. That's not important. I'd landed a few good blows, none fatal though, because of their protective armor. But after a good ten minutes, I'd been beaten. I was leaning against a tree, a dagger deep in my side.

"Hey..." I say, to no one in particular, through moans and heavy breaths. "If I don't die, you don't mind if I keep this, right? Because I'm gonna... anyway."

The ground begins to sway beneath me. That certainly isn't a good sign. Breathing becomes harder and harder, and the world begins to spin around me. Gravity has no mercy on me, putting two firm hands on my shoulders and pushing me down to my knees. I can't move, I can barely breathe, and it takes everything in me not to scream out in pain. I won't give them the satisfaction.

"You'll be fine," Daman says, dismounting from his horse, and kneeling next to me, before turning his attention to the guards. "Tie her up, there's a carriage waiting to take her to Cazlamenta."

"With all due respect, Your Highness," One of the guards, with rose gold plating on his shoulder, speaks up, clearly from Couteau. "We have direct orders from the king and queen to return both princesses to Caeara."

"Really?" I jerk my head up to look at him, making things spin more quickly.

"Calm down, and yes, they did, but I can't let you go back there my love," Daman says quietly, before whipping around and sternly saying, "If you knew what was best for you, you'd learn your place and only speak when spoken too. This isn't your territory after all. If they want her back, they have to deal with me."

176

"Actually," says a familiar voice. "If any of you think you're going to take Veronica against her will, you are sadly mistaken."

All of them immediately drop to the ground. Jinx steps into view, frantically looking around. Eventually, she spots me, and in a blur, she's beside me.

"Are they dead?" I ask, growing more and more woozy by the second.

"Luckily for them, I have a personal no-murder rule. They're just unconscious. Oh... darling," Her voice becomes distant, as her gaze falls upon my wound.

"It hurts," I whisper. "It hurts so bad, and I'm light-headed, and everything's spinning, and I can't move and– oh, stars, I'm going to die, aren't I?"

"Not if I have any say in the matter," She says, scooping me up.

Within seconds, we are in the cave. I don't think I'll ever get used to vampire speed. She sits me down on the countertop of the kitchen.

"Alright, I'm going to pull out the dagger. It's going to be quick, alright?"

I try to shake my head in protest, which only prompts a *massive* headache. She wraps her hand around the dagger, then winces and jerks her hand away. Silver handles. That's a new one. She frowns and shakes out her hand. She pulls her sleeve down over her hand, covering it the best she can. She wraps her hand back around the dagger, hand now shielded by her sleeve, her eyes meeting mine.

"Tria... duo... unum," She says softly, before pulling out the dagger. "Ibi imus." *Three... two... one. There we go.*

She wipes the blood off the dagger with the fabric of her long, black paneled skirt. She sets the dagger beside me. She screws open a kettle and pours water on a scrap of cloth she finds in a drawer. She cuts fabric off from around the area of the wound, before gently dabbing it. It stings.

"I'm... I'm sorry," I murmur, trying to keep my thoughts straight.

"Did you start the fight?" She asks, unphased, still focused on what she is doing.

"Yeah," I mumble.

"Exactly, so you have no reason to ap– pardon me?"

I look away, as she threads a needle.

"Veronica, what?" She stammers.

"I'm sorry," I mumble, unable to look her in the eyes. "I thought I could do it."

"Why on *earth* would you do that?" She asks, with a genuine amount of concern that I wasn't used to, especially from her.

"They were gonna hurt you," I mumble as Jinx stitches my wound closed.

"I'm immortal, you're not, that was a foolish decision," She says.

"So you'd've rather I let–"

"Absolutely! Because I'd rather you *not* be in harm's way!" She yells.

"Well, I couldn't let that happen!" I yell back.

"And why not?" She says, finishing the final stitch.

I don't respond. She nods, disappointment and anger written clearly in her expression. She doesn't prod me further. Instead, she begins dabbing around my eye with the wet cloth. It stings. I wince, and she softly apologizes. She takes a look at my eye once again and sighs. She then dabs at my lower lip, which has been split open. Her finger brushes against my upper lip. I nearly suffocate then and there. She's upset, but she's so gentle. It's not fair.

Why not? Her voice echoes in my head.

It's too late to answer. The moment is over. It's too late.

Why not?

I can't admit it. Not to her. Not to myself. I'm a coward.

"Because Aella was right!" I shout, everything boiling out at once.

There's no going back from this. I take a breath.

"I am fond of you," I admit. "Far beyond fond of you, I think there may even be a part of me that loves you. A part of me that falters when you smile or laugh, melts when I see the real parts of you. A part of me that wants to stay beside you in a way I've never understood. I wanted to deny it for so long, but it seems as if I cannot."

And there I am. I've poured it out, laid it bare. Stars, I'd give anything to take it back. I can't tell what's making me hyperventilate, the panic of what I've done, or the results of the fight. Jinx isn't saying anything. Why isn't she saying anything? Oh, stars, is she going to kick me out now?

"Please say something," I breathe.

I watch as her face turns a disturbingly purple color, and she releases a breath. She looks at me for a moment, something seeming to hang on her breath. She holds my face in her hands, eyes seeming to dart around, but always landing on my lips. I hold my breath. Her lips part like she's about to speak, but she instead squeezes them shut. Her thumbs brush my cheeks. Her eyebrows flick upwards, and she blinks quickly. She sighs and drops her hands, lowering her head.

She walks away, dropping every piece of me with her, and shattering it to the ground. She stops at the door, then turns and looks at me for a good while. Within seconds, in a blur, she's in front of me again, holding my face, looking at my lips. She just stands there, staring.

I stare at her lips. She won't move.

I've ruined enough, haven't I?

I press my lips against hers.

She doesn't pull away, instead pulls me closer, leaning into the kiss.

Daman never kissed me like this.

We pull away, breathing heavily, foreheads resting together. She's still holding my face, kissing my forehead, the tip of my nose, every facial injury I'd obtained during the fight, then one last light tap on my bottom lip. She pulls away, looking almost dazed. I awkwardly pat the side of the counter beside me. She nods and hops onto the counter beside me, fingers brushing against mine.

"Well, this is absolutely not how I expected this evening to go," Jinx says.

"Me neither," I say, and we both laugh a bit. "So... what do we do now?"

"We figure it out. Together. Likely when you're not feeling the effects of blood loss."

I turn my palm over, and slowly, her fingers thread themselves through mine. She squeezes my hand, and I turn to look at her, she's looking at a wall with a kind of grin I've never seen before. I haven't had the feeling of butterflies in my stomach since a few years ago, back when Daman knew how to pretend to be kind. Now it was out of the open. The butterflies have been released.

And we'll figure this out.

We do. The rumors are true, relationships with women do seem to move faster than with men. Aella says that we're the most annoying couple the Two

Kingdoms has ever dealt with. I just stick my tongue out, and we lightly bite thumbs at one another. It's a quiet night, four of us sitting on top of the cave. With all the constant planning of usurping the Couteau throne, it was nice to have a final quiet night. A night before things got far more complicated.

Noah is here with us, sitting criss-crossed, Aella sitting in his lap. Jinx and I are sitting across from them, my head resting on Jinx's shoulder, her arm around me. She's holding my hand with that same arm.

"I'm just saying," Aella says. "If you were gonna run into battle like that–"

"Shut up," I smile.

"I'm pretty sure that's physically impossible," Aella says, and then shifts positions so that her head is in Noah's lap.

Noah sucks in a breath, looking distant. Aella doesn't notice, and if she does, she doesn't seem to care. Jinx laughs, and suddenly I'm in no place to make fun of Noah. Feelings like this... they're a silly thing. It's a cold night, in late October. I will turn eighteen on the twenty-third, which is in a week and a half. I would've never expected any of this a year ago. I lift my head off of Jinx, and she looks bewildered for a moment, but then shrugs and plants a kiss on my forehead.

Stars, butterflies are swarming from Cupid's piano. Her eyes catch something in the distance, yet nothing all at once. She smiles a particular smile of knowing warmth and lets out a whistle that pierces the sky. She extends her arm and begins to pet the air. She scoots closer to me, and I put my head back on her shoulders as she puts her free arm around me.

"Edgar?" I ask.

"...Edgar?" Noah asks, after pausing a moment, looking at Jinx.

"Yes," she smiles.

Noah smiles, leaning back on his hands.

It's all too calm. All too nice. And it's only for a night.

After tonight, everything would change again.

Chapter 20
Veronica

"Please, promise me you'll be careful, darling," Jinx says softly into my ear, her arms wrapping around me.

"Always am," I say.

"We are both very aware that statement is complete and utter bullshit," She whispers.

"Okay, okay, fine. I promise I'll be careful."

She releases me. I give her a quick kiss on the cheek and quickly move to meet Aella outside the cave. Aella grins, and I throw her a jacket. She slips it on, and luckily for the two of us, it's long enough to cover not only her wings but also the small satchel hanging down at her waist. After this, there's no going back, and we're both painfully aware of that. We're going in as a team, and at least we have that.

Through the dark, through the siren territory, and dangerous woods, we venture somewhere we once swore we'd never dare return.

We make it there at sunrise. Let's just say there were a few unexpected complications on our way to the castle. Such complications are; sirens, trees, poisonous vines, and not to mention nearly getting stabbed by horses that had grown horns out of their heads. The whole thing. Fun. Very fun.

Despite that, here we are, in front of the white gates covered in lilies and vines. Just up the hill from the gate stands Caeara, a pink castle surrounded by fruit trees and all kinds of plants that peasants would never live to afford to even see in their lifetimes. It's infuriating. It once was home. Now it is a prize to be won with guts and glory.

We stood outside the diluted cyan doors leading to the throne room. They seem to be a mile high, towering above us surrounded in thin gold rectangular accents, with white concrete floral adornments. My hand lingers over the gold handle on the left door, Aella firmly gripping the handle on the right.

"Here we go," I breathe.

"Never thought I'd return to this shithole by choice," Aella said. "I don't think I've been in this area of the castle. The lab was always so dark and brown and bloody."

Before I can get the chance to respond, she turns the door and pushes through. I follow her lead and step into the room, the doors closing behind us without so much as a squeak. The room had always seemed so big, and I'd always felt so inconsequential.

The walls are a light lavender, the pillars topped with busts of previous rulers, all trapped in an ivory concrete prison. Blue, purple, and pink light spills from the curvilinear tracery windows and onto the white marble floor. The brightly colored shadows stretch onto the velvet burgundy strip of fabric that leads to the stairs to the thrones.

The frame of the larger throne is a twisting thorn bush of cyan and silver. On the blush-colored seat sat my father. His golden crown sitting upon his ebony twists. Beside him sat a smaller throne, the frame on this less thorny and twisted and complicated, molded into a heart of rose gold. There sat my mother on a pink cushion, a rose gold crown atop her cascade of golden curls.

They're both just like the castle. So sickeningly, horrifyingly, deceitfully beautiful. My father's dark brown skin remains completely unscathed, as did my mother's peach skin, aside from hidden scars on her stomach from when Aella and I were born. My father's rich purple and navy blue garments coupled in silver have not a single wrinkle. My mother's dark pink and purple dress doesn't have a single stain. If you'd looked at the two from afar, you'd see not a flaw, not a single flaw.

182

But we know.

We know. We know, and we share their blood. My light blue dress is torn, blood-stained, mud-stained, and ragged, as is Aella's white collared shirt, her black pants torn, revealing scales and scars. Aella has my father's nose. I can lie, like my mother. Yet, despite it all, the only thing Aella and truly I share with these monarchal monsters is a last name.

I am unprepared for their reactions. My mother gasps and steps up from her throne. She traps us both in her arms. Aella immediately pushes her aside and swears at her, stepping away. I'm paralyzed. My mother never hugged me before. Not once in my life.

Whatever it was, it was too late now. Her fate was sealed.

"We were worried sick about you both," My mother says, before turning to me. "My stars, look at you, you're all scratched up, oh you're absolutely filthy, Victoria. We're going to have to fix that right away. We've missed so many months, but we're going to get you back on track."

"My name is Veronica," I say, firmly, shrugging her off of me.

Aella pats my shoulder with approval, putting an arm around me.

My mother pays me no mind, immediately turning her attention to Aella. Typical.

"Aella, carissima, what on earth were you thinking? I cannot believe you were out with those horrid, horrid monsters again. They've corrupted you, they're setting you off your path, for stars sake, look at your hair."

"Yeah, good to see you too, Evsaphine," Aella mumbles.

"Don't be smart with me. Not only that, but you dragged... Vic- V... your sister into this."

"Nice," I say, bitterly. "Well said, *mother*."

"Veronica, watch your tone," My father says.

"Funny how you only remember my name when it's convenient," I respond.

Aella gives me a quick squeeze around my shoulders but doesn't let go. This time, we're in it together. They may have separated us, they may have pinned us against each other from the start, but here we were, against all odds. We've come as karma. If I have to become karma, so be it. No matter the risk, no matter the cost.

Now listen, mind control is hard. My head is already loud enough as it is, the additional buzzing and the agony of someone else's thoughts, and resistance and ambitions are enough to give anyone a splitting migraine. The whole morality of it never sat right with me. I just have to remember, and I have to keep running the words, no matter the cost, through my brain. Aella can hear it too.

No matter the cost, her mental voice booms through my mind, as she gives my arm another squeeze.

This is not a confession. I am certainly not confessing to having any influence on the berries that were picked by the servants, nor any influence on how they got in the drinks. We just happened to be in the right–wrong place, at the wrong time.

May the record also show that the fact that our shared last name is Belladonna, and the fact that reports will show the king and queen were poisoned with deadly nightshade, also known as Atropa belladonna, is in fact a complete coincidence and not at all prompted by my girlfriend. After all, my hands are completely clean, like Aella's, and Nightshade is notorious for her personal issue with murder.

"You both are back now, and that's all that matters," My mother says. "We'll get everything back on track."

"By that you mean neglecting your entire kingdom, being bigots, and treating us like shit, right?" Aella asks.

"Bite your tongue," My father says.

"'Kay," Aella grins, sticking out her tongue and biting down on it.

Aella raises her eyebrows a bit and lays both thumbs against the bottom of her sharp teeth.

She bites down so hard that her teeth lodge their way through her thumbs, blood leaking from the wounds.

I suppose Aella does have blood on her hands. Let that not be shown on the record. She pulls her thumbs out from her teeth and sets her hands at her sides, returning to biting down on her tongue, grinning madly.

The whole display causes horrified gasps from both of my parents. She just laughs in response, angering them more. Stars, to have her bravery.

"What?" Aella says, through a burst of mocking laughter. "I did as I was told, didn't I?"

"Your attitude is unappreciated," My mother says.

"Kinda unfair of you to say that, you don't really appreciate anything," I say, and Aella knocks her fist against mine. "Also, you're really bad at everything you do. So, take that."

"What she said," Aella says with a wicked grin, snapping and pointing at me.

The doors burst open right as both of our parents open their mouths. My mother returns to her throne. Someone steps into the room, a rose gold dish in their hand, two matching challaces sitting upon it. They quickly bow approaching my parents, setting the plate between the two thrones, and leaving just as quickly as they came.

"Took them long enough," My father says. "We'll rid ourselves of that one later."

Aella and I share a look. My father takes a sip of his drink, and my mother follows suit. Everything appears just fine. They don't seem affected. Part of me begins to wonder... as I let the buzzing in my mind silence, trying not to collapse from exhaustion. As previously mentioned, mind control is incredibly draining. Again, not a confession. After all, this is all up for you to interpret, not me. So we wait, wait, and wait.

"Dearest," My mother says to my father, though it seems difficult for her to get words out without slurring. "Did you also notice something... off about that servant?"

"Her eyes..." My father mumbles. "They were pink."

"Dearest, are we flying?" My mother whispers.

Her eyes roll behind her head. My mother used to sit with such perfect posture. I used to have to sit with my back like a board, and if she noticed me long enough to catch me slouching, I would have to skip the next meal of the day. But there she is, laying vertically to the left, eyes wide open. The crown slips off of her head, knocking the chalices off their plate. Those stains will likely never get out.

"M'lady!" My father cries.

He stands, venturing to see what happened to her. He begins to sway and is attacked by a fit of coughing. He falls to his knees. He swore he would never fall to his knees. Not even when he proposed to my mother. He collapses face-first onto the steps in front of him. His crown bumbles down the steps with several loud clangs, before rolling and hitting my foot. I shudder, nudging the glass away with my foot.

"Oh no," Aella mumbles, completely deadpan.

I find myself walking toward my mother.

"Veronica?" Aella asks, concerned.

I put a hand up, and keep walking, stopping just before her body.

I remember one night when I was young. I had gotten home from a few nights in Cazlamenta, and clearly my parents had gotten into an argument. My mother was bruised in the face, the neck, and very clearly drunk. She'd put a hand on my shoulder and told me I was beautiful. She told me my beauty was a curse, something I should be wary of. She taught me my girlhood was something to be ashamed of, in an in-depth, drunken lecture. She told me to fear men, especially men in power. She told me though I must serve Daman, as his wife, but to be cautious of him.

She saw a lot of herself in me, I suppose. She wanted to ignore it. She was ashamed of it, just as I'm ashamed of how much of myself I see in her.

And now she's dead. A woman stuck in a horrible position.

I drop to my knees. I can hear Aella distantly yell my name. My hands touch the floor, and in a daze, I find it.

Her crown is *mine* now.

I place it on my head, the rush immediately hitting me. It's heavy, but stars does it feel right. I place it on my head, and slowly, turn to Aella.

"Oh no," I say, unable to keep myself from grinning so widely that my face hurts. "Clearly, this was a horrible tragedy, and one we must quickly recover from."

Aella looks at me like I'm an entirely different person. I don't mind it.

I look at her, feeling all too much at once, but ultimately, numb. "What do we do now?"

Chapter 21
Veronica

Our parents *mysteriously* died a month ago. We were crowned the day after, I turned eighteen within the following week. Aella and I were now ruling together. To quote Aella specifically, "We inherited a shitfest, but c'est la vie."

She's sitting on the dark purple table beside me. The strategy room is just as disgustingly beautiful as the rest of the castle. A large gold fireplace is trapped between two baby blue bookcases. There are rose gold chandeliers covered in purple candles, and bubblegum portraits of the constellations. On the left side of the room is a cyan couch outlined in gold floral frames. Raven's entire body is spread over the couch, head on Sage's lap, legs on Hazel's. Icylyn is near the top of the sliding ladder to the bookshelf, Beckett creeping behind, about to push her to the side. Icylyn pays him no mind. She's been silent since we entered the room, just grinning widely and fluttering her hands. Jinx is standing by the other bookshelf, a copy of *The Castle of Otranto* in her hand.

"I'll tell m– Rebecca," Icylyn warns, staring down at Beckett, speaking for the first time.

"Oh come on, you won't fall," Beckett grins.

"Fine," Icylyn says.

She switches her position so that she's only holding on with her right arm and leg, the rest leaning to the side, wings spread.

"Do your worst."

Beckett raises his eyebrows, and they both laugh. He grabs the rung nearest to him and takes a few steps backward. He runs forward and

187

eventually lets go. She whoops and laughs, leaning backward and then grabbing it with her other hand.

"No killing each other!" Aella yells. "If either of you die, Becca will never let me hear the end of it."

Just then, Icylyn looks as if she's about to hit the wall. And she just goes through it. Yet another secret about the castle that I was completely unaware of. Sabine is standing somewhere in the corner.

"Did you know about that?" I ask her.

"No," Sabine says, eyeing the wall Icylyn went through.

"Guys!" Icylyn yells giddily from the other side of the wall. "There's more books in here!"

"Well... that's incredibly infuriating but..." Jinx says, and then within seconds, she's on the other side of the wall.

You never do get used to vampire superspeed. Beckett takes off after her, and Hazel follows calmly soon after. Aella laughs about it all from beside me.

"Nerds!" She yells after them.

Beckett runs back into the room, lightly bites his thumb at her, and slowly backs into the fake wall. Aella laughs, lying on the table. I can't help but laugh as well. There's a lot more responsibility involved now, but things finally seem calmer.

We'd been prepared for riots, protests, and war, but so far in our first month of ruling there was nothing but smooth sailing. We were actually able to make progress, which was incredibly important, as, like I said before, my parents didn't do shit. We started from the ground up, fixing the economic structure where we could, trying to put in laws to give more people homes and food, and got to work fixing supernatural rights, as well as rights on gender and sexuality. Again, we prepared for backlash on this front, but through sheer luck, none seemed to come.

Aella moved out of Rebecca's house, but we invite Rebecca, Icylyn, and Beckett for dinner every night, and on occasion every two weeks usually... the rest of the rebellion. Jinx moved out of the cave and now shares my bed.

No one outside of Rebecca, Sabine, some of the staff, and the rebellion knows we're dating yet. We're not ready to tell them. We're already lucky we're not getting rocks and torches thrown through our windows, we're not going to push it. Maybe one day we'll tell them if we're still together in the long run. For now, everything is more or less hypothetical.

But isn't life a hypothetical in itself? Jinx's voice booms through my brain.

Inamorata, stop reading my mind, I transmit back to her, holding back a laugh.

Jinx walks out of the room, a slight smirk on her face. Oh no. She appears next to me in a second. I jump off the table. She twirls me around and offers her hand. I gladly take it. Aella slides off the table and follows us, Sabine, Sage, and Raven following behind. There literally is no wall. I expect to hit something, or at least feel something there, but there's nothing. We step into the room, a large room that seems to reach just slightly less than a redwood tree, a room of small width in which every wall is lined with bookshelves.

"Hey, Ice, come check this out," Beckett says, standing in front of a bookshelf on the other side of the room.

Icylyn makes her way over to where Beckett is and stands beside him. She's completely shaking out her arms at this point, and I don't think I've ever seen her grin so wide, eyes carefully trailing over every book. Beckett taps his feet against the floor, thumb sliding over his pocket watch, as Jinx fiddles with her hair. Beckett points at something in front of him, and Icylyn turns to look.

"Do you see the dust on the shelves and the spines and pages of the books?" He asks.

"Yeah. It's really sad that–" Icylyn starts.

"Agreed, but not the point," Beckett says. "Do you see how this one has significantly less dust on it, and how the spine–"

"The spine looks worn, oh my stars, you're right," She says, and the two of them share a look.

As Aella said before, nerds. Most thirteen-year-olds do not get excited by the lack of dust on particular books. Most thirteen-year-olds don't notice. But there they are, seeming to get more excited by their discovery by the minute. Something we all disregarded.

"So–" Beckett starts, and Icylyn cuts him off.

"This book is obviously–" Icylyn starts.

"Oh, it definitely is hiding something. The rest are completely disregarded!" Beckett starts.

"Clearly, and since it can be easily hypothesized that this one is more frequently used–"

"They were using it to hide something shady," Beckett and Icylyn say in unison, huge grins on their faces.

Beckett puts his hand over the book, and Aella whips around before he grabs it.

"Hold on, whatever it is, it could be rigged," Aella says.

"It doesn't feel rigged," Beckett says, then signs. "Also... does anyone else feel a really weird humming coming from the other room?"

There are general headshakes.

"I do," Sage signs. "Felt it near that wall, the fireplace, and by the couch."

"I feel it too," Hazel nods. "Felt it in the same places, and near the weird room I got my guitar from."

"You mean where you saw the weird tech stuff, right?" Raven asks.

"Yeah," Hazel nods.

Most elves, as stated before, have knowledge absorption, laser eyes, control over a maximum of two elements, and as we're about to discover, technopathy. Technopathy was previously unknown as our tech is very archaic.

However, The Woods slowly began opening up Mortem Venenum about a year ago, and have been trading... something, in return for modern equipment that never, ever leaves the castles. Maybe one day it will. In that room is where Hazel found her butterfly-shaped electric guitar but barely escaped with her life. At that time, she began manifesting her powers, and of course, the Woods caught her. As punishment, she was tied to their electric chair and electrocuted until they deemed that she had 'learned a lesson.' That's why she can control lightning rather than the elements, being the first and as of now only elf with the ability to do so. But that's all just lore.

Aella eventually lets go of Beckett's hand, and he sets it on the book. We expect that he'll just slide the book out of the shelf, open it, and we'll find out whatever information is important within the said book. But, as with most things, it does not go as planned. The book stays latched to the shelf, only tipping a bit. Beckett removes his hand, and the wall slides to the side. What lies there– none of us could quite comprehend.

190

Large rectangles, each with moving portraits of different rooms in the castle. The pictures cast a slight glow into the otherwise completely dark room. Beckett, Hazel, and Sage seem to tense, and Hazel puts her hands over her ears as Beckett winces.

"What... the... fuck?" Aella exclaims.

"It's a computer," Beckett says.

"What's a computer?" Icylyn asks.

Beckett opens his mouth, then closes it and frowns. He shakes his head, and his eyebrows knit together. He taps his foot a bit, before sighing and covering his ears. Sage and Hazel exchange a look, but they seem just as perplexed as Beckett.

"I'm gonna be honest, Ice, I have no idea," he says.

"Then how do you know what it is?" I ask.

"It told us," Sage signs, blinking slowly as she realizes how odd this all is.

Beckett just nods in confirmation. Aella opens her mouth to say something stupid, and Jinx gives her a warning look. Aella nods and backs off. Beckett sits in front of what we now know were screens, and hovers his hands over the keyboard.

"Oh... *mierda*," Beckett says.

He seems to pale as he turns toward us, fiddling with his pocket watch. He clicks it open and snaps it closed. Then once again, clicks it, snapping it closed not less than a second later. Snap, snap, snap, snap. Hazel pales, and Sage's eyes narrow, biting hard on the inside of her cheek.

"What is it?" Jinx asks, slow and cautious.

"We... found... graphic confirmation on what they're trading outside countries for imports," Beckett says.

"No," I shake my head.

Beckett nods at me.

"Potions," Hazel stammers. "Potions and other things made from–"

"They are trading parts of supernatural corpses," Sage signs.

We'd found more of this new technology in hidden crevices all across the castle. Through more research and the elf trio's long discussions, things gradually became understandable. It was a slow process, but it was progress nonetheless. Some things made sense. We'd discovered that the fake wall in the "Plotting Room" and the adjacent fireplace were projections. Beckett, Sage, Hazel, and even Icylyn took up more time better studying the new technology, and Beckett started trying to replicate and advance upon it.

Despite that curveball, things are continuing to go suspiciously well. I'm not complaining, this was rather appreciated, seeing as we're trying to fix a crumbling kingdom that's been abused and neglected for over a century.

So the rest of the rebellion is now in the castle more often. Beckett and Icylyn got permission from Rebecca to sleep over at the castle so they could get more time to figure out the new technology we'd found. There was barely any sleeping done, as they often get so hyper-focused on what they are doing that they forget to do basic things. Sage is the same way. Hazel is usually making sure the others are doing basic things such as hydrating, while also assisting in the science aspect where she can. The rest of us were there for moral support. None of us are strangers to all-nighters, especially not Jinx. Part of me wonders if Jinx ever slept before I met her. That's just what happens when you date a vampire revolutionary, I guess.

Such is this particular evening, all of us in the castle. Beckett is asleep with his head resting on the table, a wrench in one hand, his pocket watch in the other. Icylyn is sitting on top of the table next to him, scratching something out on the piece of paper she was holding. She looks on the verge of passing out. Every so often she'll hand the paper over to Sage, who'll scribble around what Icylyn has, and occasionally the two will sign something to each other.

Raven is in the corner snoring rather loud, Hazel's head resting on their shoulder, also asleep. Aella finds a stack of every caffeinated beverage she could in the kitchen and continues to mix several drinks before downing them in one gulp. Sabine says she'll laugh when Aella gets a heart attack, and the two nearly get in a fist-fight.

Jinx is drinking tea and reading a book in front of her as it floats midair, occasionally giving directions or breaking up a fight. I'm sitting on the couch beside her, running a brush through her hair.

Beckett suddenly shoots up, and Icylyn jumps a bit, snapping to attention.

"Divide the mass by sixty–" He says, then stares off for a moment. "I fell asleep?"

Icylyn nods. Beckett makes a face and sits up on the table. She hands him her notes and he looks over them. Aella hands him a mug, and he drinks it. He immediately makes a face, and Aella bursts out laughing.

"¿Qué carajo?" He asks, still seemingly half asleep.

"It's coffee. We found it in that extra room," Aella says.

"It's so bitter," Beckett says.

"Can't be worse than Sabine," Aella winks.

Sabine glares at her. Beckett slides off the table and walks out of the room, Icylyn close on his tail. They're gone for a while.

Well, this is boring," Aella says. "Anyone wanna play a game?"

"We just found out world-shattering things, you have a kingdom that's falling to pieces, and you want to play a game?" Sabine asks, incredulously.

"Alright Sabine, let's play a question game. Starting question, how far does the stick up your ass go?" Aella asks.

Sabine raises her eyebrows, and I see her unconsciously reach for her sword. Her fingers tap the metal but she doesn't take it out. I get off the couch, and I can hear Jinx quietly protesting. I make my way over to Sabine and gently nudge her shoulder.

"Hey Sabs," I say, softly. "Look, I'm scared and confused too. But we're all working the best we can. I know Aella can be... Aella-"

"Hey!" Aella yells.

Aella half-heartedly throws a pencil at me, and I dodge it. I make a face at her, and she sticks out her tongue until we're both flipping each other off. Aella eventually cedes, laughing and picking up a stack of papers. Queen responsibilities.

"As I was saying," I roll my eyes, turning to Sabine. "I know you two don't get along great, but she's trying her best to lighten the mood. Trust me, this is hard for all of us. Believe me, I know a thing or two about my entire world being flipped upside-down."

Sabine relents. She puts her hands behind her back and lowers her head. She sighs and looks back at me.

"I *suppose* you're right," She says.

"Always am," I smile.

"Bullshit," Sabine, Aella, and Jinx all say.

I roll my eyes and sit down on the couch next to Jinx, slowly sliding closer and closer to her. She wraps an arm around me, pulling me in. I rest my head on her shoulder. Aella and Sage are having some silent conversation, and Sage is now laughing. This, in turn, wakes up Hazel. I find myself battling to keep my eyes open, especially as Jinx gently strokes my head. I fall asleep. *Shit.*

A few months pass. It's late January now, a new year has begun. Things are starting to look up in the kingdom. I know deep down I should get up and get to work, but I don't want to leave my bed. It's cold, and my mind is still foggy with sleep. I'm buried under covers and one of Jinx's wings. She's close, holding me from behind, her right arm tightly curled around me, her hand resting on my chest. If anywhere is my safe place, it's her. Funny how things change like that.

Though once a glance would send an icy chill down my spine, she is now warmth. She is laughter, she is cuddling close against a fireplace on a winter night, she is moonlight. And, *stars*, she's mine. Though at first touch, her fingers felt like icicles, her clutch felt like death, the brush of her lips against mine is reminiscent of the secure warmth of hands loosely gripping a warm cup of tea. Her touch is cold, yet she fills me with warmth. She defies logic and reason.

I was once scared to lay with the man I was going to marry. I was scared of most things about him. But Jinx? I never want to leave her. It's a rare occasion in which we find moments like this. Life is hectic, to say the very least. Most nights I fall asleep over a pile of legal drafts and letters, sometimes waking up in a puddle of ink. Most nights she refuses to sleep, as she always had done. Not to mention that things go wrong when we sleep. I kick in my sleep, and I scream. She'll start levitating out of nowhere. One or the other, if not both, will often wake up from a nightmare. But this? This is bliss.

She pulls me closer. I don't protest. She is still very, *very* asleep. I can feel her heart slowly patter on my back. She'd once asked me if her heartbeat. I told her it did, just really slow. And even now, it beats really slow.

"What time is it?" She murmurs softly, her voice warping and echoing.

As a result of being a shadow-blood, her voice naturally was distorted and would echo itself as she spoke. She'd learned to control it, to hide it. Occasionally it'll pop out, when she was trying to be intimidating, or when she laughed, or even now as our sleepy brains are slow to process things. A reminder that now, at this moment, we have no reason to rush, no reason to hide. And... if I'm going to be honest? While her voice was already pretty hot, being low with a slight rasp, a cockney accent, and a hint of a lisp, the echo thing just ramped it up.

"I don't know," I respond, turning to face her.

"Mmm," she hums. "Well, anyway, good morning, darling."

"Good morning, amor meus," I mumble. "We should probably get up... I have things I need to do."

"You're right... we probably should," She says.

Neither of us gets up. We gently smile at each other and laugh. We lay there for a bit longer. Just a bit, but sink into every moment we can. It isn't until we hear a rap on our door that even consider getting up.

"Hi Sabine," I answer.

"You awake?"

"No, I'm afraid we're both very much asleep," Jinx says, with a smart look on her face.

The other side of the door is quiet. There's a short, annoyed sigh.

"Aella wanted me to tell you both to hurry up," Sabine says.

We can hear her footsteps plunk down the hall. Both of us groan and dramatically flip up the covers. I accidentally bury her in my covers as I jump down from my side of the bed. She rolls across, and still covered in blankets, grabs me from behind.

"No!" I squeak as my feet lift off the ground.

She laughs triumphantly, flopping back onto the bed. She holds me there and kisses the top of my head.

"What're you going to do, bite me?" I tease. "C'mon, I got work to do, love."

She relents, letting go of me. I turn and can't help but laugh at the mess of blankets she's trapped under as she slowly peels them off. She stands up, and I offer my hand. She bows and kisses my hand. She's a dramatic bitch, but she's my dramatic bitch. And my stars, did I love that dramatic bitch.

"O mi stupri sidera," Aella remarks as I sit down beside her. "Are those bite marks?"

"Whatever happened to 'good morning?'" I ask my face now incredibly hot.

"Oh my stars," Aella laughs, nearly falling out of her chair. "They are. They totally are."

Jinx's face goes bright purple. I bury my face in my hands. Sabine mutters something under her breath. Aella is still losing her shit, now doubled over with laughter.

"Look I can explain," I say. "It was yesterday night–"

"Is that why you were wearing the dress with the one collar that–"

"Yes, okay look I woke up from a nightmare, and accidentally woke her up, and she realized she was hungry and I didn't want to be alone so..." I shrugged.

"Oh, my fucking stars," Aella snorts. "These bitches are gay! Good for them! Good for them."

Sabine coughs, and I mumble that we should probably get to work. Aella is still laughing. Aella is still laughing for another good three minutes. I want to spontaneously combust for another good three minutes. Scratch that, three horrible minutes.

"You called us in here for what?" I ask.

"The Woods sent us a letter, and I didn't want to open it without you," Aella shrugs.

"Wonderful," I sigh.

This would not be fun. I slide onto the lavender bench beside Aella, and Jinx plops down beside me after closing the curtains from afar. Aella breaks the seal and all four of us cringe. Slowly, we open the content of the letter, and Aella hands it over for me to read aloud. It's, of course, a threat.

Addressed to our formal names, from none other than Isolde herself.

Whatever secret funding our kingdom had been getting from Cazlamenta would now be void. She says to expect war shortly. She singles me out specifically, telling me she had high hopes for me, and I've not only betrayed her family, but the will of the stars. She tells us to step down, that we're not ready for this. She threatens that if we don't not only will her kingdom attack, but they will first strike at the people we most hold dear.

Shit. I collapse onto the table and groan. Aella inhales and roars out every curse that she can think of in both English, Latin, and even some French. I sigh, before sitting down, and inspecting the letter once more. I slouch in my chair, crumpling the letter into a ball and tossing it to Aella. The letter lights aflame and immediately turns to ash in her palm. Jinx walks to the back corner of the room, tossing on her hooded cloak, mask, and bow, securing her quiver into her belt. She'd begun braiding her hair the second Aella announced the letter. I immediately jump up off the bench and stand in front of her, taking her fingers in my hands.

"Hey," I say, gently, as her eyes move away from me. "Where are you going?"

"Only to take care of business, darling," She gives me a half smile, tucking her mask into a pocket.

"*Please* don't do something irrational," I beg her. "Please don't do what I think you're trying to do–"

"Hey," She says. "Everything will be alright, I promise. I'll be back soon."

She leans down to kiss me on the head and exits the room, disappearing before I get the chance to protest.

Chapter 22
Nightshade

I absolutely do not want to return. This is only out of necessity. This is for the rebellion, for the people, for my friends, for Veronica. So I return. I return to Cazlamenta. Something I promised myself I wouldn't do until I was completely ready. Until I could find a non-fatal, humiliating, life-ruining way to take them down.

After all, I was told if I ever returned one of two things would happen:

A. I would be killed.

Or B, they'd use me in a way they saw fit. And both sound horrid.

Nevertheless, I persist.

The hallways are filled with ghosts. Ghosts in the most literal sense, but also with the ghosts of memories. They still have portraits of me as a little girl on their walls. My hair that they'd made me dye black, the crown that was always too heavy. None of them show the burn scars from the electric chair in the hall, the burns from when I was forced to stand in the sun, the fear, the emptiness I kept hidden behind my eyes. As I venture down the hall I notice my face has been scribbled out or scratched in most photos. I keep my eyes on the prize, not stopping to look when I see the door to my room.

I don't make the mistake of looking until I get closer to my destination. I see it in a corner. Too familiar. Standing there, I am ten years old once more.

Daman was standing in front of me. He was stronger than me. Rougher than me. He'd been trained to become *exactly* the weapon, the tyrant they wanted from the moment he was born. He'd killed Edgar a week prior to this, right in front of me, just to get me to lash out. My mother and father stood a few paces behind him, nothing more than shadows.

"Do it," My father had said.

Daman picked me up by the throat, pinning me to the wall. My throat burned. I kicked, and I choked, and I cried, and I struggled and struggled and struggled. I looked over to my mother and father, whose facial expressions were cold and stern. My mother raised her chin and crossed her arms, and my father looked askance after a while. He made a choked sound, and I realized he'd been crying.

I lowered my eyes to Daman. He was my brother. There was a time we said we'd look out for each other. Noah, Daman, and I, we'd look out for each other. Daman's views had changed and changed fast.

"Don't look at me like that," He'd snapped. "Don't act innocent. You're a monster. That's why weird things always happen around you. You're a jinx."

I kicked and struggled, and tried to push his hands away from my throat. His grip was too strong. My body was slowly going numb bit by bit, and I could see spots in the corners of my eyes. Tears started to stream down my cheek.

"You're weak. Just like they said," He said, observing my tears.

I mustered whatever strength I could to snap my fingers. He fell to the ground and I toppled down with him, his hand still wrapped loosely around my throat. I sat up, shaking off whatever numbness I could and trying to suck in all the air around me. I was distracted as my mother called for guards, and as they took me by the arms.

"He's right, you know," My mother said. "You are a monster. And a jinx. Of which are the likes of those we cannot associate ourselves with. You're a threat, a danger, and a disgrace upon our name. You're never to return. If we find you, we will kill you, or find other means of use for you, and the same fate will await you should you return."

I don't remember what happened after that. I don't remember how I stumbled upon the cave, merely that I did. I only remember the intense blinding pain of rage, loss, and despair. It was so incredibly consuming. Being ten years old, it was nearly impossible to hold all that in. I learned better how to hold in my tears after that.

Ten years old, living in a cave. Ten years old, seeing flashes of my family whenever I tried to close my eyes. Never good memories, only bad ones. Good memories were few and far between, and sometimes, I didn't even know if they existed. Ten years old, with only ghosts for company. Even the ghosts never stuck around long enough. I had to invent my own companion, but she was stronger, better. I became her when it all became too much.

Ten years old and I hungered. I hungered for blood, quite literally, but also hungered for revenge, for destruction. At ten years old, I tried to cut off all my hair with a dagger. Ten years old, I stabbed the walls of the cave, dragging my dagger across as I stepped outside. Sometimes, I can still hear the sound.

I'd climbed to the top of the cave in the nighttime, when the blanket of night had protected me from the sun. I found protection, and comfort in her embrace. The night had become my new mother.

I'd cut my hair that night, and for a good while, nothing but black fuzz sat on my head. From the vantage point on top of the cave, there was a beautiful view of Mortem Venenum. The docks, the registered vessels, the pirate ships that hid in the cove, the town square. The castle on the hill, the shops, the materialistic society that had shunned me for simply existing. A home I could never return to.

It all seemed so far away to me. So small. So insignificant. Just the way the kingdom had seen me. Just the way I'd been treated. A small, insignificant danger to the slaughter-born utopia that kingdom had been. I hated it. In my all-consuming pain, I hated everything, I hated how the flowers would glow at night. I hated the way the masts blew in the wind. I hated the castle. The dollhouse, I would call it.

I was ten years old, when one night, dangling my legs, I'd whispered to no one, "I want to set that beautiful dollhouse aflame."

I was ten years old when sleepless nights of nothing but a burning emptiness were the only thing I could rely on. I was ten years old when I thought myself a villain. I was ten years old when I refused to leave the cave, thinking myself a danger. And how could I not, when I'd been told I was? When I'd so desperately wanted the world to bleed?

I was ten years old when I wanted to burn it down.

I wanted to burn

It

All

Down.

"Ashes," I would whisper. "When I return, the people will know nothing but ashes."

I like to think I never became the villain I thought myself to be. I like to think I helped. I tried, as best as I could, at first for selfish reasons. I rescued people because the royals hated it. I stole from the rich because I couldn't afford to survive. I never had meant to become Nightshade, to be a hero in anyone's eyes. But once I did, I tried my best to give others the hope I'd so desperately needed.

Jinx was born out of necessity. I was scared of myself. I still am. Jinx wasn't scared. Jinx was confident to the point of being somewhat arrogant. She is bulletproof, fearless, someone who could make a difference. The right people hate her, and she is a symbol for others. She was who I needed to survive.

I need to be her more than ever as I step in front of the doors to the throne room. My eyes are black, my voice warping and echoing. I am too scared and too emotional to fix either of those. Whatever. The castle walls are covered in black and gold obsidian and granite. The walls bear portraits, candles, and mirrors I'd never see myself in. The floors are red. In front of two doors of carved obsidian stand two guards.

"Are you going to let me through, or are we going to do this the hard way?" I ask, forcing myself to be Nightshade.

The guards do not relent. I'd expected this, to be honest. So I take a breath and snap my fingers, watching as they fall unconscious. From there, it's easy to enter the room. Well, not quite emotionally, but the physical aspect is all that really matters. I really, really would rather not step inside. But I have to.

The electric chair sits in the middle of the room, as it always has. On thrones of obsidian and golden spikes sit my mother and father, a roaring fireplace behind them, the light bouncing off of the walls. Daman stands beside them. I step into the room, closing the doors behind me with my mind. My father almost looks scared, while my mother and Daman look infuriated. I sit down on the arm of the electric chair, resting my arm on the head, one leg resting on the seat.

"Missed me?" I ask.

"I thought we told you the consequences of–" My mother says.

"You see, I don't really care," I interrupt. "What I do care about, however, is that little letter you sent to Veronica and Aella. That does not sit well with me."

"It's simply a necessity. To protect innocent people from monsters such as you."

"I'm not the monster that you think I am," I say, voice gradually becoming more warped and echoey. "But believe me, I can become that monster and so much worse. And I'll gradually make things worse until you surrender. After all, I'm a jinx, right?"

"Lila..." My father starts.

"Save it," I snap. "This will be your only warning. Even think about threatening Couteau or any of the people I care about ever again, and you'll suffer agonizing consequences I could not even begin to describe."

"You're in no position to threaten us," Daman says.

"Oh," I tilt my head back and laugh, sliding off the arm of the chair. "Aren't I?"

My fingertips buzz and go numb, black and green fog-like tendrils surrounding my hands. My voice had clearly already unnerved them, and I swear I can see Daman wince out of the corner of my eye. I grin at him from beneath the mask, blinking my eyes back to blue. I tap the electric chair, and for a moment, just a moment, it glows a bright lime green, turning to dust.

"Just a reminder that that could be you," I say, then make my way to the nearest window.

I give a half-hearted salute as I crack the window open, leaning back and falling backward.

Stepping back into Caeara I head straight to Veronica. I don't even have time to remove my hood and mask, as after I've made my way upstairs, it's only a matter of moments before Veronica runs at me. She runs right into me, burying her face in my chest as she wraps her arms around me.

"I promised I'd be back, didn't I?" I softly chuckle, putting my hand behind her head and wrapping an arm around her.

"Didn't stop me from worrying," She responds.

She lets me go and takes my hand, and we walk down the hall together. The curtains are all closed. I don't have to wear my cloak as much anymore unless I leave the castle. After all, I don't burn with the windows closed. Lila Aylin Woods is supposed to be dead, and everyone knows Jinx Athanasia, or better yet, *Nightshade* can't stand the sunlight.

We enter back into the strategy room. I set my cloak on the coat rack, and Veronica closes the door behind us.

"Ay! You're not dead!" Beckett grinned. "Pay up, Sabine."

Sabine decides this will be a great moment to leave the room and stand guard like she's supposed to do. Veronica lets out a slight giggle. I swear for a second, I forget how to breathe. I was born undead, but *stars* if she didn't remind bits of me that I was, in fact, alive. How my breathing was slow and shallow, yet she took it away so easily. Veronica sits down on top of the table, and I join her. She rests her head on my shoulder, and Aella goes back into sorting through papers.

"Why aren't you hosting a ball, blah blah blah, because *we're doing shit*," Aella mumbles under her breath after reading one of the letters.

"There's no point to them anyway," Veronica grumbles. "The only point of it is kissing up to people to get what you want, and listening to people bitch."

"That sounds like a you problem," Aella says.

"Does *not* take away from the fact that–"

"It's not that it's pointless, you just are given anxiety from large crowds, and people in general, because you always feel watched and ignored at the same time, so you spend the entire time in an awkward anxious state in the corner," Aella says, almost bored.

"Did *not* need to be psycho-analyzed this early in the morning," Veronica mumbles.

"It's late afternoon," Aella says.

The velvet lilac and turquoise curtains are shut tightly, so it's hard to tell either way. Edgar is perched on some bookshelf, just hopping around. The doors burst open, and Raven is there, frantically. Edgar flies over and lands on their head. They give him a quick stroke before hastily entering the room, Sabine following behind.

"Yeah, so, I hate to interrupt whatever bonding time is happening, but, uh, we kiiiiinda got a problem," Raven says, their always bloody feet once again leaving trails on the floor.

"What is it?" I ask.

"Yeah, so, the wonderful people of Mortem Venenum ended up finding out that Jinx lives here... and that Veronica and Aella are both supernaturals, and let's just say the vast majority is noooot super jazzed about that?"

"How?" Veronica asks.

"No clue, heard it from word of mouth at the graveyard. Aither was in the town square earlier and heard. There's gonna be a meeting in the Castellum village," Raven says, picking twigs out of their foot.

"Ice and I can go crash it," Beckett says, sliding off the table.

"Not alone you're not," Aella says, grabbing him by the back of his collar.

Beckett grumbles under his breath. His fists are tucked under his arms which are crossed over his chest.

"And where exactly did Aither hear this from?"

"Janessa."

As previously mentioned Raven is a shadow-blood, as am I. Thus far, Raven and I get a rather good amount of intel from ghosts, seeing as they can walk through walls and not be seen by non-shadow-bloods and such. Aither is one of Raven's good friends and is a ghost. I've yet to meet Aither, but I've heard they're rather similar to Beckett.

Janessa, however, is not a ghost. Janessa is a bitch. Not that the two are mutually exclusive, but I've met many ghosts that were bitches. Believe me, ghost gossip is a whole other thing, but that's probably best left to another discussion. Janessa has some job in Cazlamenta, no one quite knows what it is, and I'm not even sure *she* knows. However, Janessa is the town gossip, hell, the gossip of the Two Kingdoms, so she spreads whatever she can get her hands on within the castle.

"Are we sure Janessa is a reliable source?" Veronica asks.

"Quite sure," I say. "In this instance. Others, not likely, but Janessa wouldn't lie about any anti-supernatural hoax she heard from The Woods."

"Yes," Icylyn seconds.

"Yep," Beckett nods.

"In situations like this? Yeah. She got info from The Woods I guess," Raven shrugs. "I think she planted the seed for the meeting. anyway, expect torches and pitchforks by sunset."

"FuuuuuuuuuuuuuuuuuuuuuuUUUUUUUUUUUUUUCK," Aella groans, tilting her head back and rolling her eyes. She flickers in and out of sight, her arms covered entirely in flame.

Veronica flops back down onto the table. Beckett yelps and slips out of his jacket, dropping it onto the tile, and starts stomping out the flame. Icylyn just blows in the jacket's general direction and the fire vanishes.

"Oh shit, sorry," Aella says as Beckett frowns at the collar of his jacket.

"I am so very appalled and offended," Beckett says sarcastically. "I don't care all that much, but I will be using this against you."

Before another word can be uttered, the fuchsia stain-glass window shatters. Rocks are being thrown through the window. Raven had received the information too late, it seems, and the attack time had apparently been moved up. Rocks now litter the floor, growing bigger and bigger they are replaced with bricks.

"Could be worse," Veronica says.

"Your majesties," A guard says, pushing past Sabine. "People are scaling the walls, our staff is overflooded."

Aella shoots Veronica a very pointed glare.

"Okay, but I wasn't wrong. If we look on the positive side, things could always be wo–"

"Stop talking," Aella says. "Every time you say those words, things get worse. You're more of a jinx than Jinx is. Full offense, to both of you."

"Well sorry for being an optimist," Veronica says.

"You're not," Aella and Sabine say in unison.

"We're getting off-topic," Sabine says.

I grab my cloak, arrows, and mask, blinking my eyes to black and summoning death energy into my fists. Not that I'd use it, but it was always helpful in getting the majority of people to back off.

I toss Veronica a dagger, and surprisingly she catches it. She pulls another one out from a holster on her thigh. My girlfriend. A subtle badass in her own right. Icylyn's eyes widen in the way they do when she gets an idea, promptly exiting the room. The room seems to grow in temperature the exact moment she leaves.

"Don't kill anyone," Veronica calls after her.

Icylyn doesn't turn around, just gives a thumbs-up and leaves, Beckett and Aella following in tow. Veronica follows after Aella, and I stay close to her, but Sabine seems bent on keeping anyone away from Veronica.

"Sun warning!" Icylyn yells.

Icylyn hops up onto a window sill, dragging Beckett with her. They rip the curtains open, opening up the reticulated windows. Beckett sits down, holding onto Icylyn's leg. He dangles his feet over the edge, scooting slightly backward and instantly retracting his legs back in, sitting criss-cross. He waves at the people scaling the walls, as Icylyn rests her hand on the outside of the castle.

Frost covers the castle, crackling and expanding. Screams can be heard from outside. People try to get down before the frost reaches them. Their efforts are futile. All of them freeze within moments. They'll live, but we're going to have to lock them up later. I can hear footsteps approaching from behind. Unfamiliar footsteps, unfamiliar scent of blood.

I grab their hand before it reaches me, turning around and flipping them upside down. More people begin filing in through the halls. Aella disappears and reappears behind several people, knocking them out. Veronica tries to help fight, but Sabine continues to grab her before she has the chance.

Raven slams their palm outwards, and three oncoming attackers fly down from the side of the hallway they came from. The whole ordeal lasts thirteen minutes. Within twenty-three minutes, all of the unconscious attackers have been locked up in a dungeon. Within forty-five minutes, those who were scaling the wall had been melted out of ice and also in the dungeon.

"That... could have gone worse," Veronica says.

"I'm going to punt you into the sun," Aella deadpans.

"Oh yeah? Do it then," Veronica says, plopping onto a chair. "You won't."

"Please don't," I say.

"So... we need a plan," Veronica says. "Because this is a hurdle we weren't prepared for."

"See, this is why contingency plans are important," Sabine says.

"How little you think of us, Sabine," Aella grins. "Of course, we had contingency plans. Besides, we have *Jinx*. Pretty sure she has like... a collection of binders of planning."

She... has me there. Planning was always my thing. To be perfectly candid, it may have become a bit of an obsessive hobby at times, but at least is was productive in my particular endeavors. It keeps me busy. It keeps my mind sharp and occupied. Distracted, yet still on guard. It helps me feel like I still have some control, even if I know, inevitably, whatever strategy I scheme, whatever plan I spend countless nights on, will inevitably go awry.

When I was little, *very* little, I wasn't allowed to have control.

Now, my mother and father were a lot of things, but they weren't naive. One of the most frustrating things about them is that they're both incredibly brilliant. Brilliant and manipulative. I digress. They knew I was a supernatural. They always told me to smile with my mouth closed, to not cry, to dye my hair black, cover my back, and cover the flower-like scars that they gave me. After all, how could they not know?

Vampires differ from other supernaturals in that it's the only species that is passed down through genes. My mother was bitten when she was pregnant with me. She never turned, that passed down to me. I was already going to be born a shadow-blood.

Back to the subject of the matter. My mother and I had been arguing for whatever reason. As of now, I can't remember the subject of the matter, only that it was growing quite heated. This was only hours before my banishment. I'd tried to keep my powers hidden as best as I could before this event. Despite that, I was foiled by my fear. I was so angry, and scared, and I didn't want to hear her voice anymore. I didn't want to be strapped down to the chair again. I was tired of being constantly scared and berated and generally unloved.

"Please stop," I'd quietly told her.

"I didn't give you permission to speak," She'd said, her icy glare still crisply digging into my mind.

I'd been suppressing the urge of tears.

"I can't, mother," I'd pleaded. "Not anymore."

"You're weak, then. How disappointing. I thought I raised you to be stronger than that, Lila," She leaned down just barely, and I winced as she cupped my face in her hand.

She brushed her thumb over my cheek. Part of me longed to lean into her, another part wanted to run. I could do neither. Some of her fingers were touching the back of my neck, and as her grasp on me got tighter, she'd slightly maneuvered her fingers. As she ran her thumb over my cheek, I could feel her nails digging into the back of my neck.

"I'm... I'm not weak," I'd stumbled over my words, throat seeming to close as my voice crackled and echoed. "I promise. But I don't want to hear you say these things anymore."

"Oh my darling little weapon," She'd mused, frowning slightly. "You're not to have your own opinions. You're to obey no matter the circumstances."

"Mother," I'd whispered. "I *can't.*"

"Shame," She says, putting her other hand on my shoulder. "Guards!"

I stood there, unable to move, not even thinking to move an inch from her grasp. I could barely think. I couldn't breathe, and my body seemed to jerk under the pressure of hyperventilating. The doors creak open, armed guards standing at the ready. They were going to bring me to the throne-room chair. I was going to sit and be electrocuted until I was ready to blindly follow whatever my mother asked of me, to listen to her spout nonsense and not be able to voice my thoughts, to fight back.

I couldn't. I wouldn't. And, if I'm being honest, I was more scared than anything. This wasn't an act of standing up against my mother, it was the only way I could defend myself. I was scared. The only times I've been brave were because I was afraid.

So I summoned the almost cold, almost numbing energy that I knew lingered deep inside of me. The doors shut with a slam. Several chairs went flying every which way. The curtains slammed closed, and a mirror fell from its place on the wall. My mother feigned horror.

Instant regret thrust out its arm, seemingly grabbing me by the hair and yanking me to the ground. I'd landed on the shards, cutting into my legs, and slicing into my palm. Something burnt me, likely the silver backing of the mirror. My obsidian blood oozed over the crimson floor. A tell tale sign of a vampire.

"You're... a vampire. And a shadow-blood," My mother had whispered.

I honestly hadn't known. I'd avoided the sunlight. My wings were just minuscule on my back, having never grown in. I wasn't allowed to run, and thus, super-speed hadn't manifested yet for me. I'd assumed the ghost in my room was nothing more than a figment of my imagination. My telekinesis hadn't activated until that very day.

I'd never realized that the fear in the eyes of some servants was for me. I'd never realized that the bite marks on their necks were from mindless midnight snacks in which my need to consume blood to remain sentient overtook all logical thinking. I'd never understood why others were scared of my voice. I'd understood that other voices didn't echo and warp and multiply as I did, but I never found it odd.

"I... I didn't know," I'd whispered, my voice shaking. "Why didn't you tell me?"

"You're a monster," She said.

"No, I'm not, I promise, I can be good."

My hand stung and I gripped it with my other, both hands now covered in warm black liquid. As always, my reflection wasn't in the mirror. It never was. I assumed it was the same for everyone. Except this time... this time I could see my eyes. Two black eyeballs shining back at me in a shattered mirror, only slightly less broken than my own reality.

Even now, sitting beside Veronica in the strategy room as we figure out how to handle this sudden attack, I cannot see my reflection. At the current moment, I can't see my eyes, so I can only assume they're "normal." Truthfully, my natural state involves the entirely black eyes and the echoed voice. Raven is the same way, though, in their case it tends to be a bit more diluted. I don't know what my other eye color is, the one that I was born with. It should be red, though I'm told it isn't. I've made the conscious choice to never let it be red. I made the choice when I was a child.

Through old portraits and paintings now torn or mangled in Cazlamenta, I can assume that at least at one time, they were blue. I assume they still are when I want them to be. Some things are obvious. As a child, my hair was jet black and always pulled too tightly into braids. Now I only braid my hair when stressed, upset, or otherwise. Which happened to be most of the time. It worked, anyway, gave me something to fidget with, and kept my knee-length hair out of the way during battle. Even now I was fiddling it into complicated braids.

"You alright?" Veronica asks, slightly nudging me with her shoulder.

"Mmm? Oh, yes, fine darling," I smile.

Veronica hums doubtfully. Her eyebrows quirk and her eyes narrow. And just then and there I nearly spill every thought out. Stars, she has me wrapped around her finger.

"We're going to talk about this later," Veronica says, pointing at me, not changing the adorably stern look on her face. "Stop smiling at me like thaaaat-"

"Oh, wow, JJ being smitten for Veronica, something definitely new and unique," Aella says, absolutely dripping with sarcasm. "*Anyway,* I think we made pretty good progress, all things considered."

"... how long was I-" I started.

"Zoned out?" Veronica asks." Honestly, I haven't been keeping track of time. We've decided we're going to send a *strongly* worded letter to The Woods, and honestly... if worst comes to worst... at least we already have systems in place. But I think their fear of exposure triumphs over most things, so I'm feeling... not super bad about this."

I'm not going to oppose it. She seems confident in her decision, and for Veronica, that is a rarity. I will simply- personally see to it that my parents don't try anything again. I know all too well that they won't be backing down. They don't back down. They fight fear with violence, by forcing those they considered an inkling of a threat into submission.

I should know. They feared me. It seems perhaps they still do.

I'm stuck in the memory once more. At some point, I'd moved from the ground to standing on top of the table. Blood was dripping down my still numb fingers, down my arms, onto the table. Just as black as the ebony table, the black walls cracked in gold, black frames holding mirrors on the walls. The only sources of light in this room were the multitude of flickering candles, protruding from the walls and the chandelier overhead. The red stained glass windows reflected upon the table, though outside the light is dim and barely existent as thunder raged outside. As terror reigned within.

"I am not... afraid of you," I had said, taking a step toward my mother, who stiffened. "And I'm not going to let you... You can't- I won't listen, you can't stop me. No matter what, I'm not going to listen anymore."

And that's what frightened her. Not only that I had power, but that I was going to use it to defend myself. That I wasn't hers to use. I was thrown out that very day.

Chapter 23
Beckett

I'd spent most of the afternoon telling Icylyn that no way on earth would I be making a blimp. Now I'm helping Veronica sketch out a blimp as Icylyn tries to rope Aella into heating said blimp. Icylyn can fly anyway, I don't see the appeal.

"Hydrogen," I suggest, then realize I'm helping. Again.

I don't like heights. It's not an angsty backstory thing, I just don't like them. Never have, never did, likely never will. But oftentimes, my need to build and learn overtakes all sense of ration in my brain. That's why I'm helping Icylyn with her project. Veronica and Aella seem to need the distraction anyway. This is all hypothetical, and will probably never come to fruition.

But if I can build it...

No, no, I'm getting ahead of myself. Though if I'm being honest, at any given moment, most of us are. I already have ten invention projects in the works, what's one more? Although... the other ten keep exploding...

I run a hand through my curls and scoot closer to Icylyn. I grab my pocket watch out of my pocket, clicking the cover open and closed... and open and closed and open and closed.

Veronica flips over the paper of my notebook, running out of room to sketch. She pauses when she sees what's underneath. Equations upon equations in my handwriting, observations written in Spanish and Latin, and English and French, again by my own hand. Sketches of past projects I'd made, or Icylyn had thought up, very few having worked. Combustion seems always to be too much of a problem.

Some work, others fail, but I'm determined to bring them to life no matter what. I grab the papers and folded them neatly together, finding pieces of blank paper and handing them over to Veronica.

"What were those?" Veronica asks.

"Unfinished projects," I said sheepishly, holding the back of my neck and continuing to click at my pocket watch.

"May I?" Veronica asks.

"Um... sure. But– but don't judge them, these are just concepts–" I start.

"You think I'm in any place to judge?" Veronica teases, grabbing the papers. "The sketch work on these is incredible."

"Icylyn did some of them," I start. "...You really think so?"

"I do. Wow, I would've never thought of most of these."

"They keep blowing up. Some of my expectations are unrealistic. Um, wait don't–"

She turns to my supernatural research page. Different symbols are scattered, weaknesses are mentioned, prototypes for the goggles I wear are present. There's several designs for cufflinks that dampen powers, and earrings with the same effect.

"That's– that's just another personal project," I say, my stomach rising into my throat. "It's not important."

"This... could actually help a lot of people," Veronica says.

"Let me see," Icylyn says, grabbing it out of her hands. "Oh my stars, yeah, Beck, why didn't you tell me about this?"

"I didn't... I was going to... once the research was more complete– but I didn't anyone getting the wrong ideas."

"That makes sense," Icylyn nods. "But knowing more about our powers, how they work, and having a limit... stars I'm already thinking about how beneficial that would be."

Sometimes having powers is really, really neat, for example, I've got some really fun powers like knowledge absorption and technopathy, which end up being really helpful because I'm able to learn things quicker. My other powers are also relatively neat, but they're also a bother sometimes, and they're a pain to control. I don't have the chance to use my hydrokinesis, but my aerokinesis can be triggered by fear, making it extremely hard to control.

I can't control the lasers shooting out of my eyes, either. Icylyn made me the original prototype of my goggles when we were younger, a few days after my family got attacked by The Red Revenge crew. They'd gotten triggered by something, and I had to sit there, eyes shut tightly as we tried to come up with things that wouldn't be destroyed by my eyes. I've made adaptations over the years, but it still kind of hurts to wear them. I don't notice as much anymore.

Icylyn's story is similar. She enjoys being a dragon. She enjoys having wings, flying, and not feeling bothered by the cold. She enjoys being able to stop time. However, she cannot withstand the heat. If she's exposed to a certain amount of heat, she'll pass out. Her powers are connected to her emotions as well. Fear, anger, sadness, all of the like, can trigger a temperature change, icicles, snow, a blizzard, you name it.

I'd assume other contradictions come from other supernaturals.

"Yeah, I gotta say, I agree with Ice-Storm," Aella says, looking over my sketches.

Aella is a fire dragon who can turn invisible and teleport.

Enough said, really.

"We'd just have to be careful," Jinx adds. "But I agree, this is all a fantastic idea, and I'm sorry you felt like you had to hide it from us. If there's any way we can help with research... and I'm sure we can find materials... somewhere."

"Thank you," I say, earnestly.

This was not at all the reaction I was expecting. I really thought if I got anywhere with this, it'd be a much, *much* harder sell. And it wasn't! Which is really neat, and relieving, to be honest.

"Beck," Icylyn says.

"Hmm?" I ask.

"Time," Icylyn says.

I turn my pocketwatch over in my palm and glance down at the time. It's 5:54. Oh. It's 5:54. *Mierda.*

"I got this," She smiles, gently, grabbing a tote bag of books off the table. "Bye everyone, a pleasure, as always!"

I barely get the chance to say, "Bye guys, love you!" before everyone stands completely still, the only ones in motion being Ice and I. Freezing time seems to be gradually getting easier for her. I pack my notebook and sheets of paper into my gear-covered satchel, and she grabs a few books off of the shelves– they won't be missed, also tossing them into the satchel. She tosses me my tailcoat and she holds my satchel as I shrug it onto my shoulders. She hands me my shoulder back, which I sling over my shoulder. I grab my top hat off the floor, dust it off, and the two of us head out.

Icylyn practically skips down the hall trying to keep up next to me. I slow down to her pace, and she walks normally. We talk for a good while, about whatever random thing we can think of. Icylyn describes the plot of some book she's reading, then abruptly stops when she sees the spiral staircase.

"Don't tell m– your mom," Icylyn says, a bit of a twinkle in her eye.

"Ice don–" I start.

It's too late. She's already jumped onto the railing and is cheering as she slides down it. I sigh, chuckle to myself, and walk down the stairs normally, holding tightly onto the side so I don't fall to my death or something. I can hear Icylyn laughing as she jumps off at the bottom. She was always the more adventurous of the two of us. Shy, but surprisingly daring.

Icylyn was the kid who ripped up long lilac dresses climbing the tallest tree so that she could read without interruptions. She still is that kid, and likely, always would be. Plants and literature and danger seemed to excite her in all the ways I'd found joy in mechanics, and science, and research.

We walk side by side in a world that lay stagnant, all the time in the world. Occasionally she'll point out a plant and start infodumping, and I'll listen intently. We walk for a good while before Icylyn teleports us to our cottage. Icylyn returns time to normal as we approach the porch. We walk in, take our shoes off, and lock the five different locks on the door. Safety precautions, living so close to the river. So close to the sirens, and otherwise.

The sirens know not to bother us, though. Let's just say that Rebecca Carmen Acosta is one of the few who's gone toe to toe with the river sirens and lived to tell the tale. My mamá's kind of a force to be reckoned with.

"Welcome back," My mamá says from the kitchen. "I just finished dinner, come on in and have some?"

"That sounds great," Icylyn smiles. "Thank you, Rebecca."

Icylyn and I sit in our room, window unlocked. We whisper back and forth, our room dimly lit by a candle on our bedside table. Her side of the room is a lavender color, filled with shelves, books, and flowers encased in frost. My side is a light brown, with clocks I made myself, and prototypes on shelves and notebooks. Behind our beds is our window, which slowly creaks open. In steps a boy about our age dressed in all black.

Dorian Lockhill. A freshly fourteen-year-old vampire with red eyes, messy black hair, an Irish accent with a slight lisp, and the best eyeliner you've ever seen in the kingdom. He, Icylyn, and I are pretty close friends. And I... may have... kind of the biggest crush on him. He lives alone in a section of the forest no one else dares to go and spends a lot of time in the tavern during daylight hours. Some nights, he sneaks into our cottage to hang out with us.

"Hey loves," Dorian says, smiling as he lands on my bed.

"*Dorian,*" I squeaked. "Um, hi, wasn't– wasn't expecting you."

"I didn't tell you I was coming," Dorian shrugs.

"Are we... are we sure this is a good– um... a good idea?" I stumble over my words, face growing very warm. "My mamá is gonna find out, and she's gonna–"

The door creaks open. My mamá steps into the room. She leans against the door, turning her attention immediately to Icylyn.

"Hey, you forgot your–" She says, before her gaze flickers toward Dorian and I. "Oh, hi Dorian."

"Hello Rebecca, wonderful to see you," Dorian smiles, waving at my mom.

"Good to see you too, kid. I'll leave you guys to it then. I forgot why I came in here, Dorian, the offer still stands."

"Thank you very much, but I'm fine," Dorian smiles.

"Alright. Just let me know if you ever change your mind or need anything," Mamá says, then leaves the room.

I slowly blink, and I share an utterly confused look with Icylyn. Dorian just chuckles and tells us not to worry about it. He leans against the wall, picking at his black nail polish. Icylyn grabs a book off the shelf and starts reading it, cozying up in her bed.

Dorian shrugs off his jacket, setting it behind him. His bat-wings peak out just slightly from the holes in the back of his black long-sleeved puffy blouse, low cut and laced in the front. Although, I notice his wings were... mostly gone. Torn off, it seemed, perhaps burned in some areas. Much worse condition than Jinx's wings, practically nothing more than tiny stubs on his back. I scoot closer to him. His attention is focused elsewhere, his red eyes gleaming in the path of the moon as he observes an orange tree right outside of our window.

"I've uh... never seen your wings before," I say, choking on my words.

"Nothing really to see," Dorian murmurs. "I'd be happy to put my jacket back on if it makes you uncomfortable, love, it was just so warm in here."

I put my hand on his jacket to stop him, accidentally putting my hand over his. My face seems to light on fire, and he goes subtly purple. We break eye contact immediately, he coughs and I clear my throat, and we both scoot away from each other.

"No, no, they're–um, they're neat," I say, my voice cracking.

"You're just saying that," He runs his hand through his messy black hair. "I appreciate the gesture though."

"I wouldn't've said it if I didn't mean it," I say before immediately being cut off by Icylyn.

"That's true," She says, nodding.

"Oh. Right. Thank you, then. They're a bit... broken," Dorian says.

"The cool– erm, the beautiful thing– thing about broken things, is that there's an opportunity to build up from them."

Nice, Icylyn's voice booms in my brain, only this time, she's being genuine.

"You-you know, um, I could... always make like... working ones if, uh, if you ever wanted that," I say, my throat closing up.

"Yeah?" Dorian asks.

"Yeah," I say.

"I'm going to go talk with Rebecca," Icylyn says suddenly, snapping her book closed.

She stands, awkwardly, and moves stiffly out of the room. She carefully shuts the door behind her, closing it all the way. She doesn't look at us throughout the entire process.

"Bumbóg?" Dorian asks, tapping his knees.

"Yeah?" I ask, painfully aware of my voice cracking.

"I like you."

"No," I panic.

"...Did you just say no to me confessing my feelings to you?"

"...Wait, hold on," I say. "Let me just– I like you too. You like me? *You* like *me*?"

"Yes," Dorian laughs.

"I like you too," I say. "I want-I–"

"You're busy," He smiles, ruffling my hair. "When you're done with your big-shot science work, I'd like to go out with you."

I sit there, utterly in shock. He raises an eyebrow and I nod, almost frantically. He laughs and puts his coat back on. He opens up the window and leaves one foot on the windowsill. He winks at me.

"When you're free, you know where to find me, bumbóg."

"BOOMSHOT!" I scream, the second he's out of earshot, pumping my fists into the air.

The first thing I do is tell my Mamá.

It's a few days later now. Everything just feels too perfect. The sun is shining lightly through the treetops and onto the snow. I'd found a dry patch of dirt beside a white tree. Icylyn is sitting up in its branches, ebony puffy curls tied into a light purple headscarf. It's quiet for the most part, besides the rustling of leaves, my pen against paper, Icylyn flipping a page and quietly humming to herself. It's a relatively calm moment. One that was not meant to be ended so abruptly. But then Raven, Sage, and Hazel walk by.

I should've told my mom. We should've told *someone*. Apparently, this was Sabine's idea. But she didn't show up, just convinced the others. And then Ice and I tagged along because we figured it'd be a safer bet. It isn't. It definitely isn't. And... okay *maaaaaybe* I was curious about the tech.

Yeah, I went for the tech.

Ice stops time right outside the gates, allowing us to get inside unnoticed. We get pretty deep into Cazlamenta before Ice can't handle the strain anymore. The plan is simple. Raven will act as a distraction if needed. Sage and Icylyn will sneak out whatever hidden dirt or plans they can find, as Hazel and I dismantle weapons and steal whatever tech we can carry. It goes well at first.

It isn't long before the familiar buzzing sensation returns, and I can tell that Hazel senses it too. Closer and closer we creep, until we make our way to the door. I am, quite literally, shaking with excitement, fiddling with my pocket watch as I shake out my other hand.

Until we are both grabbed by approaching guards.

Chapter 24
Nightshade

Something had felt off about that morning. Aella was arguing with Sabine about something down the hall. Veronica was sitting on her balcony, sketching birds as they passed. Things had gotten overwhelming for her, and she was trying to calm herself down, taking a few minutes away from the problems in the kingdom that fell at her and Aella's feet. I stepped out as clouds moved in and covered the sky, blocking out the majority of the sunlight.

"I know I should be doing things," She mumbles quietly, absently. "I just need a break."

"Take your time, darling," I say, holding her from behind.

"I need to get to work," She mumbles, seeming to struggle with the words. "But– my chest hurts, and I feel like I can't breathe, and I'm light-headed, and I feel like I'm gonna throw up but we're on a time crunch and I don't have time to be feeling like this and I'm sorry and I know Aella can't do it alone–"

"Hey, hey," I say quietly, spinning her around to face me, and holding her gently.

"It happens a lot, I should be used to it by now," She mumbles, shutting her eyes and stepping back, shaking out her hands and walking back and forth.

"Don't invalidate your feelings like that, darling," I say softly. "Is there anything I can do?"

"I don't... I don't know– I'm sorry– I'm being dramatic... it just hurts and I can't stop it."

"Veronica, hey, I promise you, you're not being dramatic. This happens to me too sometimes, and eventually, it'll pass. Take a deep breath. Can you see that tree over there?"

She sucks in a breath and exhales as she nods, still rocking on her heels and shaking out her hands.

"Could you count the flowers on it?" I ask.

"Jinx..." She groans.

"Please?" I ask.

She grumbles but then does. The shakiness in her voice seems to slowly dissipate as we move from tree to tree. We continue until her panic seems to pass. She turns toward me, slipping her arms around my waist, and rests her head against me. I hold her tightly.

"No matter what your brain is telling you," I whisper to her. "You're doing wonderfully, and I'm proud of you."

It's a good quiet few minutes before someone else steps on the balcony.

"Your majesty, there's an issue."

Something is wrong. Something is definitely wrong. I send out messages to the rest of the rebellion telepathically but to no avail. Something is wrong. I'm standing on Veronica's balcony, as she'd told me to wait there, she'd be right back. Her balcony is high enough to even see across to Mortem Venenum.

At first, I take no note of the snowstorm approaching Mortem Venenum. After all, it is February. Only, the clouds seem to be gathering closer and closer towards the castle, and the mass of snow is far greater than usual. Odd, but I've seen odder, so I pay it no mind. What is weird, is that I could hear Aella scream from across the hall. A pained, guttural scream. I turn to investigate, but then I see Beckett standing there.

"She's fine," Beckett says, unable to look me in the eye.

There's something off about his voice. There's a slight echo to it, the way mine echoes on occasion. It's all too familiar. Barely noticeable and not nearly as drastic as mine. Beckett runs his hand through his hair and leans his hand against the doorway. Veronica runs past him. She's hyperventilating and pulling at her braids. Tears are forming in her eyes.

"Did... did you get the transmission?" Veronica's voice is strangled.

"No, everyone has been completely silent. I've been trying to reach them for–"

"Something came up. They... they– they broke into Cazlamenta. Raven and Sage were taken, Hazel, and Icylyn managed to escape but...they can't find Beckett."

I look over at Beckett, who swallows and seems almost wobbly on his feet. He still can't look me in the eyes. He's crying now. He's terrified. Absolutely terrified. Oh. Oh no.

NIGHTSHADE

Chapter 25
Icylyn

I hate being right. I told them we shouldn't split up, I told them we should go in with a plan, I told them we should at least tell someone what we were doing. I had a feeling something would go wrong. I had a feeling someone would get hurt.

Stars, I *hate* being right.

I barely escaped the castle. I wouldn't have been able to if it weren't for my invisibility. Others weren't so lucky. Others... definitely fared worse. As I tear down the hall, an arrow narrowly misses my shoulder but tears through my wing. I have to think on my feet. Previous plans of jumping out the window, well, fly out the window. All that matters is getting out alive.

Eventually, I made it out of the castle, spotting Hazel not far from it. I allow myself to reappear in front of her. Tears are streaming down her face, as she leans against a tree, sliding to her feet. We'd made it out. Where are the others?

The wind begins to pick up around us, and Hazel immediately stands. She grabs me by the arm, holding onto a tree branch.

"Sage and Raven were captured," She says over the wind, voice strained.

Sage and Raven were captured. Oh, stars. I really, *really* hate being right.

"Where's Beckett?" I ask, seized by panic.

Chapter 26
Beckett

Relief hits me all at once. I really didn't think we'd get out of there. I can't tell if it's the adrenaline, relief, or the newfound buzzing I feel around current technology, but something electric pulses through my veins, making me feel more alive than ever before. It's an incredible feeling, one I can't wait to tell my mamá about. I can't wait to show her the computer either. She didn't completely believe me when I told her about the one we found in the castle. Well, more like she couldn't comprehend it, I think. She'll be so proud of me, going on a mission, just like she did as a teenager. I mean, sure, I'll get a little bit of a lecture, but it'll be worth it. I mean, she can't be that upset, I'm coming out of this completely unscathed. Now I just have to find Icylyn and get home, I'm sure Hazel, Sage, and Raven are already out by now.

I have an added skip to my step, and I stop humming as I cup a hand to my mouth. I let out a whistle, doing my best impression of a Rehliyth bird. It's a soft pink bird in the Sturnidae Family and is a symbol of safety and good luck. It's an easy call to learn, and one my Mamá taught us after the Red Revenge...

Actually, that story is kind of a mood-dampener. I don't want to talk about that right now, not when everything's on such a high note.

I wait a minute. Icylyn doesn't whistle back. I stick the computer into my satchel, carefully latching the button. I adjust my satchel so that the strap is secured by the left side of my neck, the bag hanging from my right side. I cup both sides of my mouth, whistling louder as I walk further out. There's the sound of birds crying in the distance, and the sky turns black as crows shriek and circle and disperse. I step backward, a twig snapping beneath my feet.

I look down at the brown leaves beneath my feet and catch my breath. I always found brown leaves the prettiest. They're my favorite color after all. I clutch the soft leather of the satchel that once belonged to my mamá and look towards the black sky. The crows circle, their screams nearly deafening. I can barely take my eyes away, jackrabbit heart bouncing in my chest, veins seeming to twist from my chest to my stomach. Where's my sister?

I start feeling spacey, my throat growing dry.

Mierda. I can't afford to have a seizure right now. Where's my sister?

I struggle to whistle, and I can't. I sit down, and I sit still. I drop the strap of my satchel, sitting it beside me, unbuttoning my shirt to loosen it. The crows dissipate, and I can hear a sharp echo of my whistle.

"Icylyn," I sigh, the vines within me untangling and settling back into their designated spots.

"Guess again."

My heart skips a beat. I stumble to my feet, tossing my satchel over my neck and shoulder. I twirl my finger, gathering wind, and flinging it in the direction of the voice. Daman simply grins, pressing his back against a tree and holding on.

"Oh no, no no," Daman taunts. "I know your tricks... what is it that reptilian trash calls you? Nerd boy?"

"She's *not* tr-trash," I say, silently cursing myself for stumbling over my words. My mouth grows dry, my tongue feels all too large in my mouth, and none of the languages in my brain are sounding even close to coherent. "*You-*trash, you're trash. You're the one who's trash."

"Here I was thinking you were supposed to be the clever one," Daman says.

"I am."

"If you were clever, you would've run."

I back up slowly, my body not wanting to cooperate with my quickly scrambling brain. I run as fast as my feet will allow, not thinking to use the force of the wind. I barely register the sound beneath my thoughts, the pounding of my feet against crunching leaves and unsettled sticks, the wild whistling from all around, crows fleeing the scene.

All too singular, all too fast. I didn't register the explosion.

I feel it though. Not all at once, I barely notice until it is all that I can notice. I hit the ground, hissing. The pain is more than I can manage. I've never felt anything like it. I crumble within myself, pressing my palm against the back of my leg, hardly registering that the bullet passed through my kneecap.

"Did you really think you'd get away?" Daman shouts over the howling wind.

He finds the muddy spots in the ground, and sticks his shoes deep, allowing himself to move forward against the wind.

"Tell me," He steadily demands. "Tell me you knew you couldn't get away from me."

"Stop," I plead.

"Say it," He raises his voice.

"No!"

"Say it, or I'll expand the wound and rip out the tendons in your star-forsaken leg," Daman commands.

"Vale, vale," I all but whimper, holding up two shaky hands. "I knew I couldn't get away, will you please let me go now?"

Daman kneels beside me, pressing his gun against my shoulder. He presses it down, forcing me to lay flat on my back. Pain tears through me like a knife slicing easily through a ripe fruit. The drying, sticky red liquid painting my hands and dripping down my legs almost feels reminiscent of days spent cooking with my family in the kitchen or eating the fresh fruit I'd grown on early summer days, the taste of the sun melting sweet on my tongue. I can't see the sun now. There are too many crows, and Daman's blocking my light. My mouth tastes dry and bitter and not sweet at all.

Mamá would know how to get out of this situation. She's probably worried now. Icylyn and I need to go home now. I can't find Icylyn, and my vision is getting all spotty.

"You have something of mine," Daman says, the glint of his crown nearly blinding me.

"You can have it," I scramble to sit up, unclasping the button on my satchel.

"Give me the whole bag," Daman says, rising. He presses the gun to my forehead. It's warm. My leg throbs and it takes everything in me not to scream.

"My mamá made it," I say, tears blurring my vision.

"My mama made it," Daman repeats, in a mockery of my voice, exaggerating the way my bottom lip is wobbling. "I don't care. Give me the bag, freak."

"I'm not a freak!" I shout, laughter seeping into my tone.

"Is something funny?" Daman asks, stone cold.

I break into hysterics. I can't stop laughing. I can't stop crying. I'm hiccuping, and I'm giggling, and I'm wheezing and I'm sobbing and I'm snotting and I'm bleeding and I'm cackling, and it all comes out all at once and I'm terrified.

Where are my sisters? Where's my mamá?

I reach for the tie to my goggles.

"If you take off your goggles, I will shoot your precious brains out," Daman says. "Understand?"

I drop my hands, and not even sure what sounds are escaping me, I hand him my satchel. It feels like a betrayal, but I know she'd prefer me alive.

"You won't kill me, right?" I plead. "I'm thirteen. I'm not even a threat, I'll– I'll quit the rebellion, I'll be quiet, I promise, it'll be like I don't even exist!"

"Like you won't even exist?" Daman echoes.

"S– Yes, yes Your Highness," I say.

Daman chuckles under his breath. He secures my satchel, removing his gun from my forehead. I heave a sigh of relief, holding a hand to my wound, and waiting for him to leave.

"Like you don't even exist," Daman repeats as if tasting new words for the very first time. Smiling as though it intoxicates him. "I quite like the sound of that, freak."

"I'm not a freak," I protest.

"Of course not," Daman says, pacing. "You're not anything at all. It's like you said. You don't even exist."

There's another explosion, and a pain much, *much* worse than before. It's between my ribs. It'll be much harder to fix this one. I'm slipping, I can feel it. Colors blend around me, and the only sensation I can remember is pain. I forget the concept of breath, and I can barely taste the sensation of my name in the back of my throat. I can't do this to my mamá, not after all that's happened. And Icylyn, Aella, Dorian, I can't do this to them either. I can't do this to my friends.

With the last bit of mental energy I can hold onto, I send a transmission to Icylyn. It all swirls around me, and I don't think she'd like this painting very much. The colors I've loved since childhood, differing shades of brown and black and red, all seem so twisted and cruel.

I don't want this. I want to live.

My mamá used to hold my head every night after it happened. Every night as she sang me to sleep, she'd press her forehead against mine. For a while, her tears used to fall onto my cheeks as she held me close. She'd tell me I had a light, hidden just behind my eyes. She told me that no matter what, I couldn't lose that light.

I know all too well what the eyes of the dead look like. I'm going to disappoint her now.

Someone grabs me by the collar of my jacket. It's familiar, and it settles the vines twisting in my chest, thorns that dug too deep into my jackrabbit heart. It feels like the warm embrace of the sunlight after an unforgiving winter that's well overstayed its welcome. It's hard to register reality as what it is, beneath the slipping of my thoughts, my blood watering the saplings beneath the ground, the pain that only announces itself louder with every bump we hit. But everything's fine now, she came to take me home. I'm going to be okay.

"Lo siento, Aella," I murmur. *I'm sorry, Aella.*

Daman's laugh doesn't sound like his anymore. It sounds like the tangled colors of the laughter of everyone I've ever loved. I can't tell anything apart in the twist of pain and my final savior, the final graces of my once damning imagination.

Chapter 27

Icylyn

Hazel's eyes widen when I ask about Beckett. I ask her again. She opens her mouth, and no words come out. She winces, and I look down and notice frost forming around her arm. The wind picks up, and I hit a tree.

I swear I can hear him. Just barely, but I can hear him. I swore I could hear him. I could've stopped time. I could've stopped time, right then, right there, and found him. But it was too late.

A gunshot is barely audible over the screams of the wind.

"Beckett!" I yell.

The winds die down instantly.

No. No. No, no, no no, no, no. No.

I call out for him again. There's no response. There's nothing. Nothing. No, no, there can't be nothing. I can't allow that, I won't allow that. I'm not going to leave my best friend to die. I'm not going to let my other half, my brother, die. I call out his name again. Silence. Complete silence. Until...

Hey, Ice, um, I've got... news, his voice blasts into my mind.

Where are you? I respond.

I'm pleading. Please, anything but this.

I can barely see. I've been shot.

Hang on, I plead with him. *Please hang on. I'm going to find you. We're going to get help. It's going to be okay.*

I'm scared, Ice, he transmits.

My throat is burning. Clouds are forming around me, and it's hailing. It's my fault. I don't care. I don't care about any of that right now. I need to find him.

Beckett?

I'm sorry.

It goes quiet. Completely quiet. I try to transmit back but–there is nothing but emptiness. Something inside me feels empty. I can feel something draining from me. Which meant...

He is dead. My best friend in the whole world is dead. I fall to my knees and scream as the hail stops overhead. I don't notice as icicles spike up from all across the forest. He is dead. He is dead. He is dead.

Deeper and deeper I sink, as snow storms above me. I scream and scream, and scream, but it doesn't do anything. It doesn't bring him back, it doesn't fill the empty void that is so insistent in dragging me down.

I don't remember walking through the forest. I don't remember finding the well, I don't remember how I figured out he was down there. I don't remember getting him out of the well.

All I remember is kneeling beside the well, on my knees, cradling him in my arms. I remember lifting his goggles off of him and setting them on the ground beside him. His eyes are empty. There was no life, no practical joke. This isn't just some twisted prank. He's gone.

His hand is in mine, though bloody and cold. I stay with him as long as I can. I can't leave him. He doesn't like to be alone. He hates being alone. It scares him. I have to stay with him. I can't just leave him here. He hates being alone. I promised. We promised. We promised each other that we'd never leave each other, no matter what.

No matter what, even if that means my sweater will forever be stained in his blood. Even if it means my tears turning to ice as they fall into his curly brown hair. Even if it means cradling his corpse as close as I can, trying my hardest not to freeze it. Trying my best to keep my broken promise.

"It was supposed to be me and you till the end," I whisper. "Im ' sic paenitet, Beck. Reliqua facile, mi carissimi amicus." *I'm so sorry, Beck. Rest easy, my dear friend.*

Chapter 28
Aella

"Yeah, okay, Sabine, come talk to me when I care," I say, walking out of the room.

Beckett and Icylyn will probably be here in an hour. I'm not gonna lie, I miss living with them. But... don't tell them I said that. Anyway, I'd tampered a bit with the holograms in the room, under Beck's direction. He and I had made a plan to prank Ice the other night. Everything is looking out to be great.

Until I get a transmission from Icylyn.

Aella? Her voice booms in my mind.

Hey Ice. What's wrong?

It's Beckett.

Everything in me feels a rush of cold. I can't see my hands in front of my face, and back up from the table in case I lit on flame. I open up a window, prepared to go save him if I had to.

Aella... he's dead.

Something inside me just shatters. I drop to the floor, weighed down completely. I open my mouth to scream, and nothing seems to come out. Tears evaporate off of my cheeks, everything seeming to be ripped from me.

Aella? Icylyn's voice returned. She sounds equally devastated, scared, and alone.

Please tell me this is a joke.

I wish it was.

It wouldn't be too far off if it is. But then again, it's Beckett. Beckett would never go this far. Not even for a prank, not even to get back at me.

What I wouldn't give for just one more day. I'd tease him a bit, sure, but I'd hug him tightly, I'd tell him he and Ice meant the world to me. But fate didn't seem to have those plans for us. At least... not now.

No... no. I wasn't going to take no for an answer. No matter the cost, we have to bring him back. There has to be a way to bring him back.

Chapter 29
Veronica

It's been a month since Beckett died. Since Raven and Sage were taken. Since everything turned upside down all over again.

"If we're going to do this," I say. "We're in desperate need of a strategy."

"Why are we in charge again?" Aella grumbles, rubbing the sleep out of her eyes.

"Because mom and dad were neglectful tyrants," I say.

"Oh... right... screw them," Aella yawns.

It's like the spark that had ignited Aella died with Beckett. She'd lost all her energy, and it was very rare she left her room. She spent most of her time either asleep or clinging to Icylyn. Sometimes she'd find me and just sit with me like there was something she needed to say. Then she'd go back to her room, go back to sleep.

I admit, maybe we are a bit over our heads with this whole situation. We're trying to fix our collapsing kingdom whilst trying to fight a battle against bigotry, as well as preparing for the incoming war with Mortem Venenum.

Not to mention that all we wanted to do was rescue Raven and Sage, and revive Beckett. With any priority, *that* came first. Stars, I should've never been put in this leader position. People don't say it, but I know they think it, and I think it constantly.

We'll be able to bring Beckett back. I'm going to hollow Daman's throat. No one will mind trading Daman's life for Beckett's. Beckett hasn't moved on yet, and since he is stuck in a limbo of unusual circumstances, it should be possible to bring him back. It all seems so impossible, and so big, and I have to walk the line and pretend I'm seconds from collapsing at any given moment.

"I don't think I can sneak us in again," Icylyn mumbles and the room gets colder. "I failed last time."

"Hey..." Hazel says, squeezing Icylyn's hand. "That wasn't your fault, not at all. We knew the risks, your powers aren't supposed to strain for so many people for so long. You did your best. It's not your fault."

"*Maybe* you shouldn't have snuck off to do something you weren't ready for without telling anyone," Sabine says.

Now– Icylyn is *not* a violent person. Her powers are often uncontrollable and responsive to her emotions, but she would never willingly harm anyone. She is also never one to be easily angered, and she often chooses reasoning before anger. But just then, she creates an icicle out of ice, likely subconsciously, and jumps onto her feet, an unseen fire in her eyes.

"No," Hazel says calmly, grabbing her by the arm.

"...Sorry," Icylyn says softly, sitting down.

"Wait, wait," I say, stepping off the table, and immediately tripping over a chair, being caught by Jinx. "Ouch. Anyway, does anyone know what just happened?"

"It was Sabine's idea," Icylyn says quickly, before slamming her mouth shut.

"You weren't there, Icylyn. I didn't make the plan. I suggested ideas, yes, but I never said we should act on them," Sabine says, firm yet somewhat sympathetic. "Although, yes I do think we could be acting quicker in some areas, not a critique on anyone here... it's just... some people I'm very close to have been really suffering for a long time."

"Okay," I take a breath, sitting on the table. Jinx squeezes my hand. "Okay. Okay, okay, okay– alright. Okay. Okay. Okay, so we're all– on edge, but we need to stay united. We can't be pinning the blame on each other, we just need to understand that we're all doing our best."

"... what she said," Aella nods.

I lay my head on Jinx's shoulder and take a deep breath.

"Okay. We're bringing him back," I say, finally.

"And then we're taking The Woods down," Aella says, standing beside me.

"Once and for all," Jinx says.

Oh, how we were so confident.

"Oh! You're... *both* here!" Hazel said, eyes darting between Aella and I.

The remaining members of the rebellion gathered together outside the front of Fear Forest. While it may have been a better idea for Aella and I to stay behind, when have we ever gone with the reasonable decision? Jinx stands beside Aella, posture rigid, all Nightshade.

"We left Sabine in charge," I say.

Icylyn crosses her arms, face turning sour, and frost rises on the surrounding trees. Hazel frowns at the situation, tightening her guitar strap. I'm still not sure why she brings it everywhere. Maybe it's a symbol. Maybe it's a weapon. Maybe it's a reminder of something to her.

"Look," Aella says to Icylyn, hand on her shoulder. "You, Beck, and Becca are the closest thing I had to a family for a *long* time. The Woods have toyed with a *lot* of people, and I can't sit back and watch it anymore, especially not when they're getting my family involved. So, I'm coming, no matter what. Even if it means having to trust Sabine."

"... And Veronica?" Icylyn cautiously asks.

"Other than her very apparent main character syndrome and need to be included?" Aella teases, nudging me in the rib. "She's one of our bes–"

"I got this," I nod, before I can get flustered. I'm not used to Aella being directly nice. "The Woods had me under their influence for far too long a time. They hurt Beckett– they *killed* Beckett, they killed so many people. All that, and they had me convinced that I wanted to be part of their so-called family. I still have scars from each of them. I want them to pay. I want them to pay for what they did to Beckett. To everyone. And with this... I just want to be there to help give them what they deserve."

Hazel and Icylyn seem to relent. We continue on. After all, at this point, it's all we really can do. And that has to be enough. We walk away from Fear Forest, not daring to go inside, as we make our way toward Cazlamenta.

Chapter 30
Nightshade

Veronica's thoughts are always loud. Louder than most, to the point where often I hear her thoughts even when not intentionally reading her mind. We walk hand in hand through the forest, crossing the river in the neutral territories that border Couteau and Mortem Venenum. Her grip gets tighter and tighter as we grow nearer to Cazlamenta. I can hear her heartbeat just slightly, beating to the tune of her thoughts.

I'm going to kill Daman. I'm gonna do it. I'm gonna kill him. She thinks.

I don't say anything for a good while. I brush my thumb over her hand, hearing her breathing become staggered. Our shoes squish against blue, dew-covered blades of grass. Icylyn nearly slips several times as she frosts the grass over. Veronica's thoughts continue to grow louder and louder, panicked, angry, nearly screaming.

I'm gonna kill him. I'm gonna kill him. I'm gonna kill him.

Just slightly faster than the tempo of her hummingbird-like heartbeat.

I'm gonna kill him. I'm gonna kill him. I'm gonna kill him. I'm gonna kill-

Well, you get the picture.

"Darling," I say softly.

She lets go of my hand and walks faster. I match her pace. We don't say anything for a good while.

Darling, you are aware that my parents have trained Daman in combat for the purpose of becoming a merciless warrior king, yes?

You're forgetting that I had to teach myself to fight you, She responds. *With that and the countless dance and etiquette lessons I had to endure growing up, my body is basically its own weapon at this point. And I've got knives. I brought a lot of knives. Knives are a good weapon.*

"Hey," I said softly, my fingers finding their way back between hers.

She stops walking. I cautiously step in front of her, and she shakes off a breath, looking back at me. Her eyes were full of tears that she clearly was trying to hide. Storm clouds. Her eyes are storm clouds growing too heavy, storm clouds breaking down, sprinkling blood onto the dry cracks of the ground. Heavy rain of the many faults of the Two Kingdoms, of the world. The problems that Veronica believed so strongly that she could stop. Problems she guilted herself for when she couldn't bear the weight.

I cup her face in my free hand, and she leans into it, a single tear falling onto my finger. I feel a sharp jab into my stomach as if her pain was transferring into me. Veronica squeezes her eyes shut and sucks in a shaky breath, turning away and continuing to walk. Aella jogs up to her, and puts a hand on her shoulder.

"You okay?" Aella asks, far, far gentler than usual.

"Yeah," Veronica nods, and I watch as she forces a smile. "I'm fine."

After several hours, we make it. I remember when I was younger, I swore to myself I'd die before returning willingly. Well, here I was again, having been back not long ago. We walk across a bridge, high, high above a fog-covered ocean, a bridge the color of skulls. It's almost as if they'd used the victims of the rotting corpses hidden within and around the castle as inspiration. Dark towers jut out from the castle, sharp, agonized, seeming to scream the anguish and horror it witnesses inside its walls.

I used to be barricaded within those walls. I used to call them home. And yet it sat, a castle on a cliff, a doll upon a shelf. A porcelain doll, no flaws, no cracks. But even dolls and dollhouses hold their secrets deep within, never to tell another soul. Still, the childish dream to set that dollhouse aflame reverberates in my mind. One day.

Beckett walks beside me, eyes staring wildly at the castle. Darting to the forest in which the well resided.

"Just... be careful. Please," Beckett says, flicking with his pocket-watch.

"No promises," I say.

Beckett looks over at Icylyn and Aella, then me and Veronica, then Hazel, then at his slightly glowing hands and sighs. I feel guilty bringing him here, but it's the only way to keep him tethered to me. The only way to keep him from floating away, moving on before we can bring him back.

"Hey... Jinx," Veronica says, slipping her shaking hand into mine. "We should... we should..."

"I know," I say softly. "I know."

Darling, I transmit. *Before we do this, I need to tell you something. It's something I meant to tell you much sooner before we even began dating, but-*

Tell me afterward, she transmits.

Are you sure?

Yes.

We continue on.

We stay out of sight. The others start to sneak into the castle, but I stay behind, hiding in a bush, just to make sure Veronica is alright. Aella sits beside me, but she's anxious to go. Veronica looks sickly, terror-stricken, as she squeezes her eyes tightly and quickly pounds on the door, stepping back quickly as if the door were made of flame. The door slowly creaks open, and surprisingly, Daman steps out.

"Veronica..." he says, somewhat surprised. "You're... here."

"Yes. I've realized," She says, stepping toward him, leaning against the door, pouting just slightly. "I was wrong. Without you I'm nothing. Nightshade... she-she filled my head with lies, and I'm so confused. Please. I'm sorry. You were right."

She takes a step forward, throwing herself into him.

"Please take me back, please fix me."

He slides an arm around her back, and she tenses. I nearly jump out of the bushes then and there.

"Hold your horses, lesbian disaster, she's got this," Aella says, holding onto me by the back of my cloak.

"Fine," Daman says, harshly, his arm tightening around her. "About time you came to your senses, dearest. Come inside, it's dreadful out there."

Veronica smiles nervously at me and gives me a wink as she walks inside. Her gaze then darkens as it falls on him, reading nothing but murder in her eyes. The large door creaks closed behind them. She's in. He'll be distracted. Aella is already out of the bushes, and running toward the side of the castle. I follow close behind, spreading my wings as she does, thankful for the cover of clouds. I lead us to Daman's room, cracking open the window door and stepping inside.

The room is unbearably red. Deep, and dark, candles flickering in the corners of the ceiling. In the center of the room, there's a chandelier, the candles resting on actual skulls.

"It's... Daman's room alright," Aella nods.

"I always hated coming in here," I say.

"I thought you used to hide in Daman's closet," Aella says.

"I hid in Noah's closet," I correct. "His room is in a different hall, next to my room. Daman gets his own hall."

"What a bastard. Mommy's boy. Not in the fun and sexy way either," Aella grumbles, chewing on her lip-ring.

"Are we sure this is the most appropriate time to discuss your kinks, Aella?"

"There's never an appropriate time to discuss them, that's why they're kinks."

"Fair point," I say,

She grins viciously, all teeth. She begins rummaging through Daman's drawers without a second thought.

"Jackpot. Hey Liles, come check this out."

She grins and holds up a leather-bound book between her fingers, waving it slightly. I turn my eyes from black to blue momentarily, just so she knows I'm rolling my eyes at her. She bites back a laugh, and I step cautiously toward her, careful not to step on anything that might make too much noise.

"Found his diary!" She whispers, far too loud, smacking it into her hand.

"Lovely," I say, insincerely, continuing to look for anything of actual value.

"Noah's gonna flip," Aella says.

I laugh under my breath. "Let's focus on this after the mission."

"I think it's funny how you pretend you have your shit together. And it actually works? Somehow, people think you have your shit together," Aella laughs.

"*Jinx* has her shit together. Scratch that, *Nightshade,* has her shit together. I, on the other hand, very much do not."

"It's probably the charisma and the accent," Aella snaps her fingers and points at me. "Because you, my friend, are an absolute disaster."

"As are you."

"Didn't say I wasn't," Aella winks. "Find anything?"

"Aside from a concerning amount of gunpowder? Nothing useful."

We keep rummaging around the room for a bit, not quite sure what to find, but finding what we can. There's an occasional sketch, Veronica's name scratched into the bottom corners of the art, of flowers, diamonds, and ballrooms. Daman keeps them in a box in a locked drawer. Aella sticks the diary in a satchel, and we head out of the room, searching for other rooms.

Chapter 31
Veronica

What is taking everyone so long? I think to myself.

I'd convinced Daman to walk outside with me, to the courtyard. Anything is better than finding myself face-to-face with Isodle and Dietrich. Even if it means having to be alone with Daman. We didn't go to the courtyard, instead he led me to the back. Not far from the cliff, the roaring waves, the wisteria flowing gently in the wind. The same place he'd proposed to me.

There's a cove and docking port below that no one was supposed to know about. However, seeing as the castle was only a short walk from the very edge of the cliff that was above the cove, The Woods knew about it. Five specific pirate crews docked there, those being The Red Revenge, Victory's Bastard, The Lobelia, The Golden Fury, and The Nox Lilium. And remaining pirate ships, including those in The Red Revenge's fleet– are forced to dock elsewhere.

Jinx has had to deal with the Red Revenge crew far too many times, due to their tendency to burn down villages and kidnap civilians simply for the sake of doing so. The Woods never seemed to mind, especially since the Red Revenge spent a lot of time specifically targeting supernaturals, run-away crew members, and those who weren't cis-gendered heterosexuals. The Woods are bigots, are we surprised? Some members of the Victory's Bastard also specifically targeted supernaturals, though the captain, Morgan Bones, didn't seem to agree to that. Though, it's said Morgan Bones doesn't have much of an opinion of anything.

"Damned pirates," Daman grits between his teeth, just under his breath, as gunfire is heard below.

I pretended to be taken aback by his "crude" language. I may be a damn good liar, but this act is getting harder and harder by the minute.

"Sorry," He says.

"You should be," I mutter, followed by, "You *will* be."

"What was that?" He asks.

"Oh nothing," I smile, sweetly. "Just mumbling about how lovely the ocean looks today."

"You should know by now that you shouldn't mumble, nor speak without being spoken to," He says, sharply. "And if you *must* think at a given moment, though highly irregular for a woman other than my mother, you should keep that thinking inside of your head."

"You forget your place, your highness, I outrank you."

Daman shuts up right then and there. And, *stars, it's* the most satisfying thing. You have no idea how many *years* I've waited for a moment like this. He stops looking at me with that stupid, dumbfounded face and his features turn into something just... utterly pissed off. Luckily for me, I have a switchblade up my sleeve.

"Oh, did I touch a nerve, dear?" I ask.

"Oh Veronica," He says, grabbing me by the throat, and pulling me closer. I tighten my grip on the dagger. "You may outrank me, but you're just the same. Naive, stupid, clueless, weak, scared, insecure. You still *need* me. Think of it, Veronica. You're drawn to power, but don't know how to handle it. You need me to pull the reins as you sit and look pretty, that's always been the deal."

"*Fuck* you," I spit.

"Isn't that why you're here?" He asks.

I kick him sharply in the dick. He falls to his knees.

"Oh, look, you're kneeling, how fitting," I say, fake pouting. "Our entire relationship was a power imbalance, Daman. Just admit it, you liked having me as a submissive object. To the point where you didn't even kneel when you *proposed.* You're a liar, you're manipulative, and overall, you're a *dick* and a coward."

Fury flicks on his gaze. His fiery features freeze over, the way they do when he finds a new way to have control over the situation.

"I know they're here. And whatever it is, you're not going to get away with it, sweetheart."

"No, *sweetheart*," I flick out my switchblade, holding it against his Adam's apple. "You're not getting away with it."

NIGHTSHADE

Chapter 32
Icylyn

If this isn't giving me major deja vu, I don't know what will. I don't like this, not one bit. Nevertheless, if there is any small chance of bringing Beckett back, I'm going to be there. Hazel and I are on a continual lookout, looking around for any potential danger to us or the plan. We'll look for Raven and Sage another time. We can't now. Not this time. Not until we are sure the plan will absolutely work. We'll come back for them, Hazel and I promise, no matter what.

We're following Veronica, and down the hall to the courtyard when we hear footsteps approaching us. Hazel stops in her tracks, and I nearly bump into her. Hazel turns to me, winking and putting a finger to her lips. I nod and imagine icicles surrounding me from the inside, staring at my hand as I turn invisible.

Several guards approach, all wearing red or black epaulets. The low glint of surrounding candles reflects on their shiny black armor, shadows burned into the red velvet wallpaper.

"Good evening, gentlemen," She smiles. "I seem to have gotten lost."

"You again," One of them groans.

"Oh, hello Finn! It's been a while! I didn't catch you last time I was here! Or should I say, *you* didn't catch *me*," She chuckles a bit at her joke. "Although, I wouldn't recommend trying to capture me this time."

"Hazel. It's my job," he says. "You defected, spied, and lied about... everything. I had no other choice."

"It was your choice, Finney," She says, with a tinge of sadness. "Ah, screw it."

She lifts her right hand up and snaps three times. I take a breath, close my eyes, and shake out my arms. I focus on the room becoming colder and colder, though I don't quite know what that feels like. Cold temperatures don't affect me. I open my eyes, and the candles all blow out.

"Haze, stop it," the guard says.

"Sorry, Phineas. But you've nearly taken me to my death before, and your people keep hurting the people I love. We made our choices."

She steps backward, and I step forward, becoming visible. I put my palm out, and she shoots out a bolt of lightning from behind me.

We liked to switch things up like that, keep 'em guessing. After a while, the wanted posters crossed out what type of supernatural the two of us were, due to the extreme confusion.

Someone shoots at me. I focus inwards, pulling everything in, slowing down what I can. I step forward, grabbing the bullet. I return time to its normal state, now standing in front of Phineas. I drop the bullet on the floor and crush it under my heel, before delivering a sharp punch to his face.

Bitch had it coming, pardon my language.

A guard grabs me from behind, arms underneath my armpits, hoisting me up. I hear him wince as he touches me.

I've been told I'm rather cold to the touch, to the point of being almost painful.

I fight him for a moment, before sighing and swinging my legs up as high as they can go. My shoes leave definite marks on the faces of two approaching guards. I go limp, leaning forward, my weight just enough to flip over the guard. I hold him down as best as I can, choking him. The hall lights up with flashes of lightning.

Hazel is pressed against a wall, before kicking her assailant to the ground. As I'm distracted, the guard I'm holding down grabs me by the hair. As I squeak out in pain, I'm tossed into the wall. I grunt and try to get up, but I'm too exhausted, and crash right back down.

I can feel the hairs on the back of my neck pick up, and frost runs up the walls. Electricity seems to completely light up Hazel, her gold eyes and freckles now completely glowing, lightning bits spreading from her shoulders, down her arm, crackling at her fingertips. She takes a sharp inhale, and apologizes before kicking the head of the guy who threw me, zapping the remaining guards. They spasm on the ground like fish out of water.

Hazel sighs and shakes off her shoulders, smiling and giving me a thumbs up. I heave out a breath and laugh, shaking my head at her. The lightning fizzes out, and though the hair is still raised on my skin, all that's left glowing is her eyes and freckles.

"Nicely done, Ice," Hazel says.

"Are you kidding? You were incredible!" I grin.

"We both did good," She smiles and holds out her hand to help me up.

The second our fingers touch, I feel a shock. We both jolt backward, yelling "Ow!"

"You shocked me," I say, as she says, "How on *earth* are you that cold?"

We both shake out our hands and laugh. She goes to help me up again, and once again I take her hand, only to the same effect. I resolve to just use the wall behind me, and my wings to prop myself up. We follow down the hallway, but by then, Veronica and Daman seem to be long gone until...

We catch sight of a lancet window, of which's reflection bleeds red all over the deep, dark, crushed velvet boysenberry tile. We approach the window, keeping close to the curtains, to avoid being seen. All seems to be going well, that is until Daman has Veronica by the throat. We watch as Veronica kicks Daman in the crotch, and puts a switchblade to his throat. By the looks of things, Veronica went off-script and Daman got upset. This won't end well. Hazel turns to me, seemingly trying to mask her concern. She puts a hand on my shoulder, and informs me:

"I'm going to call Aella and Jinx for back-up."

Chapter 33
Veronica

"Oh, you fool," Daman chuckles.

I kick the side of his head, knocking him to the ground. I was always good at lying. I was always good at putting on an act. Especially if it meant I got what I thought I wanted. But I can't, not with him, not anymore. I want him to hurt exactly the way he hurt me, the way he hurt everyone else.

He's in my head long before I can think to get inside of his. I step back, wiping away tears. Daman stands up, and grabs one of my shoulders, clutching far too tight as he brushes my braids off of my shoulder, brushing my chin with his thumb.

"Dearest," he says, looking into my eyes. "You didn't think you could actually do it, did you? That's so much hope, so much heartache for one person. We both know this is too much for you. If you were mine you wouldn't have to face so much. We'd take care of things you'd have the benefits, even though you're... well, you know."

He lifts his hand and I flinch away, so he grabs my shoulder tighter. I take a deep breath, and wipe my tears. This was no time to let him break me down.

"Look, you self-righteous bastard. You are a vile, perverted sordid excuse of a human being. You can choke on shit and die for all I care, or get trampled by your own horse– or– or get burned alive in that *stupid* shirt. You don't give a damn about anyone but yourself. You think that we're evil? That we're some unholy beings? Go take a look in the star-forsaken mirror, and maybe think about something other than dicking down on some poor girl that *clearly* isn't interested in you. Don't think I didn't know about the other girls you were trying to make advances on while we were engaged, I know all that shit. I'm not as stupid as you think I am, Woods. You can say I need you, just so you can keep fucking it up, over and over again. What do you want, a prize for constantly fucking it up and running to mommy and daddy to spin the truth and say your misdeeds are 'heroic acts?' Because you aren't going to get one."

"Vile talk for a lady," Daman spits. "Where on earth did you learn to speak like that? You need to watch your mouth before–"

"Drag his ass, V!" Aella yells, running out of the castle, Jinx close in tow.

"Get your filthy hands off of her," Jinx says, eyes going black, voice echoing and repeating.

Before I can stop him, before I can do anything, before I can even think, he pulls out a small gun.

And he shoots Jinx in the lungs.

Jinx's eyes go wide, and the black film over them dissipates, revealing not blue... but red. She grabs onto Aella for stability, and before Aella can move to support her, Jinx falls to the ground. All the while, I'm sprinting toward her, dropping to my knees in front of her. She hisses, inhaling sharply and squeezing her eyes shut. She looks up at me with wide eyes, before quickly jerking her head away from me and coughing.

I realize she's turned to Daman.

"No mercy then, brother?" She asks.

"Thought you would've learned that by now, Lila."

...What?

Oozing black blood is projected onto bright green blades of grass, gently blowing in the only patch of sun allowed by the approaching storm clouds and surrounding fog. Time seems to slow, but not at Icylyn's doing. Not at Icylyn's doing, but at the way time slows when the light of your world begins to dim. When you can see your entire world in one person, fleeting, slipping between your fingers, blood between your fingers, hope, stability, *love* between your fingers, and it's slipping away. She's slipping away. But you can't let her. You *can't* let her. So what if she's been lying to you this whole time? That's something you can discuss later, but stars, you *need* her to live.

"It's silver," She laughs. "Would you look at that? I've handled silver before, I can take it."

"He hit your chest," I say, my own beginning to tighten, my hand against her chest.

Her blood is black. Her blood is cold. I didn't know it was possible for so much to come out of such a tiny hole. She's losing so much. I don't think at all. I can't think. She tilts her head in confusion at my panic. Her eyes slowly drifted toward my hand. She frowns, and clasps my hand between hers, lowering it to my lap and smoothing her fingers over mine, though they're now clammy and bloodstained. She heaves another death rattle, and coughs again, away from my direction, before spitting more and more blood onto the grass.

"I'm fine," She smiles, holding my face in her hand. "I'm perfectly fine. You're going to be okay, Veronica."

This is not fine. A ringing in my ears picks up, and suddenly, nothing feels real. Suddenly, nothing feels permanent. Nothing. Nothing, nothing, nothing, nothing.

Everything all at once.

"Hey, I'm perfectly fine, my love, I'm just fine," She smiles, trying to move my gaze from the wound. "Hey... hey take a deep breath for me."

I do as told.

"There we go," She smiles, as I help her to her feet. "There we go. Keep breathing just like that, you're doing wonderful darling."

Guards approach.

"Icylyn, Hazel, Aella," Lila coughs out. "*Run.*"

She walks back and removes her cloak. A few guards just stop. She's wearing a tank top... her scars are very visible. Electrocution marks, the ones matched in the paintings of artists who met the gallows for revealing the truth. Icylyn and Hazel both stop, wide-eyed, as Aella shoves them out. Lila's skin starts to make a horrid, horrid sizzling sound.

"Please don't do anything stupid, Liles," Aella yells to Lila, eyes bordering on pleading. "I'll see you in a bit."

Lila watches as they leave. I try to feel for the buzzing in my head, trying to create a mental shield around Lila and I to keep the guards from approaching.

"Nothing is going to happen to me," Lila says, gently. "But if it does..."

She pulls a stake out from behind her back. No. *No.* No, no, no no,

No

No

No

No

No.

"If Daman... tries anything. You... you take this stake, okay–"

"Lila, please," I choke out, tears spilling down my cheeks. "Please..."

"You take this stake–"

"Lila," I choke.

"Please."

She's... so desperate. And– and I swear, I swear, I've never seen her look so desperate. I'd never seen her plead so violently. She... It... it doesn't matter. None of it matters. None of it. I just want things to be okay. I just want us to be okay. And I'm so lost in that... It. It doesn't matter, let's... just...

She thrusts the stake between my hands.

"If anything happens– please. I am begging you, please. If I am to die, I want to die by your hand. And then you take my cloak and you *run,* darling. Run until you're safe."

"Lila," I beg.

"It's alright darling," She forces one last smile. "We're alright. I love–"

Her eyes widen. She catches a bullet between her fingers, right before it meets my face. She catches yet another bullet, before pushing me to the ground and ripping her cape off. A final click is heard in the distance. Daman... Daman has the audacity to *laugh.* Her black blood explodes into the wind. I drop the stake to the ground and scream, and scream, and scream until I'm quite sure that I no longer have lungs. Her eyes snap closed. She... couldn't. She couldn't have. She's immortal, for star's sake. She can't just leave me like that. Us. Us. She can't... leave *us* like that.

She looks just like a painting. That's all this is. Some... some beautiful painting that... some unthinking passerby just happened to throw black paint all over. Happened to rip into the cracks. Happened to take the painting away from everyone else.

Shaking, I tuck a piece of hair behind her ear and lean close, though, never close enough. She is so far away. I could only lean in so far. I plant a kiss on her forehead. It's cold. She's... so cold. It's painfully familiar.

NIGHTSHADE

Her barely beating heart hits its last beat in what I once thought was an infinite waltz. I hold her in my arms as long as I can, holding the cloak tightly.

If only I had one more minute to hold her in my arms.

My Lila.

Chapter 34
Aella

I felt it when she died. It's the kind of thing you don't forget. It's like feeling half of the energy drained from your body, and... you lose a *lot* of progress on being able to control your powers. There's the thought of knowing that your literal other half is... gone. And still, you have to keep going. You always have to keep going.

A snuffed-out flame never returns.

I knew when I heard the bullets in the distance. But Lila told us to go. So I kept going. I always keep going. I always do.

I didn't cry. Not for a good long time. I don't let myself process it for a good long time. It isn't until hours and hours later... When I see Veronica, I really realize that she is gone. Lila and Beckett are both gone.

Veronica's beside the hologram fireplace in the planning room, eyes puffy, face tear-stained, sitting up with her legs hugged against her chest. She has Lila's cloak wrapped tightly around her and had her fists tightly closed around the fabrics.

"She was shot because of me, y'know," She whispers, her voice shaking. "It's all my fault. I killed her."

"No. You did not kill her," I say firmly, going to sit beside her, her shoulders now shaking violently. "It was D–"

"I... I didn't st-stick... to... to... to..." She hiccups. "I'm sorry. I'm so sorry."

I put my arm around her shoulder, and she rests her head on my shoulder. She keeps trying to apologize, and I keep telling her it's not her fault.

"How long did you know?" She asks. "That Jinx is– was– Lila?"

"Always," I say.

I shouldn't have left. I could've totally taken those guards. I watch as my hands fade away, the rest of my body fading in and out of view. I can't cry, even if I try. None of it– none of it felt real. I try. I actually try, seeing Veronica there, sobbing her lungs out. I can't. None of it feels real.

In my mind, it still isn't.

The funeral is a week later, and it ends up being a joint funeral with Beckett's.

I'll admit, I did go through a period where I was quite literally on fire every day. No one is doing so hot. At all. I mean, how could we? We left Raven and Sage behind. Beckett and Lila were... y'know. Gone.

I know Icylyn and Rebecca felt empty. They still do. Veronica... Veronica shut down. She wouldn't talk until today. She rarely leaves her room.

For me, it's an all-consuming numbness that became an entirely consuming rage.

The funeral is late at night, that way any vampires that want to come can. The sirens know not to pull shit. For once, both the river sirens and the bog sirens listen when we tell them not to be hostile at night.

Noah is here too. He's here before the funeral even starts, eyes swollen, tearing up. He kisses my forehead, wrapping fragile arms around me, shaking. I nearly forget how to hold him. He catches sight of Veronica and exits the embrace.

Veronica tenses, wiping her face. He continues towards her, wrapping his arms around her. She hugs him back tightly as if her life depends on it. I look away for just a moment, letting them do their thing.

"I'm so sorry," Noah whispers.

"Thanks. I'm sorry too," Veronica responds.

Rebecca and Icylyn step into view. I haven't seen Rebecca since... before Beckett... you know. Before I realize what I'm doing, I wrap myself in flames, teleporting in front of her. I bend down slightly and hug them both.

"I missed you so much," I say. "I'm... so sorry."

"Oh, Aella," Rebecca says softly, one arm around Icylyn, the other cradling the back of my head.

This is my family. My sisters, one of blood, the other of circumstance, Noah, and the closest person I've ever had to a real mom. And here we are, saying goodbye to the two members of our family that formed it all. The two who saw a light in the world that people were too scared of. They *were* the light of that world. And now...

Well, you know.

Words are said. Songs are sung. Tears are shed. You know... the entire elaborate thing and... shit. It all happens. We dig holes for empty graves, for faces our eyes will never study again. It's revealed to the public that Nightshade– that Jinx Athanasia, happened to be the "lost" princess of Mortem Venenum.

Their tombstones lay beside each other between the trees. Their graves faintly glow at night. It's so slow, yet passes in a blur all the same. In a few years, I'll likely scarcely remember any of it.

There is... one thing, though. One thing that I'm absolutely certain I'll never forget.

An arrow whizzes through the air, hitting and sticking into Lila's headstone. There's a snap in the distance. There are staggered gasps throughout the onlookers as Noah's eyes shut. Before I register what's happening, he's fallen into my arms.

"Noah?" I ask, panicked. He's still breathing. His heart rate is still steady. Another few snaps. More people go down. There's an echoed, repetitive laugh that fills the forest.

It's familiar. Far, far too familiar.

Oh. That's why it didn't feel real.

Her hair is dyed black, her face cold, and she holds her bow under her arm. Daman stands beside her, a twisted grin settled onto his face.

Veronica looks at her stunned, only able to say one thing, and one thing alone.

"Lila?"

Acknowledgements

Creating a book, even through self-publishing, truly takes a village. I would be remiss if I didn't credit all the wonderful, wonderful people who got me here.

Starting off with Eli Piller. This is almost just as much their book as it is mine. Through this entire process, they wore so many hats. They served as the primary editor, my advisor, my alpha reader, my writing buddy, my support system, a best friend, and so much more. It's hard to imagine what this book would be like without them. I love you so dearly, my friend.

Kevin McGowen, my secondary advisor, is a good majority of the reason this book is in your hands today. His constant support, motivation, and long talks in the kitchen got me off my feet and to work. I'm forever grateful for him, and I feel as though I am one of the luckiest human beings on earth to have him in my life.

I had such an incredible team going forward. I'd like to thank my beta readers, Rose Leahy, Em Darling, and Suereya Abdella. They all went incredibly beyond what I asked, and I'm so grateful for all of their input. I'd also like to thank my lovely, lovely sensitivity reader, Remus Mo for the incredible insight, dedication and thought he put into analyzing the book.

A HUGE thank you to Rachel Sokoloski for the beautiful cover. Additionally, I'd like to thank Emily Hammill for the line art.

I'd like to thank Sophia Danis for supporting this book from the very beginning, since the summer before high school when it was an entirely different concept. They are Nightshade's first ever fan, as well as one of my dearest friends. They've stuck beside me through every step of the process, and kept me going through every step.

To Lara-May and Madeline for sticking with me and for listening to my many idea-filled info-dumps, as well as being lovely human beings in general. And no, Madeline, my dear, I will not be naming the second book Bloodraiser. Love you, though! To Lara-May for standing beside me from day one, our world domination will come soon enough.

I'd like to thank Domenic Puccio, my rival, enemy and detested worstie, for listening to me and being such a constant support.

I'd also like to thank Rowan Mayer, for being a supportive ray of sunshine. (Sorry about Beckett.)

I'd like to thank Amanda Carlisle for keeping me on track, and consistently supporting me and my writing endeavors. She is so much of the reason I never gave up on this dream. I'd also like to thank Dr. Lori Martindale for challenging me in my ideals of writing, and helping me fall in love with literature all over again.

I'd also love to thank my dear Arbel Ben-Abraham for being more lovely than humanly possible, more than anyone could ever imagine. Arbel is one of the people who has supported me the most, and they've been my love, my rock, my platonic soulmate, and one of my dearest friends for many years. Anyone who has an Ari in their life is infinitely blessed in a way that they'll never quite understand. I love you so dearly, my friend.

My dearest loves, Ari and Eels, thank you both for getting me here.

A special mention to Kaitlyn Novak (an absolute human ray of sunshine and one of the loveliest people you'll ever meet), Wren Landaverde, Theo Downey, Gabbi Smith, Kai Wallis, Sam Bonfiglio, and Brynn Schmid.

To my aunt for getting me into literature in the first place. Who would've thought reading Romeo and Juliet and Greek myths with you as a kid would've led to all of this?

To the sun and the moon for always shining through.

Thank you to everyone who picked up this book. Thank you for supporting a dream, and a story that got a weird kid through high school. Love you all!

To everyone who's been a part of my life who I might've missed, kisses to all of you. Thank you for being there. ♥

To (almost) every whisper in the wind, everyone who was once a part of my life, this book is for you too.

To Colton, who absolutely should not be reading this, I love you so much Goose. I could not have asked for a better brother. (And yes, you are probably the reason all of the little brothers in my books are ridiculously sassy and intelligent.)

Last, but certainly not least, I'd love to thank my parents. I don't know how I could ever adequately thank them in a way that will ever live up to all they've done for me, so this will have to suffice. Thank you for being my Rebecca and Christopher Acosta, my islands, my support system, the people who shaped who I am today. Thank you for being there, for being fantastic, for being you, and consistently going above and beyond to support me and my dream. I love you both dearly.

About the Author

This is Percy Cadaver's debut book! They grew up in Southern California, developing a love of stories at the ripe age of eight, when their aunt introduced them to pretentious literature. (It also helped that their teacher at the time complimented their writing). They're currently studying Creative Writing and Honors Interdisciplinary Studies at Western Washington University. When they're not yapping with their friends, or being too philosophical about nature, they love singing, watching horror movies, making tea, and spending time with their family.

Milton Keynes UK
Ingram Content Group UK Ltd.
UKHW012314060524
442290UK00005B/359